"I say the winner names the forfeit," Beatrice suggested.

Julius nodded. "I think you have planned this, Miss Fanshaw."

Beatrice raised her chin a notch. "You don't *have* to agree to race against me, Lord Chadwick. Indeed, I don't know why I entertained such a notion."

He looked at her directly and she felt her breath come a little short. "Oh, I think you do," he said quietly. "I think you know *exactly* what you want and you will stop at nothing to get it. I read people well, Miss Fanshaw, and I think you have the ability to be absolutely single-minded. You know very well why you entertained this notion."

Her smile was one of thin sarcasm. "You do a lot of thinking, Lord Chadwick."

"All the time."

"If I am as you say, then indirectly it is your doing."

"I am sorry to find that after all these years you still carry a grudge. And now all I need to do is discover what forfeit you will ask of me. And the only way I can do that is to race against you—unless you will indulge me and tell me now."

She tossed her head haughtily. To forgo propriety and do what one wished was quite liberating. "No, not before the end of the race."

"Very well. Until after the race."

* * *

Beauty in Breeches
Harlequin® Historical #313—August 2011

Author Note

All my novels are historical romances set in varied backgrounds. I enjoy writing about most periods, and the Regency period—which was one of the most romantic, glittering and exciting times in our history, when rakes and scandals abounded—is always a firm favorite with both readers and writers alike. The heroines are strong-willed young women, feisty and with a spark of life and determination—which I hope describes Beatrice, the heroine of *Beauty in Breeches*. The heroes are always dashing, masculine and forceful and also intelligent and caring—not forgetting handsome. The heroines are the most important thing in their life, even if they are antagonistic. They always come round in the end and romance flowers.

HELEN DICKSON

Beauty in Breeches

TORONTO NEW YORK LONDON
AMSTERDAM PARIS SYDNEY HAMBURG
STOCKHOLM ATHENS TOKYO MILAN MADRID
PRAGUE WARSAW BUDAPEST AUCKLAND

Recycling programs
for this product may
not exist in your area.

ISBN-13: 978-0-373-30622-0

BEAUTY IN BREECHES

www.Harlequin.com

Printed in U.S.A.

Available from Harlequin® Historical and
HELEN DICKSON

HELEN DICKSON

was born and lives in South Yorkshire with her retired farm manager husband. Having moved out of the busy farmhouse where she raised their two sons, she has more time to indulge in her favorite pastimes. She enjoys being outdoors, traveling, reading and music. An incurable romantic, she writes for pleasure. It was a love of history that drove her to start writing historical fiction.

Chapter One

Beatrice halted her horse beneath the spreading canopy of a great beech tree. The scene was like a little tableau to be viewed by any who passed by. The summertime smells of Larkhill wafted around her. She knew every tree, every meadow and bridal way and rutted track, and every stream where trout could be found. Everything around her was pulsating with life, except the beautiful old house where the squire, her father, had once ruled. The house sat like a queen in the centre of her domain. It faced due south so the sun, before it sank over the gently rolling hills in the west, shone on the mellow stone walls all day, making them warm to the touch.

From her vantage point she watched a happy group of fashionable society people stroll along the paths in the long-neglected gardens. The beautiful ladies wore high-waisted dresses, their fair complexions protected from the sun by delicate parasols, the gentlemen attired in the pinnacle of fashion. Her eyes were drawn to one of the gentlemen like metal filings to a magnet. He stood out from the others by his admirable bearing and heightened stature. She had never seen him before, but by instinct she knew who he was.

Lord Julius Chadwick—the Marquess of Maitland.

Her heart tightened with a long-held hatred and resentment. He was walking at a leisurely pace with his hands clasped behind his back. Making no attempt to hide herself from view, she continued to watch him as he strolled closer to the house. The sun's rays caught his hair. It was thick and dark and curled into his nape.

As if he could feel her eyes on him he paused and waited a moment before he turned and looked directly at her. Surprised to see her there, he broke away from the party. His handsome face was set in lines which were quite unreadable, but his amber eyes danced as though he found their meeting and the manner of her dress vastly entertaining. Below a white silk shirt, skin-tight breeches clung to her long, shapely legs above black riding boots. Being buff in colour, from a distance the breeches gave the impression that she was naked from the waist down. She had tied back her abundant gold-and-copper curls with a bright emerald-green ribbon.

Beatrice sat on her horse unmoving, as if she were some stone goddess, insensate but powerful. She gripped the reins in her slender fingers and stared back at him, defiance in every line of her young body. She was seeing this man in the flesh for the first time in her life, but she had thought of him often over the years. He had appeared in her mind like some sinister spectre, a malevolent giant, with the power to do as he liked—as he had when he'd blotted all happiness from her future.

Her head lifted and there was no softness in her eyes, which had turned to flint. Her mouth hardened to an unsmiling resentment. She had no doubt that he was curious and wondering who she was and what she was doing trespassing on his land so close to the house. He made no attempt to approach her or speak to her. Neither of them moving, over the twenty yards or so that separated them they continued to watch each other until, with a casual toss of her lovely head, Beatrice turned her horse and disappeared as silently as she had come amongst the tall, shadowy trees.

At Standish House, just two miles from Larkhill, Lady Moira Standish was taking tea in the drawing room. She was a striking woman, tall and robust with iron-grey hair, good cheekbones and a square jaw. Her husband had killed himself when he had taken a tumble from his horse during a hunt three years ago, leaving her a very wealthy widow. With a twenty-five-year-old son and a nineteen-year-old daughter, she had much on her plate if she was to see them affianced before the year was out. Her son, George, had inherited Standish House on his father's demise. The dowager Lady Standish continued to act as mistress. When George took a wife she would move into the dower house.

She had returned from London that very day, where

she had been on a short visit with her daughter, Astrid.
She sat stiffly upright on the green-and-gold brocaded
couch. With a firm hand she fluttered a delicate ivory-
and-lace fan before her heated face. Her grey eyes were
narrowed with annoyance as she darted sharp disapproving glances at her niece, who had just burst into
the room, shattering the peace. Beatrice presented a
frightful vision in her breeches, stained from her ride.
Shoving her untidy mop of hair back from her face,
the girl sank into a chair in a most unladylike pose and
yawned, doing little to hide her boredom.

As she looked at her, Lady Standish wondered if this
niece of hers would ever grow up. She was clever, intelligent, quick-thinking and sharp witted. She was also
problematical and a constant headache. Beatrice was
little more than an impoverished orphan, but she still
walked about with her head high, just like her arrogant,
reckless father before her. She was more beautiful than
Astrid would ever be, but she lived for the moment
and noticed nothing that was not to do with outdoor
pursuits and horses.

'Really, Beatrice,' Lady Standish exclaimed sharply,
wrinkling her nose as the smell of horses wafted in
her direction. 'I have told you time and again not to
appear before me dressed in those outrageous breeches.
They smell of the stables and that is where I wish they
would remain. It's high time you stopped gallivanting
about the district and occupied yourself with something
useful. I swear one would think the expensive govern-
esses we provided for you would have taught you about
behaviour and comportment. Do you forget that you are

quality born with bloodlines, breeding and ancestry? And don't slouch. It's bad for the posture.'

Beatrice sat up straight and obediently squared her shoulders and raised her chin, though she continued to fidget in her chair. Her aunt rarely spoke to her, except to lecture, criticise, instruct or command. 'It is certainly desirable to be well bred,' she remarked calmly, 'but the glory belongs to my father and his father, not to me.'

Lady Standish rolled her eyes upwards and worked her fan harder, the corkscrew curls on either side of her face almost springing to life. 'That is rubbish, Beatrice, and just another one of your absurdities. Glory? See what good his *glory* has done you—having to live off your only kin. Your father was a fool, throwing his money away without a care to anyone but himself.'

Beatrice looked at her wearily. She had heard the argument so often she knew it by heart—it failed to shake her kinder memories of her father. 'I loved him dearly,' she said simply. 'He was a good father.'

'That's a matter of opinion. The devil did his work when he made you just like him, you ungrateful girl.'

Beatrice flinched, but her aunt ranted on, turning her narrowed eyes upon her and shaking a bejewelled, damning finger. 'He left you in a fix—no dowry and now you're eighteen years old with not a penny to your name. There isn't a man that will marry you without one. The Lord knows what a task you are for me.' Lady Standish sighed heavily, as if tired of her burden. 'It's better that you were married and off my hands—and I know I shall have to provide your dowry to bring that

about, but I pity the man who would wed you. I swear
you will be the death of me—I know you will. And do
wear a bonnet when you are out. Your face is much too
brown and freckles are most unbecoming on a young
lady.'

'Yes, Aunt Moira.'

Beatrice knew she was a disappointment to her
aunt, that she had never considered her anything but
an irksome responsibility. Lady Standish tried to instil
discipline in her and to make her into an obedient, bid-
dable young woman like Astrid—Astrid had exquisite
manners, was skilled in everything a young woman of
quality should be, would sit still and work her sampler,
would stay clean and tidy—and she failed miserably.

Beatrice tried not to fidget for fear that if she moved
it would draw her aunt's attention again, but she was
weary of tiptoeing about the house and doubted her
ability to last much longer. Life was hard for her at
Standish House, but she wearily accepted the way her
aunt treated her without complaint. She had been out
since dawn, for the countryside was the only place she
could seek succour from her aunt's angry, cruel taunts.

Beatrice glanced at her cousin Astrid, whose face
was alight with intense excitement over her forthcoming birthday party in two weeks. It was to be an afternoon of enjoyment at Standish House, which was more
appealing to Astrid than a grand ball. Bright sunlight
on the windows streamed through her light brown ringlets shot through with chestnut glints. She was pout-
ing prettily and sitting poised and straight backed, her
hands folded in her lap. She was small and slender, with

china-blue eyes and rosy dimpled cheeks. She bore only the faintest resemblance to her cousin Beatrice and was cast in a sweeter, gentler mould than Beatrice's nature could ever imitate with success. The apple of her mother's eye, Astrid was in the ascendant.

'I have returned to organise Astrid's birthday party,' Lady Standish said. 'It is to be a large affair, with only the finest society people invited. You should have seen her in London, Beatrice. I think Lord Chadwick was most struck.'

Beatrice was all attention. 'Lord Chadwick? The Marquess of Maitland?' she said mechanically. She realised her aunt was watching her intently and that her face was unguarded before her.

'Of course. There could scarcely be a better match.' Lady Standish paused to take a sip of tea. 'There is no need to look so incredulous. It is quite natural. Did you not think Astrid was to marry some time?'

Beatrice gaped at her. If she had not been so taken aback by her aunt's pronouncement that made her want to shriek, she would have laughed aloud. She had given little thought to the matter of Astrid's future. She never thought beyond her own life, what *she* wanted—of returning to Larkhill, which was so very dear to her.

'Lord Chadwick—he has been abroad for several months on one of his ships and only recently returned—showed great interest in Astrid. Indeed, the attention he showed her was commented upon by several; I am hoping he will approach me to offer for her. He is of excellent family, of sound character, sharp wits, intelligence and his fortune is quite remarkable.

Through his own endeavours there is a fleet of ships flying his flag and carrying his cargo. He has mines of gold and silver that bought those ships, and his ownership of land is so vast no one knows how much. Astrid will indeed be a fortunate young woman if she manages to secure him.'

'He sounds an impressive figure, Aunt Moira, but a grand title, wealth and happiness don't always come hand in glove,' Beatrice retorted tersely.

Lady Standish gave her a sour, disapproving look. 'Any woman would be a fool to turn away from it. Astrid is certainly willing to entertain Lord Chadwick. The wedding will be a truly grand affair, with one of those new-fangled wedding tours to France and Italy, before they settle down to married life at Highfield Manor in Kent. It is an estate of some significance.'

While her aunt twittered on, Beatrice kept her face lowered, feigning interest in a magazine so Lady Standish could not see her, would not see that her face was white. She blindly turned a page so that her aunt would not be able to tell she could not control a grimace of anger and the tears stinging hot. She felt murderous. She wanted to leap to her feet and remind her aunt of the harm Lord Chadwick had done her family, harm she seemed to have forgotten, or considered unimportant when it came to choosing a husband for her darling Astrid. But Beatrice had not forgotten.

Beatrice wanted Lord Chadwick to suffer all the torments of the damned and crawl to her for forgiveness for being the architect of all her misery. She simply could not bear the thought of Astrid being the Marchioness of Maitland, Lady Chadwick, living her life in grand style, while Aunt Moira would have Beatrice married off to the first suitor who chanced her way.

'Of course, should Astrid marry Lord Chadwick it will be a perfect match. If he offers for her now, they can be betrothed before the little Season starts in the autumn.'

Astrid had come out the year before and had been the toast of the Season. She had received several offers of marriage, but Lady Standish had considered the young men who made them too low down the social ladder and not rich enough for her daughter and had declined their offers, hoping for better things, a brilliant match, and to that end she had in mind Lord Chadwick.

'If he does indeed offer for Astrid, it will be a spring wedding.'

Beatrice was unable to keep quiet a moment longer. Blinking back angry tears, she looked at her aunt. 'But, Aunt Moira, how can you let such a thing happen? He alone is responsible for all the misfortunes that have befallen me. I shall neither forget nor forgive what he did to Father. Would you not feel as I do?'

'That is in the past and you would do well to put it behind you since nothing can be done about it now.' She gave her niece a watery smile. 'If you think of your scriptures, Beatrice, you will remember being taught that Jesus told us to love our enemies?'

'Jesus hadn't met Lord Chadwick,' Beatrice retorted bitterly. She glanced at Astrid's crestfallen face and dared to ask, 'And is this what Astrid wants—marriage to a total stranger?'

'He will not be a stranger to her by the time they are married. The marriage of my only daughter is of great importance.' Her aunt's face was stern, her eyes as hard as steel. 'This is family business, not sentiment.'

'But—Lord Chadwick has not offered for me and he might not,' Astrid said quietly, hesitantly—the old habit of obedience and deference to her mother had a strong hold on her. 'He has shown kindness towards me and nothing more. I—think you read too much into it, Mama.'

'Nonsense.' Lady Standish waved the objection aside. 'It's early days, I agree, but he did pay you a good deal of attention. It shows real promise. He saw what a gem you are. The party must be a success. It is a perfect opportunity to demonstrate to Lord Chadwick that you are, at county level, well qualified to be his bride. We must ensure that you spend as much time in each other's company as possible at the party.'

'But—Mama, he may not want to.'

Her mother shot her a dark look. 'Don't argue, Astrid. I do know what I am talking about. Marriage is not something you can settle for yourself. You are young, you can't decide these things. You have to be guided. In the end it will be down to me. I will decide where you wed.'

'But Lord Chadwick is hardly a suitable candidate,' Beatrice dared to voice. In this instant she refused to sit with her head bowed as Astrid always did. She sat with her head high, one dark eyebrow slightly raised, and she met her aunt's level gaze as if she were her equal. 'Do you forget what that man did to my father—and that my mother was so ill and distressed by the whole sorry affair that she died of a broken heart? The man should have been horse-whipped for taking advantage of a man in a weakened state.'

Lady Standish looked at her coldly. 'How dare you speak to me in that tone, Beatrice. Know your place. But since you are so eager to have your say, I will tell you that I do not forget and I do not like it that you feel you must remind me. But I do not hold it against Lord Chadwick. Your father—my own dear husband's brother-in-law—was lamentably weak. His weakened state, as you put it, was brought about by an over-indulgence in alcoholic spirits. It was his fault that he lost Larkhill and shot himself. It cannot be blamed on anyone else.'

Her aunt's cruel words cut Beatrice to the heart. 'I blame Lord Chadwick absolutely,' she persisted firmly. 'I always will. Anyway, what is he like, this noble lord? Does he have any afflictions?'

'Not unless one considers shocking arrogance an affliction,' Lady Standish answered sharply. 'Of course he has every right to be so, with friends constantly following in his wake. Why, if it were up to females to do the asking, Lord Chadwick would have had more offers of marriage than all the ladies in London combined.'

'I can't see why,' Beatrice remarked in a low, cold voice. 'He is absolutely loathsome to me.'

'Oh, no, Beatrice,' Astrid said breathlessly, rising quickly to his defence. 'You do not know him. He is

handsome and charming; I know you will think so too
when you meet him.'

Only the prospect of another dressing down from
her aunt prevented Beatrice from saying that she had
already encountered the odious Lord Chadwick at
Larkhill and was not hankering after an introduction.

From the open window of her bedroom, with her
shoulder propped against the frame and her arms folded
across her chest, Beatrice gazed dispassionately as the
titled, wealthy and influential guests gathered on the
extensive lawns of Standish House to celebrate Astrid's
nineteenth birthday, which was to go on into the night.
The terraces all around were ablaze with blossoms,
magnolias and sweet-scented azaleas.

Guests continued to roll up the drive in chaises and
carriages, many open so the occupants could bask in
the sun's warmth. A full staff of footmen were on hand
to assist them from their carriages and a full army of
servants ready to dance attendance on them as they
wined and dined. Trestle tables decorated with summer
flowers had been set up in the shade of the terrace
where only the finest food was served and bowls of
punch and chilled lemonade. Tables and chairs were
scattered about the lawns, and, for anyone overcome
by the heat, ice-cold drinks had been laid out in the
drawing room.

Standish House was no more than two hours' drive
from London. It was a fascinating, gorgeous paradise
populated by beautiful, carefree people in all their
sumptuous finery. Several of the gentlemen sported

military uniforms, a reminder to everyone of the battle they had fought at Waterloo a year ago. To Beatrice, the scene held little interest and no beauty, but there was something morbidly compelling about observing from a distance how people interacted with each other. At eighteen years old, restrained and guarded, she did not believe in the inherent goodness in anyone.

George and Lady Standish received the guests— Lady Standish, in her element, looking as if she would burst with her own importance. She presented an imposing figure in a high-necked gown of lavender-grey shot silk, with a matching turban trimmed with large purple plumes. A picture of sweet perfection, Astrid, looking like an angel in her high-waisted cream gown and perfectly coiffed hair, a bunch of fat ringlets trailing over one shoulder, was surrounded by fawning fops. Against a fabulous colourful backdrop of banks of rhododendrons, azaleas and a small lake, she was seated beneath a white gazebo. Her face was pink and rosy and glowing with happiness, the very picture of a demure young lady on her birthday as she raised her head and laughed delightedly at something that was said.

Voices and laughter and the clink of champagne glasses drifted up to Beatrice. One newly arrived guest caught her attention as soon as he alighted from a splendid midnight-blue open carriage, the Chadwick coat of arms emblazoned on the door. He was accompanied by two gentlemen and two ladies.

Julius Chadwick was as handsome as any man present, wickedly so, with his superb build and panther-like black hair. As he strolled the lawns with a smooth, elegant stride, every movement polished and assured, he was a natural target for the sighing host of young girls making sheep's eyes at him.

Through narrowed eyes Beatrice watched him. Conversations among the guests had broken off; even the servants passing among them with trays of food and drink almost bumped into each other as they paused to look at him. He was tall, rugged and muscular, with dark good looks and an aquiline nose; despite the way he casually moved among the guests, looking completely relaxed, he seemed to radiate barely leashed, ruthless power.

In contrast to the pale complexions and bored languor of the other gentlemen present, his skin was deeply tanned by a tropical sun. He exuded charm, yet there was an aura about him of a man who had seen and done all sorts of things—terrible things, dangerous things, forbidden things—and enjoyed it, and Beatrice could not deny that if she had not already determined that he was her enemy, she would have liked to get to know him.

He was elegantly attired in a beautifully tailored dark-green jacket that clung to his wide shoulders. His pristine white cravat was folded precisely and secured by a winking gold pin, and dove-grey tight breeches outlined his long, muscular legs above highly polished Hessians—the perfect outfit for a wealthy gentleman meeting his neighbours for the first time.

Beatrice was distracted when Lizzie, one of the

chambermaids, came in bearing an armload of freshly laundered linen.

'Great heavens! Miss Beatrice! Why aren't you at Miss Astrid's party? Why, it's a grand affair and it's high time you went out and enjoyed yourself.'

Beatrice shrugged and turned to survey the scene once more with little interest, her arms folded across her chest. 'You know I'm not one for parties, Lizzie. Besides, I doubt my presence will be missed. And why Astrid insisted on Aunt Moira inviting half of London society to Standish House I cannot imagine. It's such an extravagance.'

'Is it, now?' Lizzie said, in total disagreement. 'Your cousin is a young lady of considerable beauty and consequence. Her mama will be hoping she will attract the attention of one of the wealthy young men she has invited.' Placing her burden on the bed, Lizzie raised her brows and stared disapprovingly at Beatrice's breeches. 'Perhaps if you took more care in your appearance, you, too, would attract the same kind of attention. You are a very beautiful young woman, Miss Beatrice, and you should socialise more.'

Beatrice accepted Lizzie's well-intentioned rebuke with cheerful philosophical indifference. 'I'm not so vain that I allow my looks to concern me. It would take more than silks and satins and powder and paint to make me into a proper lady, Lizzie.'

All Beatrice's hopes of becoming a lady had been dashed when she had been thirteen years old. She was an only child, the daughter of Sir James Fanshaw. She'd been raised at Larkhill. Apart from visits to Standish

House when she was allowed to play with Astrid, her parents had kept her isolated in protective gentility, hidden behind the high stone walls of Larkhill like an enchanted child, waiting for the magic of a prince charming to set her free.

And then one day her prince did come, but not in any magical way like the one she had read about in her story books, on a white steed and as handsome as a Greek god, but in the dark forbidding form of a thief of the highest order. Her papa had lost Larkhill to that man in a game of cards; afterwards, unable to live with the shame of what he had done, he'd shot himself.

The humiliation, shame and heartbreak of it all and being forced to live in shabby, penny-pinching gentility on the charity of her mother's brother, Lord Standish, was too much for her mama. Unable to come to terms with her husband's suicide, ill and distressed she had taken to her bed and retreated into herself and did not speak to anyone. Just six months after coming to live at Standish House, she had followed her husband to the grave. Even now Beatrice felt the wrenching loss of her parents.

Aunt Moira was a woman of strong personality who had despised Beatrice's father's weakness and despised even more her mother's inability to come to terms with her loss. Unable to turn Beatrice out since her husband would not allow it—and if she did it would reflect badly on her—she had grudgingly endured her impoverished niece living at Standish House with the intention of finding her a husband and getting her off her hands as soon as possible. But her strong-willed niece had other ideas and they did not involve a husband.

Beatrice had a mop of unruly chestnut-and-copper curls, a small, stubborn chin, pert nose, and a pair of sooty-lashed, slanting sea-green eyes that completely dominated her face. Her face was lightly tanned from being outdoors riding Major, her precious horse given to her by her uncle before his tragic accident, or fishing and shooting with her feckless and charming, though eternally loyal, rogue of a cousin called George. Even though she lived in a house full of people, Beatrice was her own person and as isolated as she had been as a child at Larkhill.

'Do you know that man, Lizzie—the one with black hair and wearing a dark-green coat—the arrogant one? Who are those with him?'

Lizzie, a young woman who always knew everything, came and peered over her shoulder, her eyes settling on the object of Miss Beatrice's interest. The gentleman in question was conversing with others close to the house. 'Why, that's the Marquess of Maitland, Lord Julius Chadwick—and as handsome as a man can be, don't you think?' she uttered on a sigh, as struck as all the other females drooling over him. 'According to Miss Astrid, he's been off on one of his sailing ships to some far-off foreign place I've never heard of. Came back last month—much to the delight of the ladies of the *ton*. He's staying at Larkhill and has brought a small party with him. That's Lord Roderick Caruthers he's talking to, and his wife, Miranda. Sir James Sedbury and his sister Josephine are also in his party. I heard Lord Chadwick is extremely rich.'

'Apparently so,' Beatrice said with derision. 'Most of his wealth has come from what he can attain from others. He's a gambler—and good at it. I know that for a fact.'

Hatred and an odd sense of excitement stirred in her heart as her interest in Lord Chadwick deepened. Of course she'd already known he was at Larkhill with guests, but she could not seem to check her desire to find out as much as possible about him. As if he could sense her eyes on him, he paused his conversation with Lord Caruthers and looked up and Beatrice was caught in the act of staring at him. His light amber eyes captured hers and Beatrice raised her chin, looking at him coldly, trying to stare him out of countenance. A strange, unfathomable smile curved his lips before he looked away and carried on his conversation. She might as well have been invisible for all the notice he took.

'It would be a feather in your aunt's cap if Miss Astrid managed to capture that particular gentleman. She's counting on it and has made no secret of it either,' Lizzie prattled on as she busied herself storing away the linen. 'What a match that would be—to have her only daughter a marchioness and married to a man of such wealth.'

'I'm sure you're right, Lizzie,' Beatrice murmured drily. What Lizzie said was true, but Beatrice knew they were ill matched and that marriage to a man of such strong character would terrify her gentle cousin when the time came for her to walk down the aisle.

'Now he's back and being a man still in his prime, I imagine he will be looking for a wife.' Having finished packing away the linen, Lizzie came and peered over her shoulder. 'Look at Miss Astrid. How beautiful she is—and enjoying herself. Whereas you, Miss Beatrice—volatile and moody, that's what your aunt says you are. Now why don't you put on something nice and get along down there and join in the celebrations?'

Deep in thought, Beatrice continued to lean against the window frame as she watched the man she truly believed to be the architect of all her misery. A man in his prime, Lizzie had said, and probably looking for a wife. But who said that wife had to be Astrid? Beatrice had dreamed of Larkhill, of one day returning to live there. She did not dream now. She started to think. In the back of her mind a plan was forming to give her back her home and to forge out some stability for her future.

Suddenly she was presented with an idea that brought her up straight—an idea that was as preposterous as it was splendid and she congratulated herself on having thought of it. Her mind was racing like a ferret in a cage to find the spring on the trap that would catch Lord Chadwick. She let the silence ride and watched him with renewed interest, her green eyes as inscrutable as a snake's. So, they thought she was moody and volatile. Well, let them. After today they would know just how moody and volatile she could be.

As the afternoon wore on, the more liquor the guests consumed and the more boisterous they became.

Beatrice observed Lord Chadwick's popularity as people rushed to speak to him. He talked and joked, speaking to those around him with lazy good humour. He threw back his head and laughed loud at something her aunt said to him, his even white teeth gleaming between his lips, causing everyone within close proximity to turn their heads in his direction, such was the effect this handsome, most popular bachelor of London society had on others.

She particularly watched him when he conversed with Astrid, noting that he never betrayed any emotion other than polite interest, and there were moments when he observed the festivities that his expression slipped and he looked bored, as if he would prefer to be elsewhere.

Beatrice folded her arms across her chest. Already she had decided to use this handsome lord in her desire to return to Larkhill. She could not help her aunt's dreams. She had her own dreams. Someone had to be disappointed. However, she did consider what Astrid's feeling might be on the matter and she would speak to her first, but an opportunity had presented itself that she did not intend letting slip away. This was the time and the place. The way to capture Lord Chadwick was to surprise him before his conscience was awake, not to let him prepare and consider and reject her in advance.

With Henry Talbot, the son of a close neighbour by her side, Astrid wandered away from Lord Chadwick and Beatrice saw her aunt's bright, demanding stare, prompting her daughter to make herself available to Lord Chadwick once more. Beatrice saw Astrid's shoulders slump and watched her walk back to him. Her cream parasol trembled over her fair head as he stepped forwards to meet her. He bowed low and took her gloved hand, but Beatrice knew, with keen insight, that it was not the heat of passion Lord Chadwick felt for Astrid. And what was her silly cousin blushing for? Why was she trembling?

'What's happening now?' she asked Lizzie when the maid returned to the room. 'It looks as if some kind of debate is taking place at the far end of the garden.'

'And so it is. One of the footmen told me in the kitchen that the main topic of conversation just now is the racing at Goodwood and about Lord Chadwick's acquisition of a horse he purchased recently at Newmarket. Apparently he's challenged anyone to a race who thinks they have a mount that can beat his. As yet no one's been brave enough to take him up on his challenge, but it still stands.'

A slow smile curved Beatrice's mouth and her eyes lit. 'Well now, that is most interesting.' At last she'd heard something that caused her to turn from the window. Despite the impropriety of what she was about to do and her aunt's wrath when she found out, she would seize this God-given opportunity before it slipped away. 'You're right, Lizzie,' she said, with more enthusiasm than she'd shown all day. 'Perhaps I should go down. Help me dress, will you? My green, I think. I must look my best for Astrid's party.'

Assured of her beauty, the green of her gown making her hair glow more golden and her eyes to

shine brighter, she was endowed with a boldness
second to none. The beautiful setting, the laughter and
the warmth of the day spurred Beatrice on through a
sea of nameless faces to carry out her scheme to its
limit. She was quite mad, of course, but that neither
concerned nor deterred her from her purpose. She was
not about to act like a rider who falls from their horse
before the race was done.

With a false smile pinned to her face, she followed
the pretty path that wound its way through the attractive garden drenched in warm sunshine, her eyes on
the large group of people at the other end. Some of
the fashionable, overdressed gentlemen were sprawled
out on the lawn, drinking champagne and talking and
laughing much too loudly as the liquor loosened their
inhibitions. Beatrice was confidently aware of the
gleam of her silk dress hinting at the contours of her
long shapely legs as she walked. Long gloves encased
her arms and her shining hair was caught up at the
crown in a mass of thick, glossy curls.

She was surrounded by other ladies, beautiful ladies,
but when Beatrice put her mind to it only she had that
perfect self-conscious way of walking. She moved as if
every man present was watching her. She walked as if
she were irresistible, such was the power of her convic-
tion that she would achieve her goal in what she had set
out to do. Even the diamonds adorning the throats of
the ladies winked at her like bright-eyed conspirators as
they caught the sun. A certainty stronger than anything
else assured her that her hour of triumph was near.

She was aware of the stir she created as she

continued to advance, with a strange sensation of fatality and enjoying a kind of immunity. A lightning bolt of anticipation seemed to shoot through the crowd, breaking off conversation and choking off laughter as some two hundred guests turned in near unison to see where she was heading.

In the surrounding haze Beatrice no longer saw anyone but him. Her attention was focused entirely on him. She looked at him fixedly. Had she wanted to look away, she could not have done. She was not even conscious that people were watching her, feeling they were about to witness something surprising.

Never had Beatrice seen such a figure of masculine elegance. Lord Julius Chadwick looked so poised, so debonair. His movements, his habitual air of languid indolence, hung about him like a cloak. With his dark hair tousled by the breeze, he looked every inch the well-heeled businessman and landowner—and a great deal more dangerous than the average country gentleman.

The perfect fit of his coat and the tapering trousers accentuated the long lines of his body. It was impossible not to respond to this man as his masculine magnetism dominated the scene. A slow half-smile curved his lips and she saw him give a careless shrug. He raised his fine, dark eyebrows at some remark. She completely ignored the young women in the knot eyeing him with encouraging, flirtatious glances over their fans, tittering and giggling. Where other women might have succumbed to the irresistible pull to see behind the cool façade and start uncovering the man beneath, Beatrice could feel the palpable danger around him. She was never a rational person, but this time she knew she should have the good sense to heed the warning and turn and walk away. But her mind was made up. Too much was at stake.

Lord Chadwick cast a pair of laughing eyes over those around him; his gaze came to rest on a pair of jade-green eyes in which gold-and-brown flecks blazed, a sure sign that their owner was under some urgent compulsion, staring at him with a fixed intensity. He stood watching her in silent fascination, then he smiled slowly. Julius was easily moved by the beauty of a woman and the calm boldness with which this one was looking at him intrigued him.

He saw a sculpted face of unforgettable beauty, with high, delicately moulded cheekbones, a perfect nose and generous lips. It was a strong face, but essentially feminine. Her hair was burnished gold by the sun. Bright curls clustered in artful disarray on the top of her head, a few gilded wisps wreathed about her delicate ears and nape, drawing attention to her slender neck. There was something unusual in her attitude. A strange sense of shock quivered through him when he recognised her as the woman he had seen at Larkhill some days past, and again today when instinct had drawn his gaze to an upstairs window of the house. Who was she and why did she watch him so intently?

Beatrice faced him with outward calm. She looked at him for a long, thoughtful moment, as though estimating her chances. The corner of her mouth rose insensibly as her eyes narrowed. Now that the moment of confrontation had arrived she was strangely relieved.

'I hear you have offered a wager to anyone who believes their horse can beat yours. I will accept your challenge,' she announced clearly. A loud gasp ran through the guests as they gathered about, parting for her to pass through. At the sight of Beatrice Fanshaw the frosty eyes of the hopeful young ladies pierced her back with a thousand darts; those young ladies fanned themselves with growing annoyance.

Lord Chadwick excused himself and came forwards to meet her. Her face was uptilted; as he looked at her, deep inside, he felt something tighten, harden, clarifying and coalescing into one crystal-clear emotion. Taking her gloved hand, he gallantly bowed over it. As she lightly rested her fingers in his, he brushed them with a kiss.

'Whoever you are, you look extremely beautiful, a rare jewel adorning the garden.'

How dashing he is, Beatrice thought, smiling triumphantly at him as he looked at her searchingly. The warm liquid of his amber gaze missed nothing as he became caught up in the excitement of her presence. She totally ignored the other women struggling to maintain their composure as they tried to hide their hostility towards her.

'What it is to be so popular, sir. I thank you for the compliment,' she said coolly, lightly, withdrawing her hand, as if his compliment meant nothing to her at all while secretly feeling a trifle flattered that a man should find her attractive, 'but I have an aversion to flattery.'

His eyebrows lifted at her forthright remark. 'Really? I am surprised to hear that since every female of my acquaintance welcomes adulation from the opposite sex.'

'Do they?' she replied airily. 'Flattery and false praise are much the same in my book.'

Curious about her casual, cool manner, yet undaunted, his smile was humorous. 'I assure you that my flattery was genuine and well meant. It is not flattery to tell the truth.'

Beatrice glanced around. 'You appear to have attracted a great deal of attention yourself. Why, ladies surround you like moths around a candle.'

He tilted his eyebrows with amusement and leaned forwards so that only she might hear his words. 'Many moths, but only one rare butterfly. Besides, I have never been partial to moths,' he murmured, and Beatrice read in his face such evident desire that heat flamed for a moment in her cheeks. A curious sharp thrill ran through her as the force between them seemed to explode wordlessly, but she did not forget who he was or why she was here.

He took a step back from her. 'So, who have we here?' he asked, regarding her down the length of his aristocratic nose. Her body was slender but rounded in all the right places and disturbing in its femininity. The swell of her hips was outlined softly beneath the soft folds of her gown and her breasts, exposed just enough above the low neckline, hinted at their firm shapeliness. He had not been so intrigued by a woman in a long time. 'Will someone not introduce us?'

Beatrice stiffened as his challenging and impertinent eyes sharpened and narrowed in amusement. And did his gaze actually linger on her breasts pushing their way up out of her bodice, or was it only her confused imagination that made it seem that way?

With Henry Talbot by her side, Astrid glanced up at him shyly and said breathlessly, 'Oh, this is Beatrice, my cousin, Lord Chadwick. She is quite mad about horses. Indeed, she can think and talk of nothing else from morning till night. It comes as no surprise that she is interested in taking you up on your wager.'

Julius arched a brow, smiling. 'Beatrice?'

'I am Beatrice Fanshaw,' Beatrice provided, lifting her chin proudly and looking directly into his narrowed amber eyes. Her own were glowing with brilliance and fire, her gaze never wavering from his face as she awaited his reaction to her announcement.

In a split second his smile was wiped clean from his face and his eyes were now sharp and penetrating with interest and something that resembled shock. The young lady who had so intrigued him a moment before had suddenly taken on a whole new identity. 'Ah! Fanshaw! Of course. How very interesting. I do recall the name.'

'You should. My father was Sir James Fanshaw.'

'I remember your father. However, I was not aware that he had a daughter.' Already nettled by her cool attitude, Julius delivered his reply with a small bow and an exaggerated show of disdain. 'It is obvious you know who I am, Miss Fanshaw.'

'You are Julius Chadwick.' Her words were firm and measured as she failed to address him with the courtesy of his title. 'The same man who ruined my father.'

'And is that what all this is about? You are here to beg me to retrieve all that he lost?'

Something welled up in Beatrice, a powerful surge of emotion to which she had no alternative but to give full rein. It was as if she had suddenly become someone else, someone bigger and much stronger than the woman who had joined the party. Her eyes flashed as cold fury drained her face of colour and added a steely edge to her voice.

'Those who know me know that I never beg, Lord Chadwick, and by my oath I intend to take more from you than an old man's loss.' Her promise was made with an icy, threatening calmness.

Julius looked at her, his face a mask of indignation, but then he was so taken aback by her outburst that his superiority evaporated. He stared down at the lovely young woman whose fury turned her eyes to a darker green.

'Dear me, Miss Fanshaw. I can see I will have to watch my step.'

'More than that, my lord. You are the man directly responsible for my father's death.'

Her attack took him so completely by surprise that he looked startled for a moment and more than a little uneasy, then a hard gleam entered his eyes, for his conscience was sore with the irony of trying to protect the reputation of his own undeserving father while—at least where Miss Fanshaw was concerned—damaging his own. 'I don't think so,' he replied, aware that those around them had fallen silent and were watching and listening with an uneasy, open curiosity. 'Your father brought about his own death.' He smiled. 'It was easy to beat him. He had no skill when it came to cards.'

'Then why did you allow him to stake Larkhill? You certainly didn't want it—indeed, you have not spent a penny piece on it since, for it is crumbling with neglect. Do you enjoy taking things from people who are weaker than you—humbling people? In my opinion that is the mark of a coward.' She took a step towards him and was pleased to see him take a step back.

Not discouraged and ignoring the gasp that went up from the crowd, he gave a bark of laughter. 'You call me a coward?'

She smiled. 'Only a coward would do what you did. You knew he couldn't win. You knew his loss would destroy him. Didn't that worry you?'

He shook his head slowly. 'Not unduly. He was a grown man. He knew perfectly well what he was doing when he staked a house and estate that was already mortgaged up to the hilt.'

Beatrice stared at him in disbelief. 'I might have known you would say something like that to discredit my father, but I do not believe you.'

He shrugged. 'You may believe what you like, but it is true. I do not lie. I did not find out myself until later—when I had to find the finance to pay off the mortgage.'

Beatrice looked at him directly, finding what he said hard to believe and wondering what sort of man this Julius Chadwick actually was. 'My father was a man without deceit, a man you could trust, who had fallen on hard times. And you, Lord Chadwick, took advantage of his weakened state. Larkhill meant more to me and my mother than to be put on a gambling table in a seedy gentleman's club.'

'It was a private gentleman's club,' he countered, needlessly provocative. 'There was nothing seedy about it.'

'A gambler would say that. So now you have two homes.'

'Three, actually.'

Momentarily thrown, she stared at him in amazement. 'Three? How can one person live in three places at once?'

'I don't. I travel a lot,' he stated by way of explanation. 'Miss Fanshaw, must I remind you that we have an audience. Might I suggest that you lower your tone? You embarrass us both with your show of emotion. I understand your antagonism towards me, which must have increased a thousandfold as you have allowed it to fester over the years. Indeed, I would feel very much the same were the situation reversed.'

'I'm glad you understand,' she uttered scathingly, 'although it doesn't alter the way I feel. I am not like my father. If you are a courageous man, you will allow me to accept your wager.'

'If nothing else, you are forward and recklessly bold, Miss Fanshaw.'

'I always believe in being direct and I enjoy walking on the wild side. I am sure you find it shocking and unfeminine that I have interest in things beyond *petit point* and fashion, but that's the way I am.'

'I do, but in your case I will overlook your unfeminine interests—but will your aunt, Lady Standish?'

'I don't doubt she will flay me alive for daring to intimate that I am anything less than a perfect lady. But a perfect lady I am not and never will be. You are staying at Larkhill?'

'I am. I've been out of the country for several months; now I'm back I intend spending more time in London. I found the time was ripe to visit Larkhill, to look over the property and decide what is to be done.' A subtle smile curved his lips. 'There are many factors which might influence how long I stay.'

'Then I hope you enjoy your stay. So, Lord Chadwick, what do you say? Will you accept my challenge?'

'I am a huntsman, Miss Fanshaw. I enjoy the chase.'

'Aye, and once the prey is caught, the sport is over. You should know better than to gamble against my good friend Julius at any game of skill,' Lord Roderick Caruthers warned. Like everyone else he had been listening to the interesting altercation between these two.

Beatrice looked at Lord Caruthers coolly. 'Lord Chadwick and I are not acquainted, sir, so how could

I possibly know that? But I am sure that if he is as skilled as you say he is, then he will have no qualms about me taking him up on his challenge.'

Chapter Two

Julius smiled at her words. His smile was the same smile that caused Astrid to flush and tremble—but it would take more than a smile from Julius Chadwick to have the same effect on Beatrice.

'So, Miss Fanshaw, are you really serious about taking me up on my wager?'

'I would not have put myself forward if I wasn't—unless you have an aversion to accepting a challenge from a woman, afraid of how it will look should I win.'

'Win?' His lips curved in mockery. 'Do you seriously think you can beat me?'

'I stand as good a chance as anyone else.'

'I see. Then the answer is, no, I do not have an aversion to a race between us.'

Common sense told Julius not to encourage her, and yet, confronted by her challenge, he was intrigued and was unable to resist the temptation. He was compelled to take her on, merely to see how well she could ride. He stared at her profile as she turned her head slightly, tracing with his gaze the beautiful lines of her face, the curved brush of her lustrous dark eyelashes. Yes, Miss Fanshaw was quite extraordinarily lovely. She had an untamed quality running in dangerous undercurrents just below the surface and a wild freedom of spirit that found its counterpart in his own hot-blooded, temperamental nature.

'The place and the distance will be of your choosing and we shall meet at eight o'clock tomorrow morning.' He turned to George. 'Arrange it, will you, George? Who will you place your bets on?'

George laughed. 'Now there's a challenge in itself. Were it anyone else, Julius, I would certainly back you, but be warned. My cousin has a special affinity with the equine species, preferring them to people. She would rather throw a saddle over a horse than attend a ball. She'll do anything for a dare and is a demon on a horse. Her own is no dainty mare, but a brute of an animal—a gelding. On such an impressive mount she stands to win.'

Beatrice threw Lord Chadwick a challenging look. 'Perhaps Lord Chadwick considers it most improper for a young lady to ride a gelding.'

An eyebrow jutted upwards. 'Young lady? My dear Miss Fanshaw, you are the most controversial and exciting woman I have ever met in my life; I suspect that your vitality is such that you are a menace to everyone you meet. It does not surprise me in the least that you ride a gelding.' A roguish grin tugged at his lips. 'If you told me you rode an elephant, I would believe you. As it is I shall take my chance.'

The wager had attracted a good deal of attention and others began to place their bets.

'I'll back you, Chadwick,' someone shouted. 'Fifty guineas you win.'

Julius turned and grinned as interest in the race began to mount. 'See what is happening, Miss Fanshaw. You have fallen among desperate gamblers.'

'I already knew that before I accepted your challenge,' she uttered, not bothering to hide her sarcasm. He gave her a cold look, but chose not to comment on her provocative remark.

'Seventy-five guineas,' another voice shouted.

'A hundred.'

'My diamond necklace,' a lady from the back of the crowd piped up.

And so it went on until the stakes reached heady proportions. But neither participant was listening as they continued to watch each other warily. Beatrice's gaze was ensnared by the glittering sheen of the amber eyes.

'And us, Miss Fanshaw?' Julius murmured. 'What will we forfeit?'

There was a deathly hush. From beneath the gazebo Lady Standish watched what was happening in appalled, stony silence, unable to believe her niece's shocking behaviour. The look in her eyes was as potent as a spoken curse.

'I say the winner names the forfeit,' Beatrice suggested.

Julius nodded. 'I think you have planned this, Miss Fanshaw.'

Beatrice raised her chin a notch. 'You don't *have* to agree to race against me, Lord Chadwick. Indeed, I don't know why I entertained such a notion.'

He looked at her directly and she felt her breath come a little short. 'Oh, I think you do,' he said quietly. 'I think you know *exactly* what you want and you will stop at nothing to get it. I read people well, Miss Fanshaw, and I think you have the ability to be absolutely single minded. You know very well why you entertained this notion.'

Her smile was one of thin sarcasm. 'You do a lot of thinking, Lord Chadwick.'

'All the time.'

'If I am as you say, then indirectly it is your doing.'

'I am sorry to find that after all these years you still carry a grudge. And now all I need to do is discover what forfeit you will ask of me, and the only way I can do that is to race against you—unless you will indulge me and tell me now.'

She tossed her head haughtily. To forgo propriety and do what one wished was quite liberating. 'No, not before the end of the race.'

'Very well. Until after the race.'

There were loud guffaws from the crowd. 'Careful, Julius,' Roderick Caruthers shouted. 'Be careful what you commit yourself to. You are a gentleman, remember, and gentlemen never renege on their word.'

He grinned. 'I'd better win, then.'

'And should I win, you will give me your word to honour the forfeit?' Beatrice asked, holding his gaze.

'I do.'

Her expression was innocent, but her eyes were hard to read. She raised her brows slightly, and said, 'I intend to hold you to that.'

'So the wager is made—but your forfeit? I think I have guessed, which wasn't too difficult considering the circumstances. Though it is immaterial since you cannot win.' Julius's grin broadened and he looked at her knowingly, holding up one hand. 'Don't tell me. Larkhill.'

Beatrice gave him a level look. 'Oh, no. Believe me, Lord Chadwick, nothing I could ask from you would be as fine or as grand as Larkhill.'

His eyes narrowed. 'I am intrigued. Tell me.'

'Like I said, not until after the race—although if your horse is as splendid as you would have everyone believe, then I might well be tempted to take it from you.'

'Oh, no, lady—my horse is an exception. I have waited too long to get a horse by its sire—a winner of some top races—and I am not about to lose him now. But why are we discussing this? I shall win.'

Beatrice smiled almost sweetly. 'Then you have nothing to worry about, have you, Lord Chadwick?'

'You must be confident, to accept my challenge.'

'I would not be doing this if I wasn't confident that I could beat you.'

Beatrice would make sure that Lord Chadwick could not refuse the forfeit she would ask of him if she won the race, even while telling herself that what she was doing was foolish. Her eyes held his and she knew he would read her absolute determination to go ahead with this wager—foolish or not.

'Cousin Beatrice is no docile, ordinary young lady,' George laughingly told Lord Chadwick. 'She is a mannerless hoyden—a dark horse if ever there was is how I would describe her.' He paused with a small private smile and a playful wink at Beatrice. 'Dark horse, maybe, but she is also clever and cunning and always dangerous.'

'Really,' Julius uttered quietly. 'A woman after my own heart.'

Beatrice was so close, she had to tilt her head up to meet his eyes. 'Oh, no, Lord Chadwick,' she countered coldly. 'You can keep your heart. That is the last thing I want from you.'

He regarded her long and hard before replying. 'I shall. My heart has always been in my own safe keeping, and there it will remain. Safe. But you intrigue me, Miss Fanshaw. Already I am wondering what I have let myself in for. And I was beginning to imagine you would become unseated at the first hurdle.'

'Don't you believe it,' George told him. 'Beatrice has the best pair of hands I've ever seen. She knows horses—could whisper a horse out of a field. But should you win, Julius, what forfeit will you ask of her?'

Lord Chadwick looked at George as he considered his question, but his penetrating gaze returned to Beatrice.

Curious as to what his reply would be, Beatrice waited expectantly. The glow in her face now faded. She straightened her back.

At length he said, 'As to that, I have not yet decided. But I will, and she may not like it when I have.' He bowed his head ever so slightly. 'Until tomorrow, Miss Fanshaw. I look forward to our race.'

Beatrice had not imagined confronting Lord Chadwick would require such an effort. On reaching the house her stomach was still tied in knots and her heart had yet to find its customary rhythm. Nervousness was not a reaction to which she was normally susceptible. There was no place in her scheme of things for faint heartedness, and this afternoon she had taken the first step to reclaiming Larkhill. Recalling how Lord Chadwick had looked at her with open admiration, her lips quirked. In the circumstances, it was a definitely heartening thought.

She was about to cross the hall to the stairs when a voice rang out, halting her.

'A word, Beatrice.'

She turned to face her aunt, her brow furrowed with a twinge of premonition. She got the familiar feeling that trouble was afoot, and as she noted her aunt's sharp look, that piercing glance told her plainly that some kind of storm was brewing. It was plain that Lady Standish was both appalled and incensed over her niece's conduct.

'Beatrice! How dare you conduct yourself in this manner? How dare you? And to publicly take Lord

Chadwick to task over past grievances was outrageous—an absolute disgrace.'

Beatrice's green eyes flashed, but when she spoke she managed to moderate her tone. 'I meant no offence, Aunt Moira. Truly.'

'I know about the wager between the two of you and you forget yourself. Not only do you shame yourself, but me and our good name. I will not have it. You make yourself a disgrace. Such freakish sports are not fitting for a young lady of quality. I will not have the reputation of this family jeopardised by your folly.'

'I'm sorry if I have upset you, Aunt Moira, but I never could resist a challenge.'

'A challenge? Beatrice, this is *me* you are talking to, not a fool. You haven't the first inkling of social graces. In that I have tried and failed, for you were determined not to learn. By your activities you encourage Lord Chadwick. I see that. Why do you always take such delight in being disobedient?'

Tired of being told what to do, Beatrice averted her eyes, trying to keep her anger and frustration at bay, but rebellion was bubbling away inside her. 'Because I am old enough to look after myself.'

Lady Moira appeared undaunted. 'In society no woman is old enough to look after herself in certain circumstances—and you are just eighteen years old.'

'I am old enough and can look after myself. There's not one weak bone in my body.' Her fingers curled tightly into her palm as she tried to remain calm. 'I have enough good sense in my head to know what I am doing.'

'That is where we differ, Beatrice. Had you any sense at all, you would not have entered into this disgraceful wager with Lord Chadwick.' Her eyes narrowing, she thrust her head forwards and glared knowingly at this disappointing niece of hers. 'What do you hope for? To push Astrid out of her place? To supplant her in Lord Chadwick's attention? Though this was supposed to be Astrid's birthday party, you have stolen her attention. In fact, you have eclipsed Astrid in success. There is some doubt that Lord Chadwick will offer for her now. Are you jealous of your cousin, Beatrice? Is that it?'

A frown crossed Beatrice's beautiful face, then her anger fled and she knew a moment of shame. 'I am not jealous of Astrid. Please do not think that. I love Astrid as a sister and I would never do anything that would cause her pain. Astrid doesn't have a place in Lord Chadwick's affections, Aunt Moira, that is plain to see. You wanted him to notice her. He was polite. You saw what you wanted to see.'

'And you hate him—remember?' she pointed out coldly.

'Yes, I do.'

'Then I would have thought you would have wanted to steer well clear of him. And the wager? I do not believe in flouting propriety in this way. It is the most disgraceful thing I have ever heard in my life.'

'I am sorry if it has caused you distress, Aunt, but the wager is made. I cannot go back on my word.'

'And what do you hope to get out of it—if you win, that is,' she sneered, 'which I very much doubt, since by all accounts no one handles a horse quite like Lord Chadwick?'

'Then perhaps he has met his match. I accept that what I am doing is a risk.'

'Risk?' Lady Standish gave her a thin, sarcastic smile. 'I think that is putting it mildly, Beatrice.'

Beatrice lifted her head and looked squarely into her aunt's eyes. 'If I win and Lord Chadwick agrees to my forfeit, not only will I be able to return to Larkhill, I will also have the means to make it one of the finest houses in the county. You will also have me off your hands for good, which I know you will look on as a blessing.'

'That is the most foolish thing I have ever heard. This time you have gone too far. You will not do it. Do you hear me? Don't you dare disobey me. I will not have it. I will not be accused of being unable to keep my niece in check and made a laughing stock. Now go to your room and think good and hard about what I have said.'

'I will, Aunt Moira.' On that note Beatrice excused herself, leaving a thoroughly shocked Aunt Moira staring after her.

Beatrice returned to the party as dusk was beginning to fall. After an hour spent talking to friends and acquaintances, she went in search of Astrid. She found her listening to the musicians. They were all dressed alike in crimson coats and white trousers, seated on a rostrum hung with coloured lanterns. Astrid turned her head when Beatrice stood beside her and smiled. Her eyes sparkled and a pretty flush coloured her cheeks as she sipped a glass of lemonade cooled with crushed ice.

'There you are, Beatrice. I thought you had disappeared for good.'

'Are you enjoying your party, Astrid?'

'Oh, yes. Mama has gone to a lot of trouble and expense to make it right. Although I do find it all rather awe-inspiring,' she admitted, envious of her cousin's self-assurance.

Beatrice nodded in agreement. Looking around, she saw couples wandering away to indulge in a little starlit privacy. Lord Chadwick was watching her from across the stretch of lawn that lay like a rich velvet carpet between them. He raised his glass and bowed briefly, his smile both approving and challenging as his gaze from beneath hooded lids swept over her with practised scrutiny. She turned away to listen to what Astrid was saying.

'George is paying a good deal of attention to Leonora Fenton, Sir Philip Fenton's daughter. He always does. He's never said anything, but I think he's quite taken with her. What do you think, Beatrice?'

Beatrice glanced towards where George conversed with a slender, extremely attractive young woman in a yellow high-waisted gown. 'She's very pretty. But I wonder if your mother would agree to a match between them.'

'I don't see why not. George is of an age to choose his own wife. Miss Fenton has all the required requisites—title and money—so I don't see why Mama should have any objections. But come, Beatrice,' she said, linking her arm through her cousin's, 'I care nothing to standing still. Let's circulate. I want to have a word with you about this wager you have made with Lord Chadwick. It is quite insane—you know that, don't you? Mama is furious.'

'She's already spoken to me about it, but I know what I am doing. I will not be bullied out of it. I have no intention of backing out.'

'But—you could get hurt. Lord Chadwick is not the sort of man to take kindly to being bested by a woman.'

Beatrice stared at her. 'Bested? Yes, I might well beat him. I certainly intend to try. But does the forfeit I will demand of him not concern you?'

'No. When you accepted his wager I heard you tell him that you will not ask him to return Larkhill to you, but I suspect it features somewhere in the forfeit.'

'Yes it does. I wanted to speak to you about the race, Astrid. Your opinion matters to me very much. Aunt Moira has her sights set on Lord Chadwick as a serious contender for your hand in marriage. Will it upset you very much to see us together, racing hell for leather against each other?'

Astrid paused and turned to her cousin, her attitude one of calm resolve. 'Be assured, Beatrice, that whatever aspirations Mama has of my future husband, it will definitely not be Lord Chadwick. I will not marry him, not even to appease Mama.'

They carried on walking. Astrid said nothing else. Beatrice had expected something—a word of blame, of disappointment, of condemnation for the manner in which she had asserted herself in Lord Chadwick's eyes, but she had nothing from Astrid but a calm look which was somehow full of relief...and gratitude.

Why, Beatrice thought, seeing her gentle cousin truly, as if for the first time, *I have done her a favour.* Astrid really didn't want to marry Lord Chadwick. She never did. She was being pushed into it by her forceful mama, and she, Beatrice, was giving her a way out.

Astrid glanced across at a young man sitting on a bench in the shadow of a spouting fountain. 'Will you excuse me?' she said a little breathlessly, excitement leaping to her eyes and brightness lighting her face as she spoke. 'I can see Henry and I simply must speak to him.'

Beatrice watched her hurry away. Normally Astrid was always far too timid and serious to be giddy. And yet when Henry Talbot was near it was like the sun coming out after a dark period and she suddenly became light-hearted, foolish and gay. With a smile Beatrice turned and sauntered in the direction of the house. Her step was light as she walked slowly along a walkway lined with a profusion of fragrant pink roses that clambered all over trellising. It was a tunnel of shadow, broken at intervals by warm squares of light from lanterns hanging in the trees. With a contented sigh she closed her eyes and listened to the murmur of distant voices, a wistful expression on her lovely face. It was a warm night, heavy and sweet with summer scents.

She intended to find a quiet shady place on the terrace to sit a while before going to her room. The warmth of the evening caressed her bare shoulders and a light breeze stirred the skirts of her gown.

'Well, well, Miss Fanshaw! So we meet again.' Julius was ahead of her and, seeing her walking alone along the privacy of the arched walkway, he had paused to watch her, completely captivated by the look on her face. This was not the face of the young woman who had boldly challenged him to race his horse against hers earlier. Then her haughty manner had marked her as strong of character whereas now, with her eyes closed and a gentle smile on her lips, there was a softness about her, an elusive gentleness that declared her to be as fragile and vulnerable as the roses that clambered about them.

Clearly she was a woman of ever-changing moods and subtle contradictions, and while her physical beauty first arrested the attention, it was this spectrum, this bewildering, indefinable quality that held him captive. A strange sweet melting feeling softened his innermost core without warning, the place in him that he usually kept as hard as steel.

His appearance pulled Beatrice from the strange spell that had seemed to enclose her. She started, alarmed by the unexpected greeting, and opened her eyes. He appeared too suddenly for her to prepare herself, so the heady surge of pleasure she experienced on seeing him again was clearly evident, stamped like an unbidden confession on her lovely face.

Stepping in front of her, he towered above her. His smile was full of gentle mockery when he said, 'Are you about to retire, Miss Fanshaw?'

Beneath his impassive gaze Beatrice stood perfectly still, refusing to blush or look away, her delicately beautiful face framed by a halo of golden hair—a dainty image of fragility standing before a man who dwarfed her.

'I thought I might.'

'A sensible move, I would say. I fear if you party too long into the night you will not do full justice to the race tomorrow.'

'Your concern—if that is what it is—for my state of health is quite touching, Lord Chadwick. But worry not. If I were to party till dawn, I would still beat you hands down.'

'Your courage and confidence are to be admired, but you are going to be disappointed. I'm afraid the outcome is inevitable.'

'I don't think so,' she remarked.

'And here was I thinking you might wish to retract your challenge.' He stared at her with impudent admiration, letting his gaze travel from her eyes to her mouth, then down to the swell of her breasts. Beatrice wished she had a shawl to cover herself, as she felt her cheeks grow hot beneath his scrutiny.

'My challenge stands. Now be so kind as to step aside.'

He did as she bade, but she was not to be rid of him. As she continued to walk on he fell into step beside her.

'Will you return to the party?' he asked.

They had reached the terrace and she stopped and turned to him. 'I might, but then I might not.' Taking a deep breath, she looked up into the night sky and saw the moon, a new moon, a thin sickle of a moon. Seeing it for the first time, she closed her eyes.

Beside her Julius followed her gaze, his eyes on the slender sickle. 'Have you made a wish?' he asked.

Opening her eyes, she nodded.

'Then I hope the new moon brings you luck.'

'So do I, but I believe you make your own luck in this world.'

'That is a very cynical view, Miss Fanshaw.'

'I have a cynical outlook on life, Lord Chadwick.' She gazed up at the stars beginning to twinkle. 'I love looking at the sky at night,' she murmured. 'There are so many stars up there. To some people all the constellations just look like a jumble of stars, but they're not. See that bright one over there?'

Julius continued to look up, as if he, too, found something of interest there.

'That's Jupiter.'

'So it is—and over there is the Great Bear—and you see that faint smudge,' he said, pointing at the sky, 'that is the Andromeda constellation, which is the nearest galaxy to our own Milky Way and was named after the mythological princess Andromeda. The seven stars of the Plough are the easiest to make out, which is of the constellation Ursa Major.'

Beatrice laughed. 'You are very knowledgeable about the stars, Lord Chadwick. Do you make a study of the galaxies yourself?'

'I spend a lot of my time travelling. On board ship the nights are long and one spends many hours on deck, looking at the sky. The northern sky—which you are looking at—is very different from the southern sky and so is the sky around the equatorial zone. I'm sure you would find it interesting.'

'I'm sure I would—if I ever get the opportunity to travel. It never occurred to me that the sky would look different in other parts of the world. Do you think anyone lives up there, that any of those stars are inhabited with people like us?'

'I don't know. What do you think?'

'I don't—not really. But then, it would be arrogant of us to assume that out of all those thousands and millions of stars the Earth is the only planet where life exists. It's like saying the Earth is the centre of the universe and everything revolves around it.' She dragged her gaze from the sky and looked at him when she heard him chuckle. Her lips broke into a smile. 'What is it? Why do you laugh?'

'I am astonished. Since when did young ladies begin studying astronomy?'

'I don't know about the others, but this particular young lady began as soon as she learnt to read.' He was smiling, a smile she found almost endearing. He did seem to have a way about him and she could not fault any woman for falling under his spell, for she found to her amazement that her heart was not so distantly detached as she might have imagined it to be. Even his deep mellow voice seemed like a warm caress over her senses. For all the animosity she felt for him, she could not deny what a fine specimen of a man he was.

He took her hand to kiss it. He looked so relaxed

that she found herself responding to him. Then a glint
of mischief in his eyes reminded her of who he was.
Shaking off the effects of his winning smile, she took
herself mentally in hand and snatched her hand free.
She tossed her head proudly, but Julius Chadwick was
undaunted by her show of indignation. He touched her
arm very gently and reached so close that she could
smell the sharp scent of his cologne.

'Please forgive me,' he murmured, softly and with
disconcerting sincerity. 'I was boorish in my behaviour
to you earlier when you accepted my wager. It was
never my intention and now I heartily beg your pardon.'

Beatrice was astonished. She stared into his deep
amber eyes, looking for the mockery, the veiled contempt. She found neither. 'No more than I was,' she
conceded.

'You were angry and I understand the reason and
you intend to punish me for it. Will you not tell me that
I am forgiven?'

Beatrice found herself weakening before his smile.
Her own smile came slowly. 'Very well. You are forgiven.'

'Then I am once more a happy man and I look forward to seeing you tomorrow.' He raised her fingers
to his lips and pressed a light kiss on them. As he did
so he surreptitiously pressed a small object into the
palm of her hand. 'I would like you to have this. It is
just a small token of my respect and admiration,' he
said. 'May it serve to remind you of happier times and
of the value I place on your forgiveness.'

Beatrice uttered her thanks and watched him turn

and stride away. When he was out of sight she opened
her hand and looked down at the small object he had
placed there. Only then did her brief softening turn to
humiliation. The colour drained from her face. Damn
him, she thought. He had used subtle trickery and flattery on her and she had fallen for it and allowed herself
to become as stupid and gullible as all those silly girls
who simpered and followed him around like sheep.

What he had given her was a gold signet ring she
had last seen on her father's finger. She had not given
it a thought during all the years she had been without
him, and now she knew that this, too, must have been
among the things he had taken from her father. It did
remind her of happier times, but it also reminded her
of how those times had cruelly ended. With the death
of her mother following so soon on her father's suicide,
the deep, dark void of hollowness and sorrow was complete.

Wounded and angry, she could not even begin to
imagine the desperation that had driven her father to
part with his ring, but as she stared down at it she swore
she would make Lord Chadwick pay most dearly for
what he had done to her. She would not rest until she
had retrieved everything her father had lost to Julius
Chadwick. Nothing would stand in her way after she
had come this far.

The dew was still on the grass when Beatrice headed
for the stables the next morning with her riding crop
tucked underneath her arm. She arrived to a great fuss
of excitement. She had done as her aunt had said and

thought good and hard about the wager, but it had made no difference. Her mind was made up. Respect was everything to her aunt and what her niece was doing would have a damaging effect on her own standing in society, but in the end nothing was changed. Beatrice would not back out now.

Everyone had heard about the race and had come to watch. Major had been brought out of his stable and tacked up. The stable lad was giving his powerful haunches and glossy neck one last polish. He was by the mounting block, arching his neck and pawing the ground, waiting for his mistress.

The groom knew of her aversion to the side saddle and that she preferred the masculine way of riding astride, so Major had been tacked up appropriately. No one was surprised to see Beatrice wearing her breeches, for it was a familiar sight.

As spry as a young athlete, she swung herself up on to Major's back as George rode towards her.

'Is it all arranged?' she asked him as they rode together out of the stable yard, her horse so fresh and eager that she had to hold him in check.

'I have planned the route to your satisfaction, I hope.' Of an understanding nature, George glanced sideways at her, his brow creased with a worried frown. 'I'm sorry Astrid cannot watch the race. I know how much she wanted to, but I'm afraid Mama is incensed by your acceptance of Lord Chadwick's wager and has forbidden her to attend.'

Unmoved, Beatrice looked straight ahead. With his shock of fair hair and bright blue eyes, many were the times when she had thanked God for her fun-loving, easy-mannered, handsome cousin. He had been her friend for as long as she could remember, and she really didn't know how she would have coped without him. She would never forget the lack of welcome at Standish House from Aunt Moira, and things had not improved. She had soon learned that her aunt's love was reserved solely for her own children and that there was none for her.

'I am sorry that Astrid cannot watch the race, George—I know how much she wanted to. I am also sorry about the way Aunt Moira feels about me, but I cannot change that.' At these words George glanced at her. How typical of him to be concerned for her, she thought. She smiled to reassure him and said, 'Don't worry, George, I've grown used to it. As for the wager, it is done and too much is at stake for me to pull out now. Besides, I would not give Lord Chadwick the satisfaction. How much do you know about him?'

'Not much, as it happens. I only met him myself when he arrived back in London—from India, I believe. He is very rich, but there was a time when his family were destitute. Equipped with a clever mind, through his own endeavours and gambling everything on a series of investments, which paid off for him again and again, he brought his family out of penury.'

'If he used the same gambling methods he used on my father, then I do not care for them. It does him no credit,' Beatrice retorted bitterly, at the same time grudgingly impressed by his success. 'I suppose if he's as rich as all that, then there's little wonder people court his favour.'

'They do, but his success has come at a price. Some years ago tragedy hit his family—I'm not sure of the details. Because of it and to guard his privacy, he spends most of his time abroad.'

'I see. Tell me about the circuit.'

'It will start and end at the gate in the lower meadow. You will both do a full circuit of Larkhill, riding over the common and open ground past the village, up to the woods and through the park, where you will pick up the trail back to the meadow. It's punishing and steep in places. The full circuit will take an hour or more, but it shouldn't be difficult since you have ridden it almost every day. The hardest part will be the steep ride up the woods.'

'Have you familiarised Lord Chadwick with the route?'

'Yes. He rode it earlier and he's up for it if you are.'

'Of course. I can trust Major to handle it.'

'Lord Chadwick is already at the starting point— along with a hundred others from the house party who have come to watch and to collect their winnings.'

'No doubt everyone is expecting him to win.'

'Absolutely—although there are several who have laid bets on you.'

Beatrice looked sideways at her cousin. 'Where is your bet placed, George? I trust you remember that I am family and that you owe your loyalty to me. Were you brave enough to risk your money on me?'

Kicking his horse into a gallop, he went ahead. 'That

is for me to know and for you to find out,' he shouted laughingly over his shoulder.

The reception party was larger than Beatrice had anticipated. The entire meadow was filled with all types of people from house guests to grooms, footmen and stable hands and locals from the nearby village. The sun shone down on fashionable ladies beneath bobbing parasols, feathered hats and a colourful array of silk turbans. Curricles and chases were everywhere and those who wished to follow the race were on horseback. Everyone jockeyed for the best position, all animatedly discussing the forthcoming race.

Atop her spirited mount, Beatrice looked radiant, undeniably beautiful, as only she could do when there was something she wanted badly enough and had set her mind to getting it. She slanted an admiring look at her opponent as he approached leading his mount. He wore a tanned riding coat, a pair of buckskin breeches and highly polished brown boots.

Julius also wore a look of unconcealed appreciation on his handsome face as he surveyed her perched atop a raw-boned gelding, a giant of a horse, a glossy chestnut, its coat gleaming almost red. She presented a slender figure and it seemed incomprehensible that she could control the great beast. She met his gaze squarely, her face bright with invitation and challenge.

'Good morning,' he greeted politely. 'It's a good turnout. All it's short of to make it a fair are the acrobats and tents. Are you still up for this, Miss Fanshaw—or perhaps you would prefer pistols at twenty paces?' he teased as he leapt on to his mount with the physical prowess of an athlete.

Beatrice lifted her head, intending to treat him with cool formality, but he looked so relaxed atop his powerful horse and his smile was so disarming that she almost smiled. Confident, her expression open and her green eyes direct, she said, 'Of course I am up to it, Lord Chadwick—we can try pistols at twenty paces if I lose, which I have no intention of doing.'

'Then if a duel to the death is to follow, you'd better win if you value your life.'

She laughed lightly. 'Not only am I a competent horsewoman, I am also a crack shot, so whichever method we use, you stand to lose.'

His horse drew Beatrice's eye. It was a beautiful dappled grey gelding, its coat as smooth as silk. With sharp features, bright, intelligent eyes and a perfectly arched neck, it really was a beautiful animal, with powerful legs and shoulders. Her opponent was watching her closely and he saw her eyes gleam with appreciation.

'He is a splendid animal, is he not, Miss Fanshaw?'

'He certainly is,' she agreed longingly. 'As I told you yesterday, had I not already decided on the forfeit, I would be more than happy to take that horse from you.'

'Never. I will never part with him,' he laughingly declared.

They rode towards the open gate to the meadow where George was waiting to get the race under way. It was a bright day, but not too hot. The haymakers in the field next to the meadow leaned on their scythes and watched them pass side by side, doffing their caps as they saw the noble bearing of the Marquess, their hearts warming at the sight of their own Miss Fanshaw.

Julius slanted her a look. 'It's still not too late to pull out.'

Without looking at him, Beatrice beamed upon the crowd. 'Of course I'm not going to pull out. Indeed, I couldn't disappoint so many earnest cavaliers who have placed their bets on me.'

'Don't let that put you off. They'll get their money back.'

Now she did look at him. 'That's not the point. I am honour bound to take your wager. Besides I can think of nothing that would please me more than to beat you.' She shot him a suspicious, mischievous glance. 'Unless you have cold feet, my lord, and *you* would like to pull out?'

Julius trapped her gaze in his. 'Not a bit of it. I'm looking forward to it, though the course has many pitfalls.'

Beatrice took in the hard planes of his face, the subtle aggression in the line of his jaw, and the clear intent that stared at her from the depths of his amber eyes. A slight trembling sensation skittered over her skin. Ignoring it, she smiled. 'I dare say there will be many distractions along the way, but I am familiar with every one of them.'

'Then the fight is on. I promise you a hard race,' Julius called over his shoulder as he trotted ahead.

Maybe so, Beatrice thought, eyeing his back through

narrowed eyes. But with everything to play for, she
would win.

At the drop of George's handkerchief and with the
roar of the crowd, the two horses lunged forwards. The
two riders were galloping at full speed, crouched low
over the horses' necks. Neck and neck they left the
meadow and thundered across the common to open
spaces and up the steep track towards the woods.
One glance as they cleared a fence assured Julius that
Beatrice Fanshaw was indeed a skilled horsewoman.

Both horses held their paces well up the long, punishing slope, then raced across the rough ground at
the edge of the woods, where the undergrowth was
home to badgers and foxes. Her head down to avoid
low branches that might sweep her out of the saddle,
Beatrice kept a careful lookout for loose rocks, dangerous, treacherous roots and slippery puddles which
the sun was unable to reach and dry out. Major fell
behind Lord Chadwick's horse. Both horses were blow-
ing foam as they crested the hill. The track now lead
down to circle Larkhill.

Leaning forwards like a jockey to get every inch of
speed from Major, urging him on harder and harder,
Beatrice was after Lord Chadwick in a mad, down-
ward dash. The hooves pounded, sending divots of
earth up behind. She urged Major onwards, then there
was a giant hedge before her, white with summer blos-
som. His body flowing easily with his horse's stride,
Lord Chadwick held the advantage and cleared it
first. Beatrice felt Major's hind quarters bunching up
beneath her and with one giant leap she cleared it with

an effortless, breezy unconcern and hit the ground on the other side. Lord Chadwick glanced around and waved his hand, laughing jubilantly on seeing her several lengths behind. With a laugh in her own throat, Beatrice recovered and was off again, pounding into her fastest gallop once more.

Racing across the soft parkland grass, Lord Chadwick was just ahead of her, his attention fixed on winning the race. But Beatrice was gaining on him. She could feel the ripple of her hair as it loosed its pins and laughed recklessly to feel the wind in her face. Major's ears were back to hear her laugh, then forward as they came to another hedge with a ditch before it. She checked only for a moment and then they soared over it as one. She could smell the scent of summer flowers and crushed woodbine as Major's hooves clipped the top of the hedge and then they were moving on, even faster.

With the meadow and the finishing post within sight, there were only two lengths between them now and with a surge of energy, knowing exactly what his mistress wanted, Major, confident, trusting and elated, sailed past Lord Chadwick's beautiful grey, the crowd shouting, 'Go on, Miss Beatrice!' They flew past the winning post, at the point where they had started.

The crowd erupted, everyone laughing and cheering. Julius pulled his sweating horse to a halt and took in Beatrice's mud-spattered face and tumbling, tangled hair. Her golden skin was flushed with heat and excitement and her eyes—winner's eyes—were a sparkling, brilliant green. Dragging in a deep breath, exhilaration coursing through their veins, their wide smiles were mirror images. Julius couldn't help thinking that it was worth losing the race to see her laughing with such unfeigned delight. It was a warm, husky, rippling sound. His eyes locked on her lips, on the column of her slender throat. Instinctively his hands tightened on the reins.

He dismounted and went to her, placing his hand on her horse's foam-flecked neck. 'It was a good race. Quite splendid. You win. You rode well,' he conceded. 'Congratulations.'

She sprang from the saddle and stood close to him, her smile shamelessly triumphant. She was able to feel the heat of his body as he could feel hers. Fuelled by the breathless excitement of the race and her win, and the pleasure of standing so close to his strong manly body, she was aware that she was trembling.

It was a long time since Julius had enjoyed a ride as much, or as fast and unrestrained, with company that could handle the going as well as he. 'George was right. You're an intrepid horsewoman.'

Tossing her head, she laughed happily. 'I couldn't let you have the advantage of me now, could I?'

'I suppose not. So, Miss Fanshaw—the forfeit? What is it to be?' He stood without moving, awaiting her pleasure.

Unsmiling, she met his gaze and held it. He was looking at her with quiet patience—like a cat before a mousehole. Having puzzled on how to approach him, she chose directness, calming herself and saying, 'By his own actions my father gambled away everything he owned to you, causing him to lose his self-respect and his sanity. Now you are the only person I can think of who can help me.' She could sense he was wary, that his guard was up. There was a distance between her and this man which might never be closed. The startling amber eyes rested on her ironically.

'Of what help could I possibly be to you? What is it that I can do? My curiosity is aroused as to why you should go to all this trouble to take me up on my wager. I detect a certain recklessness in you, and if I know anything of feminine vanity it will be something of value that you think only I can give you. Will you please put us all out of our misery and tell us what it is?'

Beatrice drew a deep breath, then fired her salvo. 'That you marry me.'

Chapter Three

Julius was deaf to the collective gasps that followed this statement. Suddenly his entire body tensed. His fists clenched on his riding crop and then convulsively tightened. His features, about to relax into lines of arrogant satisfaction, froze and his face became a hard, cynical mask.

'Either you are carrying pity for me in losing the race to an unbelievable extreme, or else you're not playing with a full deck.'

'I am neither dim-witted nor crazy,' Beatrice stated, 'and pity has nothing to do with my reasons for wanting this marriage.'

'Marriage? Come, Miss Fanshaw. Think about it,' Lord Chadwick intoned in silken menace, as though his brooding eyes and smooth voice and his slight, dark smile could mesmerise any unsuspecting female. 'Admit it. You were having a lark.'

'Oh, no, Lord Chadwick. I never lark about, as those who know me will tell you.'

Gazing at her directly, Julius searched her face for some indication that she was joking, but her expression was completely unemotional. The soft pink lips were tantalising and gracefully curved, vaguely smiling. It stirred his imagination no small amount.

'Despite what you say, I think this really must be some kind of charade you play. You are asking me to do the impossible.' She remained silent, holding his gaze, and the fire that had sprung in her eyes convinced him that this was no charade and that she was deadly serious. 'Good God!' The words were exhaled slowly, but otherwise he simply stared at her. Then the corner of his mouth twisted wryly in a gesture that was not quite a smile. 'I suppose I left myself wide open for that.'

As everyone looked on with shocked, incredulous expressions, he smiled coolly. 'You must forgive me if I appear shocked. Naturally I am flattered by your proposal, Miss Fanshaw—in fact, I am quite blown away by it. Well—if this isn't the most peculiar marriage proposal I have ever heard. You are without doubt a most shameless, impulsive creature.' He was now amused. 'You expressed admiration for my horse earlier. Will you not take him instead?'

Beatrice shot him an indignant look, straightening her back. She recognised that her impromptu proposal had taken him completely unawares, but she played the game on. She shook her head, tossing the curling tresses that had become loosened by the race enticingly.

'Please have the good sense to take me seriously. Am I so ugly, sir, that you would prefer to rid yourself of your precious horse than to be wed to me?' His bold gaze stirred something deep within her and the sensation was not unpleasant.

'On the contrary,' he answered with an apparent ease he was far from feeling, 'your beauty so blinds me, I fear I must be led to the altar by the hand—should I accept your proposal. Now, about my horse. What do you say?'

Disregarding the sarcasm in his tone, Beatrice pinned a brilliant smile on her face. 'But I couldn't possibly take your horse. I recall you saying that you could not possibly part with him, in which case I would not dream of taking him from you. So I will settle for you instead. Come, Lord Chadwick? What do you say?' She flicked a glance around the bystanders within earshot. They were waiting to hear what he had to say with baited breath.

Julius let them wait a while longer as he faced the open challenge and measured the power of her will in her green gaze. There was plenty that he wanted to say, but not here, not now. In her resentment, if this young hellion thought to make a fool of him and believed she had him cornered, then she didn't know who she was dealing with. She would find out, but in the meantime he would play along with her game—for knowing how she held him in absolute contempt, that's all it could be. However, he was intrigued, all his senses completely involved with her. There could be worse things than being married to this beautiful, feisty firecracker.

'Then what can I say except that I consider myself fortunate to find myself betrothed to the most beautiful young lady in Essex.' Taking her hand, he raised it to his lips, and in so doing played the forfeit, as if young ladies proposed to gentlemen in this way every day of the week.

After a good deal of laughter, disbelief and hesitant congratulations, Julius and Beatrice, accompanied by a thoroughly bemused George, rode back to Standish House.

Clattering into the stable yard, the two men swung from their saddles and Julius tossed the reins to George, who led both horses away. Beatrice turned in the saddle, but before she had a chance to dismount, Julius's hands closed, strong and sure, about her waist. He lifted her as if she weighed no more than a child, lowering her slowly until her feet touched the ground.

Beatrice felt a blush tinge her cheeks—it was all she could do to meet his gaze fleetingly. It was the first time a man had touched her, had dared take such liberties.

'Thank you, my lord,' she said tightly, 'but the time has not yet come when I cannot get off a horse without assistance.'

Julius looked down at her, his tone slightly acid. 'The pleasure is all mine,' he said in clipped tones. 'Would you deprive me of that?' He stepped away from her. 'We need to talk.'

'Yes, we do.'

'Now would be as good a time as any.' His eyes

held hers. His face was a taut mask of controlled anger. For an instant he thought she would argue—he was relieved when she tightened her lips and inclined her head in apparent acquiescence. 'Come, let's take a walk.'

With studied calm Beatrice allowed him to place his hand on her elbow and escort her out of the stable yard and into a quiet part of the gardens. There was a controlled alertness in his manner, like that of a large cat, its strength ready to explode, but for the present docile. She was reminded of a large black panther she had seen on her visit to the zoo at the Tower of London with Astrid. In repose the panther's sinews had flexed and stretched in a fantastic rhythm of life that mesmerised. Julius Chadwick was slim, yet sturdy, and moved with almost sensuous grace. There was a sureness in his stride as if he carefully planned where to place each foot. At the moment he appeared relaxed, but Beatrice knew that he was aware of her and everything around him.

His grip felt strong and steely. A host of unfamiliar sensations passed along her nerves and her heart turned over distractingly. Such unexpected susceptibility was not, to her mind, a helpful development. She had never before been so afflicted—she hoped the effect would fade quickly. To her chagrin it did not go away when he removed his hand.

'I don't think we'll be disturbed here.'

His tone, clipped and dry, had Beatrice shifting her gaze to his face. He was a towering masculine presence in this quiet corner of the garden. 'What is it you want to say?' she asked, beginning to feel the first pangs of discomfort with the dark way he was regarding her, his gaze narrowed and assessing.

The corner of his mouth twisted wryly. 'Don't look so worried. I don't intend to harm you.' Looking down into her wide eyes, Julius saw speculation leap in their depths only to be replaced by wariness. His gaze locked on hers. 'I believe it's time for a little plain speaking.'

Beatrice stiffened. 'On what subject?'

'On the subject of your ridiculous forfeit—our future.' In an endeavour to disguise the tension that had gripped him and the way her nearness was affecting him, how he found it nigh impossible to look away from her golden hair lightened by the sun, her unfathomable green eyes and beckoning fragrance, he took a couple of steps away from her and gazed over the gardens. 'Am I *honestly* supposed to take you—I mean, this proposal—seriously?'

'I assure you, I am completely serious.'

'Then do you mind if I ask you a few questions?'

'Ask me anything you like.'

He tilted his head to one side, his face a mirror of bewilderment and disbelief. 'Are you, by any chance, under the influence of drink, Miss Fanshaw?'

'Absolutely not. I rarely drink anything stronger than watered-down wine.'

'Then am I supposed to believe that at some point you might have fallen in love with my larger-than-life reputation? That is what it would have to be since, to my knowledge, we have never met.'

'That scenario is as ludicrous as the one before it.'

'Then it can hardly come as a surprise to you to learn that I might have some objections to the proposal.'

'It wasn't a proposal.'

Julius's contemplation was steady. 'What was it, then? An order?'

'No.' The word was out before Beatrice had considered it. She tried to erase the admission with a casual wave of her hand. 'That is…'

'*Plain* speaking I believe I said. I *don't* like being forced. It goes against my grain. It is a most unwise thing for you to do. Most unwise. How dare you compromise me in this manner?'

Beatrice lifted her chin. 'I had hoped you were too much of a gentleman to renege on your word.'

'I don't have to be a genius to work out that you *planned* this. What concerns me now, what we need to discuss, is what comes next.' Leaning against a low stone wall and resting his arm on the top, letting his hand dangle limply, he caught her glittering gaze and held it. 'Tell me. When do you want the wedding to take place?'

'Why, I…' Feeling heat wash over her face, she faltered, taken off guard.

'Come now,' he pressed. 'Don't tell me you haven't thought it out. One day? Two days? A week—a month? How long?'

'As soon as possible was what I imagined.'

'Well, imagine again. If you *imagined* I'd meekly consent to this madness, you were far off track.'

'If you recall, my lord, you did consent to it. Very well, we will wed at your convenience, I suppose.'

'And *I* suppose that would be never.'

'You mean you *will* go back on your word?'

'You can bet your damned life there is nothing that would please me more. But were I to do that, I would blacken my reputation. The short of it is, Miss Fanshaw, I don't want to marry you—and if you know what is good for you, *you* wouldn't want to marry me either. Which is why I am leaving it up to you to cry off.'

She gaped at him. It was her turn to be nervous. 'Cry off?'

His eyes mocked her. 'That's what I said. It's very simple. You can let it be known that your forfeit was a joke, that you did it for a laugh, that you had no intention of holding me to my word. *You* will have to be the one to say it. Everyone must hear it from your own lips.'

'But I can't do that.'

'No? Pray tell me why not?'

'Because it would be a lie.'

'You mean you actually do want to marry me?'

She looked at him surreptitiously. 'Yes,' she replied—not that she had any idea what marriage to him would entail once she had caught him. 'I will not withdraw the forfeit.'

She would not beg him to wed her. Nor would she back down. But what a disaster she had made of it. She must have been out of her mind to think she could manage this. With that characteristic recklessness with which she tackled everything in her life, she had rushed to accept his wager without much thought to how he would react should she win the race and request his forfeit. But it was too late now. She had set the ball rolling, so to speak, and she would not back out now.

'When I named the forfeit, why did you concede by going so far as to announce our engagement?'

'Because at the time I did not take your proposal seriously. I thought you were playing some kind of mischievous game—that it was some light-hearted jest, that in some twisted way you were trying to get back at me for what you accuse me of doing to your father. I merely entered into the spirit of things. Naturally I believed you would withdraw your ridiculous proposal and it could be laughed off with no ill feeling.'

Beatrice met his look squarely. 'You do not know me. You were wrong to think that.' She glared at him. 'It was no twisted, mischievous game, Lord Chadwick. I have thought long and hard about this. Perhaps now you will realise that I was being deadly serious. Besides, after asking you to marry me in front of an audience, the scandal will be being broadcast throughout London as we speak. If you refuse to marry me, I will have ruined any chance I might have had of making a suitable marriage.'

'That is unfortunate for you, but it is entirely your own doing. It does not concern me.'

'I accept that, but you could do a lot worse than marry me. I have nothing of my own to bring to a marriage, but both my parents were well connected. I meet a gentleman's criteria of youth, good health, breeding,

I am reasonably pretty, or so I've been told, and I have an unblemished reputation.'

Julius raised a sardonic brow at her self-praise and contemplated her wickedly gleaming green eyes. 'I am impressed, but you failed to mention problematical, as bold as brass and as determined as they come.'

She smiled. 'I admit that I can be troublesome on occasion, but on the whole, you can have no objections to my suitability.'

Julius's expression was one of disbelief. He looked her over carefully, as if to judge her for her worth, and appeared dubious as he crinkled his brows. 'No objections—' he retorted sharply, then bit back the rest of his words, clenching his jaw so tightly a muscle jerked in the side of his cheek. 'I have plenty, Miss Fanshaw, and I can imagine Lady Standish will have some of her own to add. How will your esteemed aunt receive your outlandish proposal to me?'

'She will be livid, I expect. You see, where my aunt is concerned, as an impoverished orphan she has never had any regard for me. I am a duty she is forced to endure. In her world, marriages are arranged for consequence and money. She has you in her sights for Astrid. Not only are you outrageously wealthy, but you are also a marquess and we haven't had one of those in the family before, so she sees it as advancing the family cause.' She cocked her head on one side and looked at him steadily. 'Would you have offered for Astrid? Did my aunt read your attentions toward Astrid correctly?'

'Good Lord, no. Miss Standish is exquisite and quite charming, but she is not to my taste.' Julius meant it. To

anyone with experience, Astrid Standish's mere pret-
tiness could not hold a candle to Beatrice Fanshaw's
raw kind of beauty. Miss Standish could prove troublesome in her own way, but she was very definitely not
the same sort of trouble Miss Fanshaw would be. He
would never be bored with her, that was for sure. 'In
any case, you have spiked your aunt's ambitions well
and truly with this outrageous escapade.' Suddenly
curious to know more about this self-contained young
woman, although he couldn't for the life of him think
why, he said, 'Why does she resent you?'

'I think she sees me as some kind of threat to Astrid.
Against her wishes, my uncle took us in when my
mother and I had nowhere else to go. To add to our
difficulties my mother was very ill. Her illness began
immediately after my father died. Aunt Moira didn't go
out of her way to make us welcome. When my mother
died she would have turned me out were it not for my
uncle.'

'I'm sorry,' Julius said, his tone suddenly sympa-
thetic. 'That must have been an awful time for you
when you lost your mother. I am not unacquainted with
death and loss,' he said, thinking of the loss of his own
mother. 'I have not forgotten the pain of it. How was
your relationship with your uncle?'

'He always treated me kindly. Before he died he
made Aunt Moira promise to do right by me: to maintain me as one of her own children, to bring me out into
society and to ensure that the man I married was suitable. I suppose she considers she has kept this promise
as well as her nature will permit, but as soon as my

uncle died she made it plain that I should not think myself on an equal footing with my cousins. How could she like or accept an irksome alien, someone inferior and unconnected to her by any tie, an intruder on her own family?'

The softening of her manner enhanced her beauty and Julius boldly and appreciatively stared at her hard for several moments. There was a forlorn, lost look about her and he sensed she bore a deep inner pain and bitterness that had driven her to where she was now. In fact, he saw in her that which was in himself, and *that* something stirred, something moved that had not moved in a long time. It came unbidden, unexpected, born of the bleakness of his own life. Over the years he'd stifled that feeling as best he could, but it had been there just the same, telling him how he felt, and it was ridiculous, totally ridiculous, for with so much to do his life was full. But always there was something not quite right, something missing from his life.

'I can see your life at Standish House has not been easy and that you do indeed need rescuing,' he said softly.

'I have become accustomed to it.' She gave him a sideways, almost coy look. 'Will you be my rescuer, Lord Chadwick?'

He considered her remark in silence. Perhaps he should rescue her from her predicament. After all, if it wasn't for his father, she wouldn't be in this position, so maybe he should accept her marriage proposal. 'Tell me. Why do you want to marry me so badly?'

'You know why. Because you own Larkhill.'

'Yes, I thought that might have something to do with it,' he remarked drily.

'But I have no money. I can't afford Larkhill. I have nothing save what my aunt chooses to give me, which is very little, therefore it is up to me to provide for myself. I will no longer be a burden to my aunt. I can no longer submit to her opinion as a matter of course. In short, Lord Chadwick, I have decided to be my own advocate and make my own case.'

'Will that be such a hardship for you?'

Beatrice detected a mild concern in his voice. 'I hope not. I am indeed at your mercy. After this I cannot stay here. My aunt will cut me off from all connection with her family because I dared ask you to marry me. If you refuse to do this, I shall have to find somewhere else to live and an occupation to support myself.'

His eyes held hers in an enquiring glance. 'What you really mean is that your pride won't let you show defeat.'

She bristled at his light, mocking tone. 'After this I shall be regarded as low as a fallen woman—a helpless and defenceless female.'

Her words were so inappropriate he laughed out loud. 'Helpless and defenceless be damned. A woman who can ride as you do and beat me at my own challenge, a woman who can ask a man to marry her and when he rejects her can still lift her head with fire in her eyes, is not what I would call helpless or defenceless. I salute your courage and your boldness, Miss Fanshaw. You are undeniably brave—and reckless. But you are being selfish in throwing your desirable self at me, daring me to take advantage of you because you want something badly enough. You are playing with fire and it is inevitable that at some time you will be burned. I am unwilling to satisfy your wicked schemes and am most reluctant to take advantage of you—though God knows I would like to and you fully deserve it.'

'I don't know if I should be flattered or insulted by that remark, Lord Chadwick,' Beatrice retorted, her cheeks flushed with indignation.

'Take it either way. It is immaterial to me. So, it all boils down to the fact that you want to marry me for my money.'

'Your wealth does make marriage to you more palatable.'

'You don't have to go to such lengths as to tie yourself to me for life to return to your former home. When I asked you if you would demand Larkhill as the forfeit I recall you saying it would be nothing as fine or as grand as that—which makes me feel decidedly inferior that you consider me less important than a house.' He gave her a steady look. 'Why settle for me?'

'Because I need you—your money—to restore Larkhill to what it was. You have neglected the property sorely since you took it from my father.'

Shrugging himself away from the wall and thrusting his hands deep into his pockets, he began to pace. 'I understand your resentment. It can't be a comfortable situation for a woman like you, a young woman robbed of her own family, yet with your whole life ahead of you. While ever you live with your aunt you are in

Astrid's shadow—you, who are the more beautiful of the two.'

Beatrice was so humiliated by his reference to her plight that her heart clenched with the truth of it. It was such a bleak and accurate summary of her life that she almost choked at the future that opened up before her. 'That's how it is for a lot of women,' she said, stung into honesty, 'especially when a woman finds herself without a family of her own. It's not what one would choose. I don't like it and I decided long ago to find my own way out—hence the wager. Do you have family, Lord Chadwick?'

He shook his head. Pain and desolation entered his eyes, but it quickly disappeared and his expression was suddenly guarded. 'No, Miss Fanshaw, I do not. From the moment I saw you I realised that we might have something in common. Like me, you like to make your own choices. I owe no man a living and I owe no woman a duty. In short, I am my own man, free to do as I choose. That's the way I like it and how I want it to remain.'

'It's different for a woman.'

'I know. But if all you want is to return to Larkhill, you don't have to marry me.'

'No?' She looked at him warily. 'It seems to me, Lord Chadwick, that you are trying to wriggle out of your promise. You really are going to renege on your word, aren't you?' She took a deep breath, her eyes flashing daggers. 'Very well. I can't force you to marry me. Now, I think you'd better leave.'

When she tried to sweep past him, his strong hand

gripped her arm and spun her around. He hadn't known her twenty-four hours and yet somehow she already showed a talent for clouding his cool calculation. He shouldn't be angry with her—not when he was the one hiding too many dark and brooding secrets. It was himself he should be angry with.

'Devil take it, woman, I don't want to marry you! I'm not the marrying kind. I'm no good for you. Can't you get that through that beautiful head of yours?'

Suddenly he seemed enormous and very close to Beatrice. His powerful body emanated heat, matching the heat that was rising in her cheeks. 'I don't want to marry you, either. You are nothing but a—a barbarian. But I will not withdraw the forfeit. I will not make it easy for you. It is up to you to extricate yourself in whichever way you see fit.'

His eyes blazed. 'Barbarian? Lady,' he warned, his voice hoarse with fury above her, 'as yet I haven't even begun to act the barbarian. If you insist on marrying me, then let me warn you in advance that I have learned from an expert how to make a wife's life a living hell.'

His hold on her arm tightened and he looked at her for a long moment. She was so lovely, cool, virginal and stunningly arousing—and the most hair-raising woman he had ever met. He could feel himself responding, a fact that only inflamed his anger. Slowly, with menacing deliberation, he backed her against the shadowy garden wall. His grip wasn't painful, but the casual strength in his fingers was unyielding and made it impossible for her to escape his grip despite her struggle.

'Take your hands off me,' she snapped to cover her growing alarm. Giving up her futile struggle, she glared murderously at the angry light glinting in his eyes. 'How dare you call yourself a gentleman when you go around molesting women?'

'Only those who stupidly believe they can get the better of me,' he said between his teeth. 'I'm merely trying to assure you that you don't want to be my wife—to give you a taste of what you will be up against if you continue with this farce.'

One hand rose to grasp her chin, but Beatrice turned her face away, eluding capture. When his hard fingers at last closed over her jaw, she gasped with fury. 'Stop it. Do you hear me? Don't you dare hurt me! Kindly take your hands off me!'

Julius stared down at her. He hadn't missed the flare of temper in her eyes, or the fright. 'I've never hurt a woman in my life. But I mean to convince you to reconsider the forfeit you demand from me.' His gaze dropped to her soft lips, then slid lower, following the line of her throat down to the tantalising mounds beneath the soft fabric of her shirt. With her head thrown back, they quivered and thrust forwards invitingly, emphasising the undeniable fact that she was an alluring woman.

As he released her chin, his fingers unintentionally brushed her breast. He was instantly aware of the contact. So was she—he could tell by the furious blush that rose to her cheeks.

Beatrice tried to ignore the effect of his touch.

'Release me this instant,' she demanded heatedly. 'Kindly remove your hands.'

It was a supremely proper response—prim, restrained, ladylike, just the kind he would expect from a woman of her social standing, who had been taught to hold the physical side of marriage in aversion. 'Why? Don't you want me to touch you?' he murmured, deliberately running his fingers along the line of her jaw. She was so close that he could smell the fragrance of violets in her hair. 'Don't you know that as my wife I shall be able to touch you where I like and when I like, that you must accept my attentions no matter how repugnant you find them to be? Shall I give you a taste of what to expect when I exert my husbandly rights?'

Drawing her rigid body closer, he pressed it against his, and the sensation of her soft body and her slender legs encased in breeches moulded to his own acted on him like a powerful aphrodisiac. Desire surged through him, heating his blood, sending it singing through his veins, and then his mouth crushed hers with a controlled expertise that left her gasping, shocking her with his arousing warmth.

Julius finally raised his head. 'Consider it, Miss Fanshaw. You will have to learn to enjoy my lovemaking,' he warned, 'to be available to me whenever I want you, so if you still insist on being my wife, perhaps you should start enjoying it now.'

Still reeling from his devastating kiss, Beatrice stared up at him, two bright spots of colour highlighting her cheeks. His voice had suddenly grown husky with sensuality.

Julius's smouldering eyes stared back at her. She knew what he was doing and why he was doing it. If he was trying to destroy her resistance, he was succeeding. When he fitted his body to hers, she tensed with a mingling of dread and wanton longing. She hardly had time to catch her breath before his mouth descended on hers once more and his tongue plundered the inner softness in a fierce, brutal kiss that was meant to punish and humiliate her.

Rigid with fury, she clawed and squirmed against him, trying to break his hold and to drag her mouth away from the fierce possession of his lips. Her struggle only seemed to encourage him on his course of persuasion and he deepened the kiss. His arm went around her, his hand cupping her buttocks to bring her hips even closer to his. Raising his head a fraction, he murmured, 'I would take my pleasure of you any time, at my leisure, any time I choose. I would make you moan for me,' he rasped against her lips, 'moan with pleasure.'

Beatrice shuddered, seeing something primitive and terrifying flare in his eyes as his arms tightened. She jerked back, a protest rising in her throat, but his lips stifled her voice with a demanding insistence that stunned her into immobility. She had never even imagined what it would be like to be kissed—at least not in the way Julius Chadwick was kissing her, with his mouth moist and parted, warmly tasting hers, his tongue parting her lips to probe and explore with a hungry ardour and an inflaming expertise that rendered her weak.

Mindlessly she slid her hands up his chest, trying to cling for support to the very object that was destroying her balance. Confused and lost in a haze of nameless yearnings, she raised herself up on her toes, responding to the forceful pressure of his arms.

Julius groaned in response, deepening his kiss as she moulded her body against his. Her breath was so sweet, the feel of her so good he felt himself respond with that part of him that didn't give a damn about his mind, which was telling him to tread with care. In his mind he knew that what he had intended wasn't working. He was driving himself insane and losing the battle for control.

Recollecting herself when a small lance of sanity entered her mind and made her wonder at her behaviour, Beatrice tore her mouth free. She was horrified by what was happening, what he was doing to her. She should have found his kiss repulsive, but in truth she found it wildly exciting and found it hard to keep her world together. It was as if she had drunk too much wine and was giddy from it. What was the matter with her? She was neither a tippler nor a woman of easy virtue. She was a virgin, for heaven's sake. In her fury she pushed against him with all her strength. She must be out of her mind to think she could do this, could manage this charade—and him. Julius Chadwick was more than she'd bargained for.

'You beast,' she hissed. 'You filthy beast.' As she wiped the moisture from her mouth with the back of her hand, sparks of indignation flashed in her eyes. 'How dare you lay your hands on me?'

Julius stared at her as if seeing her for the first time. She was wide eyed and vulnerable and trembling. And lovely. Dear Lord, she was so damned lovely. He wanted her with a fierceness that took his breath away. His strategy to make her change her mind had backfired with a vengeance. He had begun by trying to frighten and threaten her and had ended up with his own resolutions threatened instead.

'Come now, Miss Fanshaw,' he managed to say mockingly, laughing lightly, though he himself was shaken by the moment. 'You needn't be so indignant or feel insulted.' A smile twitched at the corner of his mouth. 'It was only a kiss. You must have been kissed before. I told you, if you really do want to be my wife, that is something you will have to get used to. It's as well you know that I'm an amorous man. I would not take kindly to having a cold and unwilling partner in my bed.'

He still had his arms about her and he could feel contempt written in her straight back and imperious head. At that moment she was feeling insulted and degraded and her posture was implying that if he knew what was good for him he would go away and never come back. But no matter how much she wanted to utter the words, too much was at stake for her to utter them.

Julius let her go so abruptly that she staggered back a step, then he drew a long, audible breath. She glared at him. 'How dare you do that to me? No doubt you will say I was asking for such treatment.'

His mobile mouth twisted into a grim smile and

Beatrice had the fleeting impression that he was struggling for composure, as she was. Before this he had been a man unknown to her. She had not thought of him as anything but the man who had ruined her father and taken Larkhill and how she could use him to get it back. She'd had no reason to think of him in intimate terms. Now she saw him as a strong, attractive man who was unsettling her. For the first time in her life she felt unsure of herself.

Julius studied her, grudgingly thinking how magnificent she was. Her mouth had been sweet, warm and moist, and he was impatient to repeat the kiss. In her madness she had fought him like a lioness, and yet there had been a moment in that frenzied kiss when she had leaned against him as though the strength had gone from her and he had felt her hands, instead of clawing at him, hesitate and then slide up his chest and cling to his shoulders as though to steady herself in the havoc that washed over them both. He felt slightly bewildered by her now, almost bewitched.

'You made a grave mistake when you asked for my forfeit,' he said finally. 'However, after saying that, I don't think either of us can deny that we are *drawn* to each other.' Forcing himself to remain calm, he caught her glittering gaze and held it. 'I think we both know what we want, don't we?'

Beatrice scrutinised his expression warily. Her feelings were nebulous, chaotic, yet one stood out clearly—frustrated desire. She hadn't wanted him to stop kissing her. But she would not give him the satisfaction of

letting him know that. Holding his gaze, she drew in
a slow breath, then shook her head. 'No.'

'Liar,' he uttered quietly. 'Your eyes tell a different
story.' Turning from her, he took a moment to reflect
on her strong will, a quality he admired. He could not
escape the fact that Beatrice Fanshaw had intrigued
him from the moment he had laid eyes on her. She had
no artificial airs and graces and possessed a kind of
courage about her that was unusual in a woman. She
was also proud and independent, with bold, forthright
ways, but he considered that in the matter of the forfeit
she had acted foolishly. Looking at her now, Julius felt
her breathtaking beauty quicken his very soul, stirring
his mind with imaginings of what life married to her
would be like. He was fiercely attracted to her, yet
because of the secrets he was carrying he would have
to try to fight the attraction.

'There is another alternative to you becoming my
wife. I have an offer to make to you.' He saw her eyes
cloud with wariness and distrust at the word 'offer'.
'It is a proposition of a different kind. Once you've
considered it, I think you will agree that it would be a
sensible arrangement for us both.'

'What sort of proposition?' she asked with clinical,
cautious calm.

'That you become my mistress.'

Beatrice was so surprised that all she could do was
stare at him. After several moments of digesting what
being his mistress would involve, she fixed him with
indignant, angry eyes. 'You want me to become your
mistress?'

'Good Lord, no!' Julius took a deep breath, trying to keep his calm. 'I don't need a mistress any more than I need a wife. But I feel obliged to offer a solution to the dilemma you have so foolishly created for us both. Do you think I consider this lightly?'

His contemplation was steady. He remained silent when she moved away from him, giving his proposal careful thought. She moved with the natural grace of one who led an active life and bore nothing of the affected daintiness and fragility so often displayed by beauties of the *ton*. There was a sureness in her stride that lent smooth, fluid grace to her every movement. Julius admired everything about her; he had already set a price in his mind and only waited the moment.

At length she turned back to him and scowled. 'So I was right. You *are* trying to wriggle out of it,' she accused sharply.

'I am merely suggesting another option, one in which neither of us has to commit ourselves. I am sure that despite our many differences we would be compatible sexually. You share my bed and in return for that you will have your own house and carriage and horses. You will have your own maid, a butler and servants, gowns and expensive baubles by the dozen. In short, I will be most generous. While you remain my mistress, you will have enough money to live like a queen—providing no other man gets to share what I am paying for.'

'I don't care for baubles,' she said at length, 'although a house of my own appeals to me. Kindly enlarge on that?'

His eyes were intent. 'I would give you your heart's desire: Larkhill. Mistress or wife, you could live there—if that is what you want. What's the difference?'

Her smile was cynical. 'You may have lost the wager, Lord Chadwick, but you still have a winning way with words. There is a vast difference. As your mistress you could kick me out on a whim. My answer is no. You insult me. My aunt would be scandalised and would never allow it. And I could never accept being any man's mistress.'

He lifted his broad shoulders in a slight shrug and said in an indifferent voice, 'That is your prerogative.'

'Exactly. Lord Chadwick, are you or are you not going to honour your word given to me in the presence of others?'

His eyes boldly roamed over her body from head to toe and back to her face. 'I'm beginning to warm to the idea. Married to you, life would never be dull. When you are near me I feel there is but one thought on my mind.'

In that moment her thoughts were far from Larkhill and how her aunt would react to what she was doing; instead, they centred on the turmoil within herself. A strong feeling of doubt blasted her confidence and she was suddenly unsure of her ability to deal with Julius Chadwick.

Julius moved to stand close to her. 'Do you mean to bait me? Do you seek to punish me and, in so doing, extract your revenge for my past sins? If that is your game, then lead on. I will welcome your attention and the challenge.'

After a moment, Beatrice realised he was looking at her with a strange and tender smile on his lips. Her curiosity was piqued at his apparent ability to turn circumstances to his benefit.

'There is one thing I would like to know. What forfeit would you have asked of me had you won?'

'That was it.'

'What?'

'That you become my mistress.'

Beatrice was about to vent her indignation in his face, but suddenly his laughter rang out once more and brought quick death to her words. Strolling away from her, clasping his hands behind his back, he was as relaxed as if he were drinking with his friends in a gentleman's club. Still chuckling derisively, he turned and strolled back to her.

'I thought that might make you see the real price of your predicament. What would you have done? Would you have honoured your forfeit and become my mistress had you lost the race?'

Beatrice was surprised and shocked and intensely relieved that she had escaped such a fate, but did not show it. Taking a deep breath she nodded. 'Yes. I may be many things, Lord Chadwick, but I always abide by my word. I can only thank God and my own skill that I beat you.'

'No man or woman will ever master me, Miss Fanshaw.'

He stood gazing down, holding her eyes in a wilful use of power. Unable to look at him any longer, Beatrice averted her gaze.

'Look at me.'

Unwillingly she turned her cool, questioning eyes to his once more and found a slow lazy smile that seemed to mock her. Leisurely he passed a knuckle along the fragile bone of her cheeks. His voice was soft as he continued, but it held a note of determination which in an odd way both frightened and angered her.

'Whatever madness has driven you to this, one thing I can promise you is that the misery you have endured since your father lost Larkhill will be as nothing compared to what your life will be like married to me. Consider it and think on it carefully. As my wife you will be at my beck and call night and day—in my bed and out of it. You will be my wife not only in the eyes of the law, but in every other way as well. So between now and the day when we say our vows, ask yourself if that damned house is worth it.'

Beatrice watched him walk away. Slowly, a warm flush of triumph permeated her being. She had achieved her object, and however Julius Chadwick viewed her, he was not a willing suitor. But as she walked back to the house her thoughts were jumbled, for despite his role in her misfortunes, she had a grudging admiration for him. He was not a man to flinch from duty and that was why he had achieved so much in his life.

Despite her anger and resentment she had to concede that courage and strength ran through his veins, a strength that was in his character as well as his body. She had come away from their encounter with a feeling that he was an isolated, lonely figure without a family of his own. Surely such a handsome man should not

be alone. Well, maybe it was high time he had a wife, and, with that thought and a reputation for walking on the wild side, she fully intended to turn his life upside down. If this was how she would get her revenge, then there could be worse things.

But, she reflected, despite their unsatisfactory exchange, she owned he had many good qualities, and deep down she was quite excited at the prospect of being his wife.

George told Astrid about the outcome of the race and the forfeit Beatrice had asked of Lord Chadwick. Appalled and deeply concerned by what her cousin was doing, Astrid went in search of her. Not until the salon door had closed behind them did she speak.

'I know what happened. George told me. But—Lord Chadwick? How can you possibly marry him after the harm he has done you in the past?'

'I know, but I am going to marry him, Astrid. He agreed to the forfeit.'

Astrid frowned as she tried to comprehend Beatrice and her actions. 'But—you could make Larkhill your forfeit without going to such lengths as to marry him to get it.'

Beatrice looked at Astrid with something like pity. 'No, Astrid. What good would that be? Unlike you I have no dowry and am loathe to let your mother pay for one. She is determined to make me see my place. To obtain Larkhill I must first make myself Lord Chadwick's wife. Without wealth of my own, in no time at

all I would be forced to sell it. This way I can have it all: money and Larkhill.'

'And Lord Chadwick? You speak as if he has nothing to do with it, yet he will be your husband—a man who will be hard to ignore.'

'You should look on it as a favour, Astrid. With Lord Chadwick out of the way, you mother will cease pressurising you on the matter. Although if she had succeeded in pulling off the match, he would have soon seen through you,' Beatrice said gently.

Astrid's head shot up. 'Why, what do you mean by that?'

'I don't think he is the kind of man to marry a woman who is in love with someone else.' Astrid blushed a deep scarlet. Beatrice smiled. 'I thought as much. Anyone can see—and I know I am not wrong. You are glowing like a maid in springtime; every time Henry Talbot looks at you he looks as if he wants to eat you alive. I would put a fortune on you being in love with him. I am not wrong, am I, Astrid?'

She shook her head. 'No. Henry and I have known one another all our lives, yet it is only recently that we have become close and acknowledged the depth of our feelings for each other. But with Mama being like she is, we have had to be careful not to show it.'

'You're to be congratulated, Astrid. Even I did not suspect—until your birthday party.'

'That's because your head is always filled with other things and you walk about in blinkers, seeing nothing but what is ahead of you.'

Beatrice lowered her head. 'I'm sorry, Astrid. I don't

mean to. And please don't be ashamed of me for what I am about to do. Where Larkhill is concerned, I am prepared to throw everything—even my immortal soul—into the battle to get it back.'

'Your desire to have your home returned to you must be very powerful indeed if you will go to such lengths as to marry the man who took it away from you in the first place.'

'You will never know how powerful. And as for you, you must talk to your mama. When she realises how things really are between you and Henry, perhaps she will relent.'

'Thank you, Beatrice, but somehow I don't believe Mama will consent to a marriage between us.'

'Get George on side. He might be able to talk her round.'

At that moment the door opened and Aunt Moira came in. Her face was like a stone. Beatrice breathed in deeply. Best get this over with, she thought.

Chapter Four

'**W**ell?' Lady Standish demanded. 'What have you got to say for yourself, Beatrice? Too ashamed, are you? I am simply astounded that not only did you ask Lord Chadwick to marry you, but you practically demanded that he do so. You have behaved in a thoroughly deceitful manner and I will not have it. In one fell swoop you have broken all the rules.' Beatrice raised her head and looked at her aunt defiantly, which increased her wrath. 'How dare you humiliate me and make me look foolish in society? How dare you?' She was puce with anger and her voice rose until she was almost screeching.

'I understand that your feelings are hurt and I am sorry to have caused you so much distress, Aunt Moira,' Beatrice uttered stiffly.

'Distress? That is putting it mildly,' Lady Standish said, her aristocratic voice dripping with disdain. 'Of course as your guardian I can stop this. You do realise that, don't you?'

'But why would you want to?'

'To stop you making a fool of yourself and this family. What will you do if I don't allow it?'

Both women were facing each other. Beatrice refused to be bowed. Her sense of outrage kept her anchored to the floor.

'I'll do as I wish. You cannot stand in my way. Of late I've done a lot of thinking. I am eighteen years old—a woman—and I shall decide my own destiny. Ever since I came to live here you have wanted me off your hands. I am happy to oblige you.'

'Enough,' Lady Standish ordered. 'I am your aunt! How dare you speak to me in this disgraceful manner? I have indulged you overmuch. What other reason can there be for such behaviour? You owe me your respect. For shame! Must you always think of yourself, you insolent, ungrateful girl? You have planned this from the start. Oh, I am not deceived by you, Beatrice. You have wanted him for yourself ever since we returned from London. You seek to deny Astrid the privilege of winning his favour.'

'Lord Chadwick never had any intention of offering for Astrid. And Astrid would not favour a proposal from him anyway, feeling as she does about Henry Talbot.' She looked to where her cousin sat shrinking in a chair, watching and listening to the heated words between her mother and her cousin. 'Is that not so, Astrid?'

'I—I do have feelings for Henry,' she confessed,

which was a brave thing for her to say, for, like all young ladies of her social class, Astrid had been taught since childhood that her duty as a daughter was to marry in accordance with her parents' wishes. 'I don't want anyone else, Mama,' she said in a tear-clogged voice. 'I want Henry.'

The admission was made with such humble, hopeless misery that anyone but the hard-hearted Lady Standish would have been moved by it. Instead she glared at her. 'I think Henry Talbot presumed on your friendship and the freedom his parents have allowed him to dally at Standish House in the hope that something would come of his association with you. He is naïve to think so. That will never happen. You would be marrying beneath you.'

'I do not think Squire Talbot would care to have his son regarded as just anyone,' Beatrice dared to say. 'Henry is a fine man. He may look naïve, but I'll wager he'll make the best husband for Astrid.'

Lady Standish fixed her ice-cold eyes on her niece, her mouth twisting with derision. 'A farmer? I don't think so.'

'There is nothing to be ashamed of in that,' Beatrice argued. 'Henry loves the land and farms his father's acres tirelessly.'

'But as a younger son it will never be his. I do not like speaking ill of Squire Talbot for we have been friends and neighbours for more years than I can remember, but you deviate, Beatrice. This is not about Astrid, but about you.' Beatrice moved towards the door, but Lady Standish barred her way. 'Where are you going?'

'To my room.' With defiance Beatrice walked round her.

'And Lord Chadwick? I warn you, Beatrice. You go to him with nothing. I will not provide you with a dowry. You are a nobody and as such he will regard you like a plaything and soon tire of you and marry someone else.'

Beatrice turned from the doorway and looked back at her aunt, her brows raised in questioning sarcasm. 'Will he? And you are sure of that, are you, Aunt Moira? And this is the man you wanted for Astrid, is it—for your own daughter? Then consider yourself fortunate that he is marrying me instead.'

Beatrice was in the hall when Lord Chadwick was admitted the following morning. Their eyes met. His mood was again mocking, his eyes devouring, hers nervous and uncertain. Under his openly admiring regard, she flushed crimson. She heard his soft laugh, then he turned and went into the drawing room for his meeting with her aunt. As she followed him she noted that he was completely at ease and terribly confident of himself.

Lady Standish was seated in her usual chair by the hearth and did not trouble herself to rise when he entered. The turn of her head and the coldness of her smile conveyed very clearly that she did not approve of this marriage and that he should refuse to have any part of it.

'I think you are expecting me, Lady Standish,' Julius said in crisp tones, seeing Beatrice take a position away from her aunt.

'I am. Please be seated.'

'No, thank you,' his hard, confident voice replied. 'I am content to stand.'

'As you wish. I am interested to know your opinion about this outrageous situation concerning my niece. I am sure you will agree that her conduct is shocking.'

'I do agree, Lady Standish.' He glanced at the young woman in question with a mocking smile lightly curving his lips, wondering how she would react if he were to tell her how he had been unable to wipe her from his mind. Memories of the way she had felt in his arms, the heady sweetness of her kiss, had kept him awake all night. What a proud, spirited beauty she was. She excited him, she shocked him, and while he did not consider himself remotely in love with her, he was in her thrall.

He was aware of what she wanted and was tempted to refuse her, but the prospect of his safe, orderly life without her horrified him. It was as if she'd bewitched him, this wicked, beautiful creature, and he could not break away.

Julius had suffered hardship and tragedy throughout his life and his emotions had been stunted, which was why he had never married. His relationships with women were about sex. Just the same, he mused as he looked at Beatrice Fanshaw, life could still deliver surprises.

It was a difficult moment for Beatrice, who did not

know what to expect. She wanted to maintain an air of cool disdain, to face Lord Chadwick in calm defiance, but her mauled pride and an aching distrust of the future assailed her senses. Momentarily blinded by a rush of tears, she lowered her head, but, furious with herself that she should display such weakness, lifted it again and found his amber eyes resting on her with something akin to compassion or pity. It was almost too much for her to bear.

'Beatrice always was an underhand, quarrelsome girl,' Lady Standish went on coldly. 'She has a tendency to deceit and does not have the character and disposition of my own dear daughter, Astrid. You have given some thought to her—her idea,' she said, for want of a better word.

Beatrice knew then why she disliked her aunt so much, for it was in her nature to wound her cruelly. No matter how she had tried to please and obey her when she had come to Standish House, all her efforts were repulsed and repaid by such words as Lady Standish had just uttered. The accusation cut her to the heart, especially as her aunt had voiced it before Lord Chadwick. The unkindness painted her as some kind of artful, obnoxious creature, tainting any future happiness she hoped for.

Julius considered Beatrice a moment before replying to Lady Standish's question. 'As a matter of fact I have given it considerable thought.'

He stared rigidly at Beatrice, his profile harsh and forbidding. With a sinking heart she knew he was thinking hard for some way out of marrying her; she also knew that behind that tautly controlled façade was a terrible volcanic rage. With the silence grating on her nerves, she held herself still and waited for him to speak, his expression becoming darker and more ominous by the second.

When Julius saw her putting up a valiant fight for control, a fight she won, his temper softened. Standing before him, she looked like a proud young queen, her eyes sparkling like twin jewels.

'And have you come to the sensible conclusion that you don't suit?' Lady Standish remarked coldly.

'On the contrary,' he replied, bringing his gaze back to her, 'I think we might suit very well. In the beginning I confess to being shocked by the forfeit your niece asked of me and I did not consider it lightly. I am not usually a man of hasty decision when it concerns a lasting relationship, but I suppose you could say that Miss Fanshaw forced my hand.'

'Then you are quite mad, sir. Beatrice is no relation of mine, but you do realise that I could prevent this if I so wished?' Lady Standish rushed in, her temper getting the better of her, pushed beyond the bounds of reason by her niece's unacceptable behaviour and the scandal that would ensue. 'Beatrice is eighteen. I am her guardian until she comes of age or I consider it time that she marries.'

The room was as cold as winter in January. Julius stared at the almost demented woman, her eyes feverishly bright, her hands clenched so tightly into fists that her blue veins bulged out. She meant it, he realised. She was evidently so consumed with loathing for her niece that she would subject her to a lifetime of misery for daring to defy her by taking away the man she had selected for her own daughter.

'Why would you want to do that, Lady Standish? Because you care so much for your niece that you put her happiness first—or for spite?' he said, overstepping the bounds of politeness. 'It is obvious to me that she is no favourite of yours.' He turned his head sharply to Beatrice and studied her face as if he'd never seen her before. His granite features softened and his eyes warmed, as if he understood how humiliated she felt. 'Do you still want to go through with this?'

Beatrice gazed up into his inscrutable amber eyes and nodded. 'Yes.'

'That's all I wish to know.'

Lady Standish's face whitened at his words. 'You cannot seriously mean to go through with this—this farce of a marriage!'

A muscle twitched furiously in Julius's cheek as his angry glare took in the older woman. He loathed her at that moment. The injustice of an innocent being so harshly maligned gnawed at every chivalrous inch of his body, although he did wonder what he was getting into. 'I intend to do exactly that. From now on Beatrice will be *my* responsibility.'

'Then good luck to you is what I say, for you will need it. The girl's a liar and an ambitious schemer. She's trouble, a hellion, and you will live to regret taking her on. I will not pretend that I am happy about this ill-conceived marriage. However much it galls me, however much it denigrates my family's good name,

I must accept it. But you'll get no blessing from me,' she said, her voice tight with fury and bitterness.'

Julius's voice was scathing. 'I think we can manage to live without it.'

Lady Standish glared at her niece, noting the familiar jut of defiance in her chin. 'I cannot stop you doing this foolish thing, Beatrice. But if you do you will not get my acceptance. I will be forced to cut you off from your family and our connections. You will not get a penny from me. You will be cut off from everything you have known.'

Beatrice managed to raise her head and meet her aunt's gaze unflinching. 'I am sorry you feel that way, Aunt Moira, but I do have a right to choose my own life.'

'Choice you have, girl,' her aunt replied contemptuously. 'You have always had it, but the choice to do the right thing. If you leave this house now, you will never return. I will have nothing more to do with you. You have made your bed so you must lie in it. You will not speak with Astrid or George again. You will have no communication with them. Is that clear?'

Beatrice almost choked on the hurt this caused her, but she managed to utter, 'Yes.'

Julius's eyes had turned positively glacial during this short exchange. 'You have my guarantee that as my wife Beatrice will be supported in a manner suitable to her upbringing. It is certain she must no longer live here where she will continue to be subjected to the malice of a woman who calls herself an aunt.' These words were delivered in a cold, lethal voice, his eyes gleaming with a deadly purpose. 'Having seen for myself your unfair treatment of your niece, I suspect that, failing to get what you want, you will not hesitate to stoop to slander to soothe your wounded pride. I trust you will think twice before you resort to such vile practice. Beatrice is under *my* protection now, and believe me, you don't want to have me for an enemy.'

Lady Standish drew herself up with dignified hauteur, but exposed her fury by the way her hand gripping the arm of her chair trembled. 'Please do not threaten me in my own house, Lord Chadwick. Beatrice has only a little knowledge of the kind of man that you are, having stolen her birthright, but I have more. In time she will come to know you, to know how you treat those who dare to cross you, and then she will hate you.'

Observing the puzzled look that crossed Lord Chadwick's face, she smiled a chilling, satisfied smile, but she would not enlighten him as to what she was referring. She would save that for a later date and enjoy flinging it in his face.

'Now I would appreciate it if you would leave this instant and take Beatrice with you. Indeed, the more I look at her, the more relieved I shall feel to be rid of a responsibility that is becoming too irksome.' Seeing how Beatrice flinched under the biting remark, she was glad to know it had hit its mark. 'I can't say that she has been a pleasure to have around.'

Bemused by what she had said, Julius was pushed to ask her to explain what she had meant by it, but, impatient to leave, he turned his gaze directly to Beatrice.

Only then did he realise the gamble she had taken by
taking up his wager, which, once accepted, had started
off a chain of events from which there was no going
back on.

By asking him to marry her she had risked throwing
away not only her reputation, but her family and her
home. If he refused to marry her, with no one in the
world to lighten her cares, penniless, she would have
to leave this bizarre household and fend for herself.
As a result of that wretched game of cards, inadver-
tently, but effectively, her future, like his own, had been
destroyed. And yet, as he looked at her, he reluctantly
faced the fact that she was a far cry from a pitiable
homeless waif.

His mind made up, he said with implacable finality
that warned further argument would be futile, 'It is
settled, then.' Looking at Beatrice, he raised a finely
arched brow. 'If you have anything more to say to your
aunt, please do so, then get together whatever you wish
to take with you. I will wait in my carriage until you
have concluded your business.'

With that he strode to the door, and Beatrice caught
a glimpse of his angry, aristocratic profile, then he was
gone. Having nothing else to say to her aunt, she followed him. After going to her room and gathering the
few possessions that belonged to her, she left Standish
House for the last time.

'Now, then,' said Julius, lounging against the rich
upholstery in his elegant open carriage and crossing his
long legs in front of him, 'now we can relax.' He smiled

at the alarm which entered his companion's eyes when his driver proceeded to travel along the London road. 'Why, what is it?' he asked blandly. 'Is there something you have forgotten? Do you have something to say? By the look on your face I would wager that you have. Please don't disappoint me by holding it in. I would hate to see you explode with frustration.'

Perched stiffly on the cushioned seat across from him, and having spent a moment to adjust her skirts in an effort to avoid meeting his gaze, Beatrice now shot him a mutinous, measuring look. 'Believe me, Lord Chadwick, you wouldn't want to see me explode. And, yes, there is something I wish to say. I thought...'

Seeming to find amusement in her confusion, he laughed lightly. 'What? That I was taking you to Larkhill? Surely you didn't think we would live there. I'm sorry to disappoint you, but I'm afraid not. My companions left Larkhill for London earlier. I have pressing matters of business to attend to and I am in a hurry to get there myself. But take heart. I am sure you will find my country residence in Kent every bit as pleasant as Larkhill.'

Beatrice's fury, combined with her disappointment, was immense. 'I doubt it,' she snapped ungraciously, leaning back in her seat and glowering at the passing scenery. 'Larkhill was my home.'

'When we are married you will look on Highfield Manor as your home.' Withdrawing a thin cheroot from his jacket pocket, he lit it, bending his dark head and cupping his hands over the flame. Unconcernedly he blew smoke into the air.

Beatrice expelled an angry breath she hadn't realised she'd been holding and the sound made him glance at her sharply. His dark brows lifted a fraction in bland enquiry.

'Do you mind?'

'I've never seen a man smoke a cigar before,' she said. 'They—always smoke in another room.'

'May I offer you one?' He grinned at her sudden start of surprise. 'Why not? A number of ladies that I know are not averse to the odd cigar. I already know that you will dare anything. With your flair for doing the unconventional, you might acquire a taste for them.'

'I don't think I would and would be obliged if you would confine your smoking to when I am not present.'

'You may have failed to notice, but we are in an open carriage, so the smoke should not bother you. I enjoy a cigar—often—and I'm afraid that if you are to be my wife, you'll just have to get used to it.' Through narrowed eyes he looked at her appraisingly, the smoke from his cigar drifting slowly over his head. 'You already know the other things you will have to get accustomed to—you will recall the demonstration I gave you. Just look on this as another.'

'You can please yourself,' Beatrice told him loftily.

'Careful. Your temper is showing.'

She swallowed hard as his eyes bored into hers. It had not taken her long to throw good judgement aside and flare up at him. She must learn to control her temper and her feelings better. Setting her jaw, she glared at him, unconcerned, it seemed, with anything else he might have to say. Her eyes sparkled like diamonds and she was flushed and could barely speak through her tightly clenched teeth.

Her hair fell about her shoulders in a tangle of glossy waves and her anger had given her eyes a luminous quality. With the cigar clamped between teeth as white as his shirt, Julius watched her from beneath hooded lids; her closeness and the mere sight of her made him desire her, but he controlled the urge to drag her on to his side of the carriage and into his arms.

She was furious with him, he knew, for not taking her directly to Larkhill, and she was dying to loose a tirade at his head—he could see it in those glorious flashing green eyes of hers. The truth was that he really did have pressing business matters to attend to in London. He had delayed his departure and sent his valet on ahead to cancel some of his appointments so he could meet with Lady Standish.

'Really, Beatrice—I may call you Beatrice? And please, do feel free to call me Julius—must you look as if you want to run me through?' There was a cynical edge to his voice and a coldness in his eyes as he regarded her. 'I am about to deliver you from a barren future at Standish House, to give you what you want, and you are staring at me as though you wish to commit murder.'

'As long as I continue to stare at you as though I could murder you and not enact the deed, then you have nothing to worry about.'

Heading towards London, the greys paced in prime style. The drive through leafy lanes and picturesque villages in the lazy warmth of bright sunshine was uneventful. The journey dragged on in painful, unbroken silence. Beatrice could not trust herself to speak for fear she would give way to her angry emotions. She was utterly devastated that he had not taken her to Larkhill. Strongly suspecting that he had done it deliberately and was clearly amused by her disappointment increased her anger. And so he sat watching her like a hungry hawk, that having been snared by his sharp talons once, was tender bait for the second tasting.

Directing her gaze to the passing scenery, she let her mind wander over all that had occurred since the morning of Astrid's birthday party—the kiss Julius had given her being paramount. Her cheeks reddened with embarrassed heat at the memory of her own wanton response, when pleasure had seeped through the barrier of her own will.

From that moment nothing was the same. Her mind was unsettled, and for the first time in years, it had nothing to do with Larkhill. Mentally flaying her thoughts into obedience, she glanced across at the man who occupied them. His eyes were closed and his handsome face with a dark lock of hair falling on to his brow looked boyish and unguarded in repose. She wanted to reach out and touch him, to run her fingers through his thick hair, to have him kiss her as he had done yesterday.

A heaviness centred in her chest when she considered her future with Julius. Her aunt's remark about how, in time, she would come to hate him still rang in her ears. She was unsettled by it and couldn't begin to understand what she had meant by it. She already knew theirs would be a marriage unlike any other—without love or even liking for one another. And yet she had discovered what it was like to be kissed by a man and her discovery had marked her physically. What would he say, she wondered, if she were to ask him to repeat his actions of yesterday? Would he be shocked? Would he mock her? Or would he be willing to oblige?

She didn't know what sort of wife she would make and had given it no thought whatsoever, but strangely, she was now looking forward to it. Although perhaps Julius would spend much of his time on one of his ships and when he was home she would be a hostess and companion in his house, but she would never be able to touch his heart—and nor did she aspire to. A brief image of cosy marital bliss faded from her mind.

And yet, battle hardened though he might be by life—toughened and with an aura of hard-bitten strength—beneath it all Julius Chadwick had exposed a streak of kindness. Today he had been kind enough to rescue her and quick enough to act immediately and whisk her away from Standish House.

When they entered the outskirts of London, to Beatrice the world suddenly became an unreal place to be. It was a blur of noise and confusion. She had only ever been to London twice in her life, once with her parents and again with Aunt Moira and Astrid. With all the attention centred on Astrid, her visit had been an unpleasant experience and she had been glad to return to the country. Now she didn't know where she was going. She knew Julius had a house in Kent, so what were they doing in London?

As if Julius could read her mind, he said, 'I should tell you that you are to reside with Lord and Lady Merrick on Upper Brook Street for the time being.'

Beatrice looked at him with alarm. So, she thought, feeling as if something were shattering inside, already he wanted rid of her. 'But why? What on earth for?'

'Because you cannot possibly stay with me, alone and unchaperoned. It will be a miracle if gossip about your behaviour over the horse race hasn't already spread; if so, it will have done you immense harm. You must be prepared for that. By the time the *on dit* have circulated, your reputation will have been shredded, and if you were to live with me everyone would assume you have become my paramour. We cannot risk that sort of gossip.'

'So you mean to place me into unfamiliar surroundings with people I don't know.'

'My dear Beatrice, you have no choice.'

The casual, empty endearment made her cheeks flame with ire. 'Please don't call me "your dear". I am not that. And I do have a choice,' she said on the spur of the moment. 'I—I could go into lodgings or something like that.'

'And just how,' he asked drily, 'do you intend to pay for lodgings? You have no money.' This was the truth and she knew it, and, short of asking him for the money, there was nothing she could do but to fall in with his plans. 'Better for you to reside with Lord and

Lady Merrick for the present than risk the social stigma of living with me.'

'And that matters to you—what people will think?'

'Personally I don't give a damn what anyone thinks about me, but I am adamant that the name that I have worked so hard to repair will not be tarnished by this.' Seeing how she was looking at him with bewildered curiosity, he went on to inform her of some basic facts.

'You may be surprised to learn that our backgrounds are not dissimilar. It is no secret that the reputation of the Chadwick family has been blackened by several in recent generations. After years of declining fortunes and a few Chadwick ne'er-do-wells—the last of them being my father—the once-proud lineage became sunk into a state of genteel poverty.'

Unaccustomed to being so open with anyone, he paused and eyed his companion, searching for signs of contempt, but read none. 'To restore the family fortunes became my goal in life. With a head for business I gambled everything in a series of investments, spotting opportunities others had missed. Fortunately they paid off—and the wars with Bonaparte brought many rich pickings for investments throughout Europe. So you see, it was my own hard work and determination that has made me what I am today.'

He had failed to mention his other gambling and Beatrice wondered how much of his wealth had been acquired in the gambling haunts of Europe.

'And are you like your father?'

'No, I am not,' he replied quickly, avoiding her gaze,

his expression grim. 'He was a blackguard along with his forebears.'

Taken aback by the steely undertone in his quiet reply, she stared at him in question. When he ignored her, she decided not to press him, but his apparent bitterness about his father puzzled her.

'Thank you for telling me of your achievements,' she said. 'I am impressed—who would not be—but apart from your name, that you are a marquess, extremely wealthy and have a house in Kent, I know nothing about you.'

'Then allow me to enlighten you. I have three middle names and several lesser titles I rarely use,' he told her. 'No doubt Constance—Lady Merrick—will give you a rundown of my character. I have a great deal of business to attend to so I shall not be able to give you my full attention—and I shudder to think what you might get up to left to your own devices. You really do not have the slightest concept of the importance of appropriate behaviour, do you, Beatrice? Didn't you learn anything under your aunt's tutelage?'

'Yes, but with all her attention fixed on Astrid and knowing it wasn't important how I turned out since finding me a suitable husband was not on my aunt's agenda, I could never see the point of it.'

Julius stared into her stormy green eyes and flushed face, wondering why, from the very first, she had been able to affect him like no other woman in a long time, wondering why he felt this consuming, unquenchable need to possess and gentle her without breaking her spirit.

'James and Constance Merrick are old friends of mine and very close to me,' he told her quietly. 'Don't worry. They will like you when they recover from their surprise that you are to be my wife. Constance is a woman of enormous consequence; she shamelessly adores forcing society to bend to her will. She will not permit anyone to say an unkind word to you or about you in her presence. She is an excellent example of how you ought to conduct yourself in society. You would be wise to observe her behaviour and emulate her.'

Beatrice felt like a naughty child who had just been told it must follow someone else's example. 'How long will it be before the wedding?'

'Three weeks—enough time for the banns to be read—unless you are so impatient to become my wife you would like me to apply for a special licence,' he said with a mocking twist to his lips.

'No,' she said tightly. 'Three weeks will be fine. Where will it be?'

'It will be a quiet affair, the venue of my choosing.'

'Isn't that supposed to be the bride's prerogative?'

'Not in this case. I shall let you know when it is arranged.'

He continued to converse, questioning her about herself, about her life at Standish House, her interest in horses and her relationship with George and Astrid. What he didn't do was talk any more about himself, which, in Beatrice's experience, was what most people did best, or at least most frequently, but apart from what he had told her about his father and

how he had restored the Chadwick fortunes, his private
life remained exactly that.

Beatrice found herself in some kind of indetermi-
nate state, suspended not only in time but in emotion.
Julius had been right about Lord and Lady Merrick.
A middle-aged couple who had not been blessed with
offspring, they were warm and friendly and went out
of their way to make her feel welcome. Lord Merrick was a gentle, delightful soul, very much under his
wife's dominance. Lady Merrick was quite tall with a
majestic bearing and almost as formidable looking as
Aunt Moira. She had a pair of penetrating hazel eyes
and an imperious expression and always believed in
speaking her mind, but Beatrice soon discovered that
beneath it all she was very thoughtful, kind and warm
and was genuinely pleased to have her stay with them.

'There is no need to describe to me what happened
when Julius visited Standish House, Beatrice. I am
well aware of it as is nearly everyone else in society.
For a young lady to ask a man to marry her is not
a civilised thing for her to do. But however it came
about, I cannot suppress my exultation that, by your
actions, it has prompted Julius to take a more serious
interest in marriage. He needs my help in assisting him
to introduce you into society. I have no control over
wagging tongues, but I will do my very best.'

Beatrice was grateful for the time Lady Merrick
took arranging her wardrobe. Julius had insisted that
she be fitted out for every occasion and that no expense
was to be spared, and Beatrice was shocked to find that

Lady Merrick took him at his word and visited some of the most fashionable modistes in London. She took her on shopping expeditions to Bruton Street and Bond Street and the larger warehouses of Covent Garden and the Strand.

'I am putting you to so much trouble,' Beatrice said, feeling some expression of gratitude was due after one particular heavy shopping trip. 'I realise my wardrobe was hardly up to town standards and it is indeed kind of you to give up so much of your time for me.'

'Nonsense. I enjoy doing it, so indulge me, Beatrice. Julius is the son of my dearest friend—tragically she is no longer with us. Indeed, I will even go so far as to say he is the son I never had. His happiness is paramount.'

The word 'tragic' and the sudden pain that she saw in Lady Merrick's eyes stuck in Beatrice's mind and she wondered why. Not wishing to pry, she dismissed the thought.

The society columns were full of her impending marriage to Julius and the nuptial date. News of the race had already been splashed across the front pages of the *Times* and the *Gazette* and the journalists were having a field day with the lurid gossip surrounding this very unconventional marriage.

For two weeks Beatrice saw nothing of Julius. She was afraid to think about him—certainly to feel more for him that she could possibly help. Each day she became more settled in the Merrick household—she would be loath to leave when the time came for her to go and live with Julius as his wife and in his house, wherever that may be. The more she got to know about him from Lady Merrick, the more she began to realise the enormity of what she had done. Hidden away in the country it hadn't mattered, but here in London everything was different.

Apparently women had been throwing themselves at Julius for years, all of them eager to trade themselves for his title and his wealth. When he wasn't sailing on one of his ships to some far-off location, he was sought after by every hostess in town and every ambitious mama, and treated with the deferential respect that his immense wealth and his title commanded amongst the *ton*. He abhorred the attention he drew and rarely attended any of the major social functions, for he understood and despised the reasons why he was coveted. As a result his attitude towards any respectable female of his own class was cynical and jaded, and when he had time to relax away from his offices in Lombard Street, he preferred to spend it at his club in St James's with friends, or at the theatre.

'The longer he's remained unattached, the more of a challenge he's become to all unmarried females,' Lady Merrick told Beatrice as they sat nibbling buttered scones and sipping tea in the morning room, taking a well-earned break from the seamstresses, who had been stitching Beatrice into the taffetas, silks and gauzes that would equip her to be Lady Chadwick, the Marchioness of Maitland. 'Failing to find a woman who can see beyond his wealth and his title and his estates, Julius is convinced she doesn't exist. He merely tolerates those who trail after him and treats them with amused condescension; if one irritates him, he is capable of delivering a crushing set down that is guaranteed to reduce the unfortunate young woman to tears.'

'Oh dear. He is that bad? Well…' Beatrice sighed '…I am not intimidated by him and nor am I in awe of him, and I am certainly not dazzled by his rank, his wealth or his power—although I admit that his wealth was a deciding factor when I decided to ask him to marry me, since it will go some way to renovating Larkhill. I suppose you could also say that I did make it difficult for him to back out of marrying me.'

Constance Merrick believed her. Even though she had known her for such a short time, she had become very fond of Beatrice. Her husband and the servants were completely enchanted by her friendly, unaffected cordiality towards everyone.

'I knew your father, my dear, and from what I know, no doubt part of Julius's decision to accept your proposal owed itself to the fact that in some way he felt responsible for your plight.'

'Which he is,' Beatrice was quick to point out.

'Not…necessarily,' Lady Merrick said hesitantly, averting her eyes. She would have liked to defend Julius, but to do so she would have to divulge the truth about what really happened on the day Beatrice's father lost Larkhill in a game of cards—and the terrible events that had ensued. Julius had asked both her and her husband not to speak of it to Beatrice and Constance would abide by that. Three people were bound by a guilty secret, but it hurt her terribly to hear Julius wrongly maligned.

'Your father was not blameless in all of this. He was a compulsive gambler—but I am sure you know that. But that doesn't mean that things won't turn out for the best. You are a young lady of excellent character and breeding and considerable pluck. There is also a gentle strength about you, a compassion and understanding that I believe will make you the perfect wife for Julius. I know him well. I have seen the way he looks at you. He already cares for you a great deal—though he may not know it yet.'

'That is something I would question, Lady Merrick,' Beatrice murmured sadly.

'Nevertheless I suspect you will be good for him and that the two of you will pull off the best match in years.'

Beatrice gave her a truly dubious look. 'If our relationship so far is anything to go by, I very much doubt it. I think you are being too optimistic, Lady Merrick. Even Julius would challenge that statement.'

Lady Merrick chuckled softly, her eyes dancing with mischief as she enfolded Beatrice in a brief, almost protective hug. 'I have not always lived a life that was beyond reproach, Beatrice. Far from it. No matter what people are saying about you, I think that you are very brave. You, my dear, as young as you are, have managed to achieve that which all the other women can only dream about. To secure Julius.'

'Does he not have any family?'

Pain slashed Lady Merrick's features and she sat

back from her. 'He has no family, Beatrice—no one close.'

There was something in her voice that made Beatrice look sharply at her. 'No one?'

'There…was a tragedy—some years ago now—when he lost both his parents,' Lady Merrick told her hesitantly. 'There was a fire. Julius has never got over it. I do not believe he ever will.'

'But—that's truly awful. Will you not tell me what happened?'

'I think Julius must do that. But it may help you to understand what drives him. His life has not been easy. As a boy he was bright, with a thirst for knowledge that put others to shame. Even though his family was financially destitute—which was down to his father, who was a wastrel and a spendthrift—he had a good education thanks to his maternal grandmother. At the end of it he'd learned all he could about the world of business and finance, and, with a small sum of money his grandmother had given him on his eighteenth birthday, he left home for the Continent to seek his fortune and to bring some pride and honour back to the Chadwick name.

'He lost himself in his work with a blind, instinctive faith as his only hope for survival. His skills were quite extraordinary. Julius has the ability to calculate huge columns of figures in his mind in moments. His achievements are quite remarkable. Yes, he gambles—it is the challenge he loves best, of selecting exactly the right venture and wagering a fortune on it, not, as you believe, at the tables. His wealth has brought him many luxuries, but little joy. That is something I would like you to remember, Beatrice, in the days ahead.'

With her mind on what Lady Merrick had told her, knowing she had given her much to think about, Beatrice's heart gradually began to fill with warmth for the man whose name she was soon to bear. True, he was guarded and frequently distant and unapproachable, but the more she contemplated the matter, the more convinced she became that Lady Merrick was right—Julius must care for her a little, or he'd never have succumbed to her forfeit. But in the light of all this, the one thing that didn't make sense was his reputation as a gambler. None of what she had been told fitted with the man who had gambled and won Larkhill from her father.

'He never speaks of his past,' Lady Merrick went on. 'He is a private person. He refuses to discuss his personal life—not even with me and my husband, even though we are the closest he has to a family of his own. Julius is a man of impeccable integrity, honour, dignity and respect. His mother meant everything to him. He has been much affected by her death and by the world in such ways as few others are. He is a clever man and true to what he believes. You could not be marrying a finer man.'

Chapter Five

Julius called the next day as Beatrice was leaving the drawing room to go up to her room.

'I do hope you're not leaving on my account,' said a deep unperturbed voice behind her.

Beatrice whirled in surprise. The pleasure at seeing him again after so long and being able to speak to him was eclipsed by her growing panic about the forthcoming nuptials, a panic she'd been trying unsuccessfully to stifle for days. He stood in the centre of the hall, a tall, slender-hipped, broad-shouldered man. Attired in a tan jacket, buff-coloured breeches and Hessian boots, Julius Chadwick was as handsome of physique as he was of face. His chiselled features were touched by the light, and a gentle ache in her bosom that grew and grew attested to the degree of his attractiveness.

'I wasn't—I mean, I'm not,' she said falteringly, walking towards him.

Shoving his hands into his pockets, he regarded her with mild curiosity. 'I apologise for not calling on you before now, but I had several pressing matters of business to attend to. Since I have no engagements this morning, I thought I would come and see how you are bearing up.'

His tone was impeccably polite, impersonal and businesslike. Relieved but wary, Beatrice's reply was coolly polite, but when she raked her copper curls back from her face, her hand was shaking. 'Perfectly well, as you see.'

Watching her unconscious gesture, Julius did see and he studied her. Sunlight slanting through the windows glinted on her hair, gilding it with a golden sheen, and turned her magnificent eyes luminous bright green. The deep yellow of her gown flattered her creamy complexion and the peach tint glowing in her cheeks.

In a long-suffering voice, Beatrice said, 'Will you please not look at me like that?'

'Like what?'

'As if you're searching for all my flaws.'

'Was I doing that?' he asked absently, noting her high cheekbones, the delicately arched brows, thick sooty lashes and the fullness of her soft lips.

'Yes, you were and it makes me feel uncomfortable.'

His eyes took on a sudden gleam of suppressed laughter and Beatrice assumed, mistakenly, that he was laughing at her. She lifted her chin to its haughtiest and most obstinate angle. 'Don't do it and will you please take me seriously.'

Julius sobered immediately at her imperious tone. 'I'm going to marry you. That's serious enough— although it's hardly the most auspicious start to a marriage and don't imagine for one minute that it will be smooth sailing.'

Lady Merrick appeared and fussed over his arrival and ushered them into the drawing room while she went to supervise the unpacking of some of Beatrice's gowns that had just arrived.

Closing the double doors behind them, Julius waited for Beatrice to be seated. Instead of sitting down, he perched a hip on the arm of a chair opposite, crossed his arms over his chest and studied her impassively.

'You are comfortable here, I hope.'

'Yes, thank you. Lord and Lady Merrick have made me feel very welcome.'

'I knew they would, but if you are to be my wife you have to face society some time. Since you have a scandal hanging over your head I suggest the sooner we are seen together the better. For your first public appearance I have accepted an invitation for us to attend the Earl and Countess of Newland's ball in St James's at the end of the week.'

Beatrice paled at the mention of the scandal. 'I can't. I have no desire whatever to enter society. I can't face everyone just yet.'

'You can and you will,' he said in his determination to convince her of the feasibility and the necessity of the plan.

Unable to endure his close scrutiny, Beatrice shot out of the chair and, ramrod straight, stood apart from him. With a superhuman effort, she took control of her rampaging ire. She looked straight into his enigmatic eyes. 'A ball is not a solution. It—it's a nightmare. I really don't think I can do that—not with everyone talking about me. I shall encounter curious strangers who will watch my every move, searching for something else to gossip about. I can't do it.'

'Yes, you can.' He spoke in a tone that brooked no argument.

'And it doesn't concern you that I shall be flayed alive by wagging tongues?'

Unbelievably, he laughed outright at that. 'Not a bit. You deserve it.'

His remark made her cheeks flame. It was exactly the sort of thing she would have expected him to say as an act of revenge. 'And I have no doubt that you will enjoy every minute of my suffering.'

Relinquishing his perch on the chair arm, he stood up straight and captured her gaze. 'I may be many things, Beatrice, but I am neither cruel nor sadistic. Of course, you don't have to go through with any of this. You could bring it to an end right now and simply walk away. It's not too late to cry off.'

'No.' She was adamant. 'How pathetic and desperate I must seem to you if, after all I have put myself through, you could even suggest such a thing and believe I would go along with it. I told you, Julius, if you want to back out of our agreement then you have to do it yourself, for I have no intention of walking away now I have come this far.'

Julius shrugged. 'Then it looks like we're stuck with each other—for better or worse.'

'That's *exactly* what it looks like. But do not forget that in the eyes of the *ton* I am a shameless wanton and unfit to mingle in polite society. I have broken all the rules governing moral conduct, so if you still insist on parading me in front of everyone like some—some performing puppet, then go ahead.'

Julius gazed at the tempestuous young woman standing before him, her breasts rising and falling with suppressed fury, and his ire gave way to reluctant admiration for her honesty and courage in admitting her fear over the coming event.

'Perhaps now you will realise what you have done. Your case is extreme. Normally social prejudices exclude young women like you from the *ton*—not that you cared much about that or about what they would think of you when you connived to trap me. But as my wife these are the people you will have to associate with and it is absolutely imperative to me that you learn to get on with them. The object is to brave it out. You have spirit enough to endure what they will put you through. As my betrothed, no one will dare disrespect you—though Lord knows you deserve it.'

She glared at him. 'Why are you doing this? For what reason do you wish to put me on display? To further humiliate me?'

'I do not make sport of you, Beatrice. As I said, I want us to be seen together. It is important that we put the right face on our relationship. I don't normally attend these affairs, but I have no intention of my wife being a social outcast. Constance and James are also invited. The three of us will support you. No one will dare give you the cut direct in front of Constance and I will terrify everyone into accepting you.'

'But what to wear,' Lady Merrick said, sweeping into the room like a restless wind, suddenly thoughtful as her eyes moved over Beatrice from head to toe, her mind absorbed with dressing her in such a way that she would outshine all the rest. 'I would normally opt for glamour rather than subdued elegance, but since it's your first outing we don't want to go over the top. The lime-green tulle will be just the thing.'

Julius smiled his agreement, his eyes appraising his future wife. 'I agree absolutely. With that hair and those eyes, it cannot fail.'

In the carriage taking him back to his house, Julius leaned back against the upholstery, thinking over his meeting with Beatrice with fascinated interest. He was amazed by the gracious ease with which she had fitted into the Merrick household and the way she had effortlessly charmed James Merrick, bringing the house to life with her presence and her smile. She was fresh and unspoiled and, despite her youth and inexperience, there was a natural sophistication about her that came from an active mind. He remembered her shy responsiveness to his kiss in the garden at Standish House and the incredible surge of desire she had ignited in his body.

Beatrice was full of surprises and full of promise, he thought, with beauty moulded into every flawless feature of her face, but her allure went deeper than that. There was something within her that made her sparkle and glow like a rare jewel.

It seemed as if everyone in London was at the Newlands' ball. When Julius arrived at the Merrick house, Beatrice was just coming down the stairs. She paused and looked down at him. With a stunned smile of admiration, he took in the full impact of her ravishing lime-green gown. High waisted, it fell from beneath her breasts into panels that clung gently to her graceful hips and ended in a swirl just above her toes. Her hair was drawn back in a sleek chignon, its lustrous simplicity providing an enticing contrast to the sophistication of the gown.

Moving towards her, he took her hand to help her down the last steps. 'You look positively enchanting. After tonight, you'll take the shine out of all the London belles.'

Buoyed by confidence stemming from wearing her first London gown, Beatrice returned his smile, while deep inside she felt something tighten and harden, clarifying and coalescing into one crystal-clear emotion. Her cheeks were delicately flushed, her eyes alight, her parted lips moist and rose tinted. She thought Julius looked incredibly handsome in his evening attire. It made him look elegantly powerful. He had a certain flair in his mode of dress—a bold splash of claret in his waistcoat beneath the black coat, an artful twist to his pristine white cravat and a flourish to the ruffle at his sleeve. It was impossible to believe he would be her husband in just a few days.

When his shrewdly judging gaze swept over her once more, with a little laugh she obligingly performed a twirl, her skirts flaring.

His eyes warmed appreciatively. 'The gown is beautiful, Beatrice. But perfection can only be attained when one works with the best of raw materials.'

Beatrice's heart skittered. She lowered her gaze. 'I appreciate your compliments, Julius. It gives me confidence for what is to come. I think I shall need it.'

'I truly expected you to send me a note informing me you had taken to your bed with a headache and a dose of salts.'

Despite her dread of the evening before her, Beatrice had to bite back a guilty smile over that remark. 'I did consider it,' she confessed, smiling reassuringly at Lady Merrick who stood looking on, immensely proud of her handiwork. 'Lady Merrick talked me out of it.'

Julius nodded his approval. This young woman who was to be his wife was brave, immensely so. It was a slightly dangerous bravery that she possessed, but it was a quality in her that he admired. 'Everyone of importance will be at the ball and it will be a complete crush—which will work to your advantage. Hopefully, afterwards, when everyone has seen you with me, the gossip will die a death and you can get on with the business of being my wife.'

The four of them travelled in Julius's long black town coach drawn by four fiercely black horses. Less than half an hour later they arrived at the Earl and Countess of Newland's mansion, which was an outstanding example of opulence on a grand scale. They stepped into the brilliance of the interior. It was lit by a multitude of candles in countless chandeliers and crystal sconces that made the marble pillars gleam.

A grand staircase swept upwards to the first floor where the ballroom was located. Gaming tables had been set up in reception rooms for those who preferred to pass the evening in dice and cards, and another two large reception rooms had tables arranged for the customary light supper served at midnight.

Beatrice could feel the stares and whispers as she stood in the receiving line, but she was pleasantly surprised when their host and hostess greeted her warmly. As they advanced up the low, wide staircase, she had the strange sensation of helplessness and fatality that one sometimes has in a dream. In the surrounding haze she was aware of no one but Julius by her side, offering her his undeserved support. She was crushed by the weight of responsibility, for her stupidity, her gullibility, and all that those two traits had brought down on her. Almost all the unattached beautiful women she saw had probably aspired to be the next Marchioness of Maitland, but not one of them had behaved with wanton indiscretion as she had. She deserved to be ostracised.

Julius looked at Beatrice, noting her pallor. 'You look terrified,' he murmured. 'Feel like running away? I couldn't blame you.'

Beatrice took a deep breath and squared her

shoulders, knowing that if she turned back now, she would cover herself in further ridicule. 'Yes, but I won't. I've never run away from anything in my life. As a result of what I've done my dignity has taken a public flogging. But if I have nothing else, I still have my pride.'

Yes, Julius thought, pride was all she had left right now, and he hoped she would face them all down with her head held high. Taking her gloved hand, he tucked it through the crook of his arm. The flesh above the edge of her glove was cold. 'Your arm is like ice. Beatrice, I could never let anybody insult you in my presence. Rest assured of that.'

Touched by his chivalrous vow and the depth of his concern, Beatrice pinned a bright smile on her face. 'Thank you. I'll be all right,' she assured him. 'After all, I faced worse than this when I confronted you to take you up on your challenge.'

He watched her rally and manufacture a smile as she lifted her head and met his gaze. She meant it, he realised with surprise. 'Is that so?' he said with an assessing smile as he studied her upturned face. 'At least the memory of your brazen challenge has put some sparkle back into your eyes. It's unfortunate that my kiss didn't have the same effect.'

Beatrice made the mistake of looking at his mouth. She studied those lips for a second, then shook off the awareness that suddenly gripped her. She had to look away because she couldn't concentrate on what was happening around her. 'I wish you wouldn't refer to that. I'm not accustomed to having men I hardly know kiss me.'

Leaning towards her so that his mouth was only inches from her ear, he whispered, 'When you are my wife you will get to know me better. That I promise you.'

As they entered the ballroom where weaving lines of dancers were progressing in a hectic country dance, Beatrice's restless glance skimmed about her, taking stock of her first Grand Ball. A multitude of voices were raised in avid chatter. Silks and satins in bright and subdued colours paraded before her. Perfumes drifted and mingled into a heady haze as bejewelled ladies nodded and curtsied, while elegant gentlemen in superbly cut evening clothes inclined their heads.

Julius escorted her forwards. A huge sea of people seemed to press towards them and voices erupted as heads turned and fans fluttered and people craned their necks to observe the new arrivals. Although they wouldn't dream of giving Julius the cut, they looked at Beatrice with raised brows and severe disapproval. Knowing how conscious she was of the spectacle she offered, Julius lifted a couple of glasses of blood-red wine from the tray of a liveried footman and handed one to her.

'Drink this. It will put some colour into your cheeks and give you a little courage.'

Beatrice accepted the glass and took a sip.

They heard whispers from those around them. A stout, elderly woman, wearing a red-satin turban and standing close enough for them to overhear, joyfully remarked behind a beringed hand to her companion that Miss Fanshaw was so desperate to find a husband that she'd had to do the proposing herself. Another was heard to say that she remembered her when she had come to London with her cousin Astrid. Astrid was a sweet young thing, whereas Miss Fanshaw had such a high opinion of herself.

Julius knew the instant he looked at Beatrice that she'd heard the malicious remarks; because he couldn't offer her any comfort, he slid his arm about her waist and moved towards the dance floor where couples were whirling about to the lilting strains of a waltz. He felt anger and protectiveness begin to simmer inside him, emotions that leapt into steady flame as other venomous remarks reached his ears. He was unable to understand why women were driven to such heartless, vengeful jealousy.

'This is worse than I imagined,' he said, silencing one malicious female with a slicing look.

He understood why she would naturally dread being the focal point of so many fascinated gossips, but not until she actually lowered her head and bit her trembling lip did he realise that her embarrassment was going to be compounded a hundred times now she was thrust into the limelight.

He was right. Beatrice turned away from him as if she couldn't bear to be there any longer, but Julius caught her arm in a gentle but unbreakable grip. Instinct and experience told him that a little tender persuasion could vastly further her cause and he was prepared to resort to that, only if logic and honesty weren't enough to persuade her.

'Don't give them anything more to talk about and condemn you for.'

Beatrice stared at him dubiously. 'How can I possibly do that? I've done all I can to ruin my reputation before I even started and heaped more embarrassment on you,' she said, realising he was a person with feelings that could be hurt. 'I am being ridiculed, scorned and snubbed—and even pitied by some, which is the worst thing of all. I wouldn't blame you if you were to drag me out of here and take me back to Standish House—except that I can't go back there. Aunt Moira would take one look at me and laugh, say I told you so and close the door in my face.'

Julius hid his amusement behind a mask of genteel imperturbability. 'Dear me. This isn't like the reckless, devil-may-care young lady I have come to know. Am I to assume you've had a change of heart, and would like to be free of me?' he taunted gently.

She scowled up at him. 'The idea is beginning to have a certain appeal, but don't get your hopes up, Julius,' she replied stonily. 'I am fully committed.'

He laughed lightly. 'I thought you might say that.'

On the sidelines where she was conversing with an acquaintance, Lady Merrick, seeing what was happening, excused herself and marched towards Beatrice like a protective mother hen guarding her chick. She collected Lord Caruthers and his wife on her way to add to the ranks. Her back was ramrod straight and her jaw thrust forwards in an aggressive stance that dared anyone to question her judgement in lending her enormous consequence to Beatrice.

Julius shot the three of them a grateful look. Right now Beatrice was vulnerable and he didn't want to do or say anything that would make things worse. So, he ignored the instinct to reach up and brush back a wayward tress of shiny hair from her cheek and squelched the temptation to tell her that he had no intention of dragging her anywhere unless it was into his bed. He was not, however, morally opposed to diverting her resistance with as much alcohol as he could pour down her.

'Drink your wine and then we'll dance—and smile, for God's sake. If we are to beat the critics and quell the gossip, it is imperative that we put up a united front—in public at least,' he said in a steely voice that was in vivid contrast to the expression of bland courtesy he was wearing for the sake of their fascinated audience. His eyes shot to hers as an absolutely ridiculous thought suddenly occurred to him. 'You can dance, I hope?'

Beatrice wondered how he would react if she were to tell him that she hadn't danced since the dancing master Aunt Moira had employed to teach her and Astrid had left Standish House two years ago. Instead, with a sparkle in her eyes and a tilt to her head, the smile she gave him was quite sublime.

'Like a fairy,' she quipped.

Eventually, to Beatrice's relief, the flurry created by their conspicuous arrival died down. But when

Julius led her on to the dance floor and gathered her into his arms for a waltz, she wasn't at all sure she could do it, but the challenge in his amber eyes made demurring unthinkable. Giddiness threatened to take hold of her.

'Relax.' Julius looked down at her. She almost missed her step, but his arm tightened, holding her steady. 'Focus your eyes on me and follow my lead,' he said, steering her into the first gliding steps as the graceful music washed over them.

Of their own volition Beatrice's feet followed where he led and her mind opened to the sensations of the dance. She was aware of the subtle play of her skirts about her legs and the hardness of her companion's thighs against hers. The closeness of his body lent to her nostrils a scent of his cologne, fleeting, inoffensive, a clean masculine smell. The seductive notes of the music were mirrored in their movements and the sway was a sensual delight. Julius's hand at her waist was firm, his touch confident as he whisked her smoothly around the ballroom.

After looking at them attentively, the couples on the dance floor renewed their interest in the music. Conversations were resumed and everyone got on with enjoying themselves.

Julius stared down at the lovely young woman in the provocative green gown, her eyes as they observed the other dancers both wary and stormy. In the three weeks since he'd kissed her in the garden at Standish House, he'd made no further attempts to kiss her or embrace her. In his opinion he'd been a perfect gentleman—considerate, courteous, even casual—and the energy of a sexually aroused male, the need in him to make this woman totally his, went by her like the dancers whirling around.

Determined to have the lead in how their marriage was conducted, he said, 'There is something you should understand, Beatrice.'

She tilted her head to his. 'What is it?'

'When you are my wife, I expect you to behave as if you married me because we are in accord—that you care for me more than my title and my money, that you will never discredit my name or your own. What transpires between us in private is our affair. I will conduct myself publicly as if I were the most devoted and faithful of husbands. I will not knowingly do anything to cause you even a moment of humiliation, even though there will be times when you may have cause to regret our bargain.'

Beatrice stared up at him. Bargain? What bargain? her mind warned her in a quiet voice. The silent argument was overturned by the effect of a sombre, handsome face, a deep hypnotic voice and the powerful, tall and strong male body that loomed over her. Here was a man who, to her surprise, was offering to shield her from the world and shoulder her burdens. The combination of that and his good looks was becoming dangerously appealing, particularly because he wasn't offering love or even affection.

'In the eyes of the world,' he went on, 'you will be my cherished wife.'

Cherished! Beatrice couldn't believe what he'd

said. It was a word that was sensitive and sentimental. It didn't apply to what was between them and it was totally unlike anything she'd expected him to say.

'Of course,' he continued, 'it works both ways. I shall expect the same promises from you. Is that agreeable?'

His future wife bit her lip, considered for a moment, then nodded and with a winsome smile gazed up at him. This was better and much more than she could have hoped for, although she couldn't understand why there was a *frisson* of disappointment underlying her relief. 'If you are asking me to give a convincing performance for all the world to see that we are a truly happily married couple while continuing as we are now, then I will do my best.'

He looked irritated by her reply, but said, 'I'm glad we are in accord on that, but as my wife you will find that things will not be the same as they are now. Marriage will change everything.'

Beatrice gazed into his unfathomable eyes, seeing the cynicism lurking in the depths. 'I don't mean to pry—what you do has nothing to do with me—but I have learned from living in the Merrick household for the past weeks that you are disenchanted with life. I know I shall be marrying a man I don't love—a man who doesn't love me. That's what makes it so perfect. Our marriage won't be complicated by messy emotions. We're the perfect solution for each other. You could say this was fate—if you were superstitious, that is.'

'Which I'm not,' Julius said with a bite in his voice. 'I don't believe in fate.'

* * *

When the dance ended, he put his hand under her elbow and guided her towards the supper room where they were joined by a jolly group of Julius's friends. Over food and wine and easy, lighthearted conversation, they both relaxed. Confident that the firestorm of gossip surrounding Beatrice and Julius had subsided, Lord and Lady Merrick left the ball early with friends to attend a quieter function in Mayfair.

In no mood for dancing and suspecting that in her nervousness, to boost her confidence, Beatrice had drunk too much wine over supper, Julius suggested they get some air on the terrace.

Beatrice glanced at him in mock horror. 'The terrace? But is that proper? Should I not have a chaperon?'

'It doesn't matter,' he murmured softly, staring at her with a half-intimate smile. 'We are already betrothed— and after the amount of wine you consumed over supper, I think some fresh air would not go amiss.'

He flashed her a smile that made her heart rebel against all the strictures she had placed on herself.

'Ah,' he said in amusement when he saw her eyes darken with warmth. 'I think you're beginning to like me in spite of yourself.'

'That is merely a delusion,' she replied, fighting back her laughter.

He knew better, said his eyes.

'And don't look at me like that,' she reproached lightly. 'You can't read my mind.'

'I am older and more experienced than you, Beatrice. I see what is written on your face.'

She laughed. 'Then I shall have to learn to school it better.'

'An impossibility for you,' he said in a husky murmur.

Taking her gloved hand, he tucked it into the crook of his arm and led her towards the French doors that opened on to the moonlit terrace. They went down some steps into the lantern-lit gardens. Strolling along the paths, they nodded politely to other couples they passed. At the end of the garden they turned off the path and stepped into a shaded arbour. Beatrice stood and looked at Julius, suffused with trepidation and a tingling excitement that was the result of being alone with him in such a dark, intimate setting. The voices of others died away, leaving only distant strains of soothing music.

'Dance with me, Beatrice,' he said suddenly, his voice like rough velvet.

Beatrice stared at him, the lilting notes of the waltz floating around her. When he opened his arms, feeling as if she were in a dream, she walked into them and felt his right arm slide around her waist, bringing her close against his solid strength. His left hand closed around her fingers and suddenly she was being whirled gently about the arbour in the arms of a man who danced the waltz with the relaxed grace of one who has danced it countless times. She should have felt overpowered—threatened—but surprisingly she felt protected instead.

Suddenly his arm tightened around her waist, forcing her into closer proximity with his powerful body. 'You are very quiet, Beatrice. Have you nothing to say?

It is customary to engage in some form of conversation with your partner.'

Tilting her head back, she smiled teasingly up at him. 'What am I to say? That you dance divinely?'

Julius smiled down at her. 'That is what I'm supposed to say to you. We could engage in some kind of harmless flirtation. It is quite acceptable for couples to do that when they are dancing.'

'Why? Is it because otherwise onlookers will perceive they don't like each other? Well, don't expect me to do that because I haven't any experience with flirting—unlike you.'

'Would you like some lessons?'

'Are you offering to show me how it's done?'

Julius stared down into her dark-green eyes and momentarily lost himself in them. Desire surged through his body and he pulled her closer still. 'I'd like to try—although you're doing very well at it right now.'

'Julius, will you kindly take me seriously!'

'I'm going to marry you,' he said coolly, loosening his hold on her as the music ended. 'That's serious enough.'

'Do you realise,' she said with a winsome smile as she tilted her head to the side, 'that you become positively grim when you speak of our marriage? Are you happy—with your life, I mean? Has the breach with your father affected you very badly?'

He looked irritated by her question, but he answered it. 'Why this curiosity to know? I've already told you that the Chadwick history is nothing to be proud of.'

'That's it. I'm curious. You told me you come from a long line of gamblers. Is that what you do when you want to replenish your coffers?'

He looked at her steadily. 'You really think I make my money at the gaming tables, don't you?'

'You didn't answer my question.'

'No, I didn't.' He stepped closer, his gaze on her mouth.

Beatrice frowned, trying to ignore the tug of his eyes and his voice. 'Why is it that when you don't wish to answer a question, you divert the conversation to something else and…' Her words died as he placed his hands gently on both sides of her face, his fingers sliding into her hair, grateful she didn't favour the fashion for silk flowers and silly ribbons so many other women seemed fond of.

'Stop talking,' he whispered, then lowered his head and kissed her.

Her lips were soft and they parted slightly to receive his. Accepting her invitation, Julius deepened the kiss with ease. She was happy to submit, even though she had the feeling she was getting in over her head. She closed her eyes, exploring the sensations of delight that flooded through her. The beauty of the setting, the romantic sense of the evening and the intoxicating nearness of this man overpowered her judgement. His kiss was exquisite, transporting her to further delights.

Lost in pure sensations of wanton yearnings, warm, strong and exciting, when his mouth left hers and trailed to her neck, she melted against him, her palms sliding up over his chest. He moved against her in the most intoxicating way that sent a shiver up her spine. Lifting his head from devouring her neck, Julius let his gaze settle on her lips. Beatrice considered him the most handsome man she had ever seen; when she thought how he had manoeuvred her into the kiss, with all his worldly elegance and experience that could instruct her in every pleasure that a woman could discover with a man, she accepted he was also a silver-tongued charmer.

'Well, I'll be blowed,' a man's voice intruded. 'If it isn't the Marquess of Maitland.'

At once Julius stiffened and released Beatrice, then turned to face an old acquaintance. It was Lord Percival Canning, a ponderous, mincing fop who was dressed like a peacock in yellow coat, red-satin waistcoat and yellow-satin breeches that swelled over his protruding midsection. Two of his friends hovered behind him.

'I'm happy to see you back among us, Chadwick.' Lord Canning's eyes shifted to Beatrice. 'By all accounts we have the lovely Miss Fanshaw to thank for bringing you out of isolation.'

'Not really,' Julius replied drily. 'I've only recently returned from one of my trips abroad. It's impossible to be in two places at once.'

'So it is. Then you won't have been down to Highfield. Pity.'

'Why?'

Lord Canning shrugged. 'I hoped to discuss that little business matter with you I mentioned when you were last down there. Maybe we could meet up while you are in London.'

Julius stared at him icily. 'I don't think so, Canning. The matter you speak of is not open for negotiation.'

Anger briefly flashed into Canning's eyes and Julius's steely body tensed as the dandy drew close, striking an arrogant pose.

'Think about it. I would give you a fair price.' He turned his attention to Beatrice, his fleshy lips opening in a salacious, gargoyle-like grin from ear to ear as he ran his eyes over her in an insulting manner. 'I regret that I did not see the race at Standish House. Everyone's talking about it, Chadwick—of how the high and mighty Marquess of Maitland has been caught like a fish on a hook by a mere slip of a girl! How could you have let that happen—you of all people?' he taunted. 'I hear Miss Fanshaw beat you on a high-spirited brute of a horse. Why, I'd have put money on her myself had I been there.'

'Indeed,' Julius replied blandly. The men—Canning's companions snickering foolishly behind him—would have been dumbfounded to know that as he languidly listened to Canning, he was seething inside.

'Yes, indeed—and she's a beauty all right. Ye Gods, had she challenged me I'd have willingly thrown the race for the pleasure of paying her forfeit.'

Insulted and outraged to the core of her being by this obnoxious fop, Beatrice was furious, but, seeing the rigidity in Julius's back and knowing how he was struggling to hold his temper, she did not retaliate. But she could not bear the way he was being mocked.

'You're being very stupid, Canning—and as immature as I remember,' Julius said. 'You should know better than to bait me.'

Unperturbed and emboldened by the backup of his two friends, Canning laughed inanely and continued. 'Get the bit between her teeth, tighten her rein a bit and she'll be as docile as a lamb. I don't think you've introduced us, Chadwick.'

Julius's brows lifted. 'No.'

'It's not very sociable.'

Julius answered by slamming a fist in Canning's face that knocked him to the ground. 'I don't feel like being sociable, Canning,' he uttered icily, looking down at him with utter contempt, seeing the blood from his burst nose staining his yellow coat to match the colour of his waistcoat. His eyes sliced a warning to the stunned friends not to interfere. 'That was for insulting my future wife. Insult her again at your peril, Canning. Excuse us.' Taking Beatrice's elbow, without looking back, he strode towards the house.

Shocked by what had just happened and hoping that Canning wasn't badly hurt—although she had to admit that he deserved the punch in the nose—Beatrice was almost running to keep up with Julius's long strides. 'Julius, please slow down. Who was that man?'

'Lord Percival Canning, a neighbour of mine with an axe to grind to do with some lands he wants to buy off me. I've no intention of selling to him, but he never gives up. He never fails to take the opportunity to put my back up.'

If Julius's black scowl and rigid jaw was anything to go by, Lord Canning had succeeded admirably, Beatrice thought. But the meeting with the aforesaid gentleman made her realise for the first time what a laugh Julius's friends must be having at his expense. In the eyes of everyone who'd followed the stories in the newspapers, she had manipulated him into marrying her. She was filled with guilt and remorse over what she was asking—no, demanding—of him.

'Julius—I had no idea... I'm sorry,' she said with quiet desperation.

At those words Julius's gaze jerked to her and he stopped dead. Beatrice almost cried out at the blistering contempt blazing in his eyes.

'Julius, I—I can imagine what you must be thinking—'

He interrupted sarcastically, 'Oh, I don't think you can. If you could, you'd be quite horrified at this moment.'

'I—I didn't think—'

'What you think is not my primary concern at this moment,' he bit back coldly.

'But...I never realised people would react this way—truly. Your friends... They are laughing at you. I will call an end to it...'

'What? And shame me more than you already have? Don't even think of quitting now, lady,' he hissed. 'We play this damned charade out to the bitter end.'

'But I...'

'Shut up,' he ground out, without relinquishing his hold on her elbow. 'Let's get out of here.'

Not until they were in the coach and Julius had regained a modicum of self-control and his hard face was wiped clean of all expression did he speak.

'So, Beatrice, what have you to say about your first London ball?'

'Until our encounter with the obnoxious Lord Canning, it went better than I thought it would, although I confess I'm glad it's over. It will be a relief to be back at the house.'

Julius nodded and not by the flicker of an eye did he betray his admiration for way she had conducted herself in the face of so much condemnation. It was a pity his admiration did not extend to himself, he thought bitterly. He should have known better than to retaliate with his fists to Canning's baiting.

'Very soon you will be coming home with me.'

Looking at him, Beatrice wondered at her sudden weakness in the garden. She really had intended backing out of their arrangement if that was what he wanted. But she could see that to walk away from him now would be tantamount to jilting him and would be a slight to him and to his rank, and she could not do such a thing to him.

'When will you be taking me to Highfield?' she asked. 'Lady Merrick has told me how splendid it is.'

'My ancestors would be pleased to hear it,' he remarked drily, feeling no pride or any warm sensation in the palatial splendour that was Highfield Manor.

'You don't like it?'

'I find it oppressive. I don't often go down there—not since the demise of my parents—and, as you have just witnessed, the neighbours leave a lot to be desired.'

'You must miss them—your parents.'

'My mother, yes. As far as my father was concerned, no. We were not close.'

He turned his head and looked out of the window, but the tension pulsating from him began to play on Beatrice's nerves. She wished that he would open up to her and tell her more about his family and why he felt such antipathy for his father. She felt sure it went beyond his father's weakness for gambling and drink. Julius was locked behind a barrier and she was on the other side. It troubled her that he seemed to know a great deal about her, then shut her out when she asked for answers in return.

'Did your father hurt you?' His expression turned glacial. She knew she should heed the warning in her head, but ploughed on regardless. 'Why do you hate him?'

'Hate? Yes, I hated him.' That was his only response, but his eyes were full of secrets, as unyielding as cold, hard steel.

'Why won't you tell me what he did that makes you feel like this?' Beatrice persisted. He gave her an impatient look, a warning look, and did not reply. She knew he was getting angry with her, but she was not ready to give up yet. 'Why do you find it so painful to speak of him? It might relieve your feelings if you were to confide—'

'Beatrice, do me a favour,' he interrupted acidly. 'Do not tell me how to deal with my feelings and I won't tell you how to deal with yours. Agreed?'

She flinched at his hard tone, but she detected a turbulent pain beneath his cold veneer.

'You are such an innocent still, Beatrice, a naïve child in many ways.'

'At least I'm not heartless,' she retorted.

For the rest of the journey back to Upper Brook Street nothing more was said. Julius had his gaze fixed out of the window, aware of Beatrice glowering at him in the light from the carriage lamps. When anyone tried to get too close or attempted to pry into his past life, resentment surfaced towards his father and the terrible crime he had committed towards Beatrice's father. May God help her—and him—should she ever discover the truth.

He shoved the painful memory away, reminding himself that his father was dead. What mattered now was getting on with his life and his future with Beatrice. And yet the old barbs stuck in his flesh and posed problems, threatened what happiness he hoped for.

Beatrice wanted answers, but her questions awoke years of anger and hurt and deception and lies. To protect his father—a father unworthy of a son's loyalty—and to prevent an almighty scandal, Julius had allowed himself to be unfairly maligned. He never realised he would meet a beautiful girl who, completely innocent about her own connection to the night that had ruined his own life, would probe into his mind in her curiosity to know him better.

And now, whatever the cost, to protect his future with Beatrice and Beatrice herself, this terrible secret must remain hidden. He would carry it to the grave.

But secrets had a way of slipping out.

Chapter Six

Despite her determination to get through it without a hitch, Beatrice's wedding to Julius had a distinct aura of unreality and strain about it. At the outset, Julius had said he did not care to surround the ceremony with any pomp. This suited Beatrice perfectly, for she did not want to attract further attention to herself.

She was numb to the world about her as she stepped through the high, main portal of St George's Church in Hanover Square, Mayfair's most fashionable church. The aisle was illuminated by candles and it seemed a long walk down on Lord Merrick's arm. She had no bridesmaids, not even a matron of honour, the only guests being a handful of Julius's close friends and Lord and Lady Merrick, for which Beatrice was thankful. Never had she felt so alone. This was supposed to be the most important and happiest day of her life, yet she had no family or friends to bear witness to her marriage.

Two men rose to their feet as she approached the pews at the front of the church. One of them, his tall, powerful frame garmented regally in midnight-blue velvet and flawless white cravat, moved forwards and half-turned so that he might watch her progress. His face was stark and serious, almost harsh, and Beatrice was not to know that Julius Chadwick was fighting to control the strong rush of emotion that went through him at the sight of her in her heavy ivory-satin wedding gown.

For a moment Beatrice was tempted to turn before the vows were spoken and fly from the insanity of what she was doing. But even as she argued with herself she took her place beside Julius, to join her life with his. The amber eyes of her husband-to-be held hers, narrowing, assessing, as though he were studying the woman who had manoeuvred him into marriage.

The vision Julius saw walking towards him bathed in candlelight snatched his breath away and pride exploded throughout his entire body until he ached with it, for no bride had ever looked as lovely. He stretched out a strong, brown, well-manicured hand and offered it to her. She lifted her own and placed it in his much larger, much warmer one. Julius felt the trembling of her fingers and saw the anxiety in her large eyes. Immensely relieved that she hadn't decided to pull out of marrying him, he gave her hand a little squeeze in an attempt to reassure her. He drew her the remainder of the way to the altar steps, where he would make her his for all eternity.

Time stood still as they were swept into the marriage ceremony. Beatrice felt as if she existed in a glass bubble as she spoke the words. She could see all that went on in a kind of mist and what she said was loud enough to be heard, but the words indistinct.

It seemed only a moment before Julius was sliding a gold band upon her finger and then it was over. Not about to forgo the custom of kissing his young bride, Julius placed his long fingers beneath the delicate bones of her jaw and tilted her face to his. His head lowered and his parted lips moved gently over hers. At last he slackened his grip and stepped back and, offering her his arm through which she slipped her hand, he led her back down the aisle.

As Julius handed her up into his shiny black coach emblazoned with the Maitland coat of arms, Beatrice thought she was being handed up into the midst of paradise, for only then did she realise fully that she had succeeded in what she had set out to do. Leaving the church for Julius's town house in Piccadilly ahead of the rest, she was conscious of the man seated across from her, watching her intently. Her heart started to beat a wild tattoo and her lips curved in a small triumphant smile. She could have floated, she felt so light.

The future—a future that involved Larkhill—was as blue as the horizon. Having seen a different side to him as she got to know him a little better over the last few days, and unable to deny her growing attraction for him, she was surprised by how much she looked forward to her new life with Julius with more than a little excitement.

Only one cloud darkened her happiness—she was deeply concerned that she might not be able to live up to his expectations and would be a disappointment to him. For days now she had been apprehensive as her wedding day approached—in particular the wedding night—and she told herself that if other women could endure what their husbands did to them, then so could she. She also told herself that perhaps the marital act wouldn't be as painful as she imagined, and, since she had been the instigator of this marriage, she would bear the pain.

But as the hour when she must submit to her husband drew ever nearer, her philosophical attitude deserted her and her dread was steadily mounting. True, she had coerced Julius into marrying her, but when she'd done so, she'd been half-delirious with winning the race. Now, however, she saw with cold clarity what the results of her coercing would be.

From beneath hooded lids, Julius watched her with brooding attentiveness. The sun shining in through the windows spread a halo around her and the diamond necklace he had given her as a wedding gift shone like droplets of dew against her flesh. At that moment he thought she was the most magnificent creature he had ever seen—and she belonged to him. This delectable, golden-haired girl was his wife, to preside at his table and bear his children. She would never bore him, this he knew.

'How does it feel to be my wife—Lady Chadwick, the Marchioness of Maitland—Beatrice?'

As Beatrice met his gaze, her lips curved in a little smile. 'If you must know, I don't feel anything at the moment. It's difficult to take it all in. I feel no different to what I did before the ceremony.' She arched her brows in question. 'Should I?'

'I can think of plenty of females who would.'

'I'm sure you can, but I am not one of them. Titles are meaningless to me.'

He nodded slowly. 'That's right. Titles don't enter into your scheme of things, do they? Only a certain property.'

'You knew that from the start. I made no secret of what I wanted.'

'No, you didn't. But now I think it's about time you realised what it is that *I* want.'

To Beatrice's absolute disbelief, he leaned forwards and stretched his hand to her. Completely unnerved, she jerked back, not knowing what he intended. Annoyed because she didn't fall into his lap, he yanked her off her seat before she knew what he was about, his long fingers curled around her wrist in a painful vice. She muffled a cry as she landed in a sprawling, uncomfortable heap on the seat beside him.

'What are you doing?' she panted, unable to hide her displeasure as she squirmed against him, his glittering eyes and his mouth only inches from hers as he leaned over her, his arms holding her fast.

'This,' he said hoarsely and his mouth swooped down, seizing hers in a ruthless kiss. For several moments Beatrice was so confounded she made no attempt to stop him. His lips moved over hers, gently, smoothing, his mouth open a fraction. Within moments her tension began to melt in the heat of his kiss and her senses swam dizzily. In a kind of sensual haze, she was aware of his hand roaming possessively over the sensitive flesh above her bodice. Then she came to life, tearing her lips from his, struggling and pushing herself back from his arms.

'Please, Julius, stop it. Don't do this. I may be your wife, but that does not give you leave to manhandle me whenever you wish. I will not be forced.'

When Julius tried to reach for her again she flinched, slapping his arm hard and pushing him away with both hands, then returning to the opposite seat. For a second as he looked at his indignant, spluttering wife, he remained dazed. In what she thought was self-defence she had used the very movements of a tavern wench accustomed to dealing with drunks. He had never seen a lady defend herself in this way before. It struck him as both funny and exasperating. Did she really imagine that he was going to leave her alone? Did she really imagine he would force her?

Frowning with concern over the anxiety and tension he saw on her face, leaning forward and resting his forearms on his knees, he said, 'I am not a monster, Beatrice. I will not force you to do anything you do not want to do. You have my word on that.'

'Thank you,' she said, her tension easing a little on hearing this.

As Julius looked at her, the sight of her stormy,

brilliant green eyes, her white shoulders and that fragile neck and soft lips aroused in him a violent but unfamiliar desire, such as no woman had ever aroused in him. It was not just blind lust. There was about it a somewhat mysterious, almost sweet and gentle allure.

Something sprang into jubilant life within him and soared. Thank God, he thought, she was not going to be a submissive wife, docile and totally insensate and frozen inside, a woman who would endure his embraces with a sigh and accept that it was her wifely duty to submit to him with compliance. He sensed Beatrice was like a cat, a tigress, ready to fight like one, to match him in strength, to be his equal both in bed and out of it.

At this moment she was openly defying him, yet he was the offended one. In the beginning she had forced his hand, humiliated him as no man can bear to be humiliated without wishing the other into purgatory, so first he must show her that she was his wife, and then he would make her realise that their marriage would be conducted on equal terms, and that what they did together could be pleasing for them both.

And yet Julius would have been most surprised at his wife's thoughts hidden behind her façade of defiance and indignation. Her emotions were all over the place following his kiss. It had left her so confused she could hardly think. Why did she feel like this? she thought wonderingly. A slow realisation of what was happening, born of the moment when he had dragged her into his arms, was moving through her, making its way to her slowly thawing heart, which had been frozen for so long.

She swallowed and turned her head so she didn't have to look at the man opposite. He was so formidable, so stern, so oppressive and yet so…so what? Breathtakingly handsome? Strong, compelling and completely masculine? Yes, she thought, he was all those things. A man lean, muscular, with wide shoulders, narrow hips and trim waist, she could not help but admire the fine figure he made—near, if not, perfection. Heat suffused her cheeks and her heart was beating hard against her ribcage, as though it were trying to get out to escape the bewildering pain it felt.

Dear Lord, what was happening to her—and in such a short space of time? Why had fate turned her feelings, in the blink of an eye, from absolute indifference to this man who was her husband of mere minutes to something so painful she could not understand it? It was blurring her mind. She could feel herself shaking inside, for she was afraid of his passion, afraid of how much it would hurt in the future if she let herself weaken now.

'Fight me if you must, Beatrice,' he said softly, 'but I promise you that we will share the more tender moments of our marriage. You say you dislike force. I, too, loathe it, but I could do nothing to get out of paying your forfeit. I did not choose *you* for a wife, *you* chose me,' he reminded her, his words dripping with disdain. 'But however it came about, I do not intend to take advantage of you. Now you're angry because you will have to pay the piper, but you do not think what it has cost me to make you my wife.'

The sound of his voice brought her back to the present. Deeply troubled and confused by her feelings, furious at her sudden weakening and hurt by what he had said, she took refuge in anger. Turning her head back to him, she laughed ungraciously.

'You didn't *have* to marry me. You could have walked away.'

'So could you. I recall telling you that as my mistress you would have been treated as a queen,'

'Whereas what I have now is a master,' she retorted irately, using her anger to fortify her against her nervousness at what was to come later. 'Is that what you are telling me, Julius?'

He smiled thinly, his amber eyes nailed to hers. 'I would never be that, Beatrice. What I will say is that if you consider refusing me your bed, remember that you are only one woman among many. For a man it is easy to find relief for his baser needs.'

'And I imagine you are low enough to do that,' she said, still wondering and bewildered at the hurt and disappointment that stirred her heart.

His jaw tightened and his eyes grew cold. Did she really think she could flout him so soon into their marriage? 'There's no need to distress yourself, my love,' he said mockingly. 'You are quite safe from me for the present.'

'I sincerely hope so,' she replied, moving as far from him as was possible within the confines of the coach.

'You cannot escape me, Beatrice,' he said easily,

concerned by her distress and attempting to lighten the moment by injecting a teasing note into his voice. 'You are now and for ever mine. Marriage with me is what you wanted and that is what you shall have for the rest of your life—or mine. But fear not. You are a beauty, my sweet. I shall not grow tired of you and have no desire to leave you too soon.' He chuckled softly, reaching out and touching her cheek, relieved that she did not pull away. 'You will find I am temperamental and that I may not be termed a pleasant man to live with—but you have my word that I shall strive to be amenable at all times when we are together.'

Beatrice managed to smile and turned her head away, looking out of the window as the coach finally drew up before the house—a splendid mansion of which Beatrice would now be mistress. Julius climbed out and turned to assist her.

'Can you manage, my love, or shall I lift you down?' he asked, a smile twisting his handsome mouth.

For the sake of appearances and because the nervous fluttering in her stomach was increasing with each passing minute, she allowed him to assist her out of the coach, placing her hand on his arm for him to escort her into the house.

'Smile,' Julius said in a quiet voice while managing to smile charmingly himself for the benefit of those who had gathered to see the return of the bride and groom and to wish them well. 'Must I remind you that this is your wedding day, which is supposed to be the happiest day of your life, whereas you, my love, look as if you are going to your execution.'

Feeling that the quiet reprimand was deserved, Beatrice did as he bade and composed her features into a more agreeable expression as he escorted her inside the house.

Beatrice was introduced to the curious but welcoming servants, who bobbed their curtsies or respectfully bent their heads, though she felt such an intruder, an interloper, not one face or one name was retained in her memory.

Julius led her into a green-and-gold salon, where a long table had been prepared for the wedding feast. It gleamed with silver cutlery and crystal glasses and was festooned with flowers. Standing in the centre of the salon, a smile pinned to her lips and a glass of champagne in her hand, the bride received the well wishes of all those present. The meal went quickly—too quickly for Beatrice—who wanted to delay the time when she would find herself alone with Julius.

Seated beside her, Julius lounged back in his chair, his arm stretched possessively across the back of hers, his expression thoughtful as he watched her smile and laugh when glasses were raised in toast to the bride and groom. It wasn't surprising that everyone was in her thrall, for she looked ravishing. She was also lively and amiable in a way that not even he had seen before. She had deliberately set herself out to charm; as he toyed with the stem of his wine glass, it was that effort which both amused and exasperated him.

If she hadn't decided to make herself so delightful, everyone would have eaten their fill and gone home earlier—which was, Julius knew, exactly what she didn't want, for their presence delayed the moment when she would have to go upstairs with him and they would be alone.

Because this was her wedding day and because he knew she was probably anxious about what was to happen later, for the last hour he had been willing to indulge her, using the time to enjoy her company and to savour the anticipation of what was to come. Now, however, he was growing tired of the wait.

Leaning close to her, he said, 'I'm sorry to put an end to your day, Beatrice, but I think it's time you and I left.'

As he stood up and held his hand out to her, Beatrice realised the moment she had dreaded all day had arrived. A delicate flush spread over her features as she rose and placed her trembling hand in his. It was growing dark and, not wishing to linger without the bride and groom, the guests began to leave. Beatrice looked pleadingly at Lady Merrick when she came up to her.

'Must you go now?' she asked in a quavering voice.

The kindly woman nodded her head and gave her a motherly kiss upon the brow. 'Yes, my dear. It's time the two of you were alone. We cannot stay any longer. Be happy, Beatrice,' she said, glancing up at Julius who stood beside her. 'I know you will be well cared for.'

Beatrice watched her go. She looked at Julius. 'If you don't mind, I would like to go to my room now.'

'It's been a long day and I'm sure you must be feeling tired. I shall escort you there myself. I hope you will find it—comfortable. And there is a connecting door to my room.'

When her eyes snapped to his he straightened, his face set in lines of challenge. His lips curled over his white teeth. 'There is nothing wrong with that, Beatrice. It is perfectly natural for a husband and wife to have connecting rooms.' As he came to stand beside her, he murmured just loud enough for her to hear, 'I trust you have no objections to the sleeping arrangements. Are you afraid of being alone with me, my love, of fulfilling your part of the bargain we made?'

Beatrice coloured hotly and turned away in sudden confusion. His hand slid about her waist and she started slightly as his hard chest pressed against her back.

His deep voice seemed to reverberate within her as he announced softly, 'I think it is time for bed.'

In that moment her mind flew from all rational thought. A bolt of doubt blasted her confidence. She turned to face him.

'You—you spoke of a bargain. What bargain might that be? I do not recall having made any bargain with you.'

He raised a sardonic brow. 'Ah, but you did. Think about it, Beatrice. When you asked me to be your husband and again when you spoke your vows.' Seeing her uncertainty, he chuckled softly. 'Did you think I would have entered into this if I had nothing to gain?' He laid a hand against her cheek in a tender caress. 'I have fulfilled my part of the bargain. It is time for you to fulfil yours. It is the price you have to pay. You belong to me until death.'

Fully realising the truth of what he said, Beatrice shrank away from him in disbelief, aware of the trap that slowly closed around her—a trap of her own making.

'Tonight you will see the real price of your predicament.' His voice became gentle, almost a whisper. His eyes were hungry with yearning and touched her everywhere. 'You sought me out for a cause dear to you and I have given you my name—a high price for me to pay. Now I ask the same of you. Do you find the price too dear that you suddenly want to reject it—to deny the bargain?'

'No,' she replied stiffly. 'Of course not.'

'I am happy to hear that, Beatrice. Come, we shall go up together', and without further ado, in silence he began to lead the new Marchioness of Maitland up the stairs, along the landing in the direction of their chambers. Not until they were inside Beatrice's room and the door closed against the world did he release her, relieved to have her alone at last.

As his bride she was certainly lovely to look at. Golden strands shimmered among the carefree copper curls, crackling and alive in the light from the candles. The soft brows arched away from eyes that were clear and green—sea green in this light, brilliant against the thick fringe of jet-black lashes and as unfathomable as any sea he had ever gazed into. The soft pink lips were tantalising and gracefully curved. Under his penetrating gaze the golden skin flushed slightly.

Feeling desire stir in his loins, with a will of iron Julius clamped a grip upon himself.

With tension twisting within her, Beatrice rubbed
her arm and warily considered her husband. His face
was extremely handsome above a froth of white lace,
his dark hair smoothly brushed and his white teeth
shining in his gypsy-brown face. With a surge of admiration, she thought how ruggedly virile he looked. He
also looked relaxed as he stood watching her, his amber
eyes warm and intense, a spark flaring in their depths.

She felt the bold touch of his hungry gaze and
inwardly shivered. Her knees quaking violently, she
walked slowly around the room that was to be hers. It
was a tastefully furnished, elegant room, the bed large
and canopied in the same mulberry and gold as the rest
of the room. There was no sign of a maid to assist her
out of her wedding finery, but the bedcovers had been
turned down and the lacy white jasmine-scented sheets.

Seeing her stiffen and stare with stricken paralysis
at the bed and noting how her fingers that flew to her
mouth trembled, with long, easy strides that always
looked both certain and relaxed, Julius walked towards
her.

'Come, Beatrice, there's nothing to fear, so why are
you trembling?'

She turned and looked at him, unable to tear her
gaze from his, unable to hide her fear. 'I don't know,'
she admitted with a tremor in her voice.

'Don't you?' he asked softly, one eyebrow raised in
question. 'You do realise what is to happen between
us, don't you?'

She nodded. 'Yes.'

'And is it now your hope to avoid keeping the bargain we made?'

Lifting her head, Beatrice faced him, trying to tell herself that the act she was about to commit wasn't sinful or anything like that, that in submitting herself to her husband she was actually doing something noble. But confronted with his size, his strength and his indomitable will, Beatrice found her reasoning did nothing to quell her fear.

Instead of lying to him, which Julius half-expected her to do, she surprised him by saying instead, 'It is my hope, but I am prepared to become your wife in every sense. I will not deny you the rights of my own vows. You will have what I promised you.'

'Yet you fear it.'

'Yes.'

'Do you fear me?'

'No—only what will happen. But I will submit—if that is what you want.'

'Submit?' Julius repeated, annoyed by her choice of word. 'The marital act is not some kind of punishment to which you should *submit*. Don't fear it,' he ordered softly as his fingers caressed her cheek. 'And for God's sake, don't fear me. You've never feared me before. Don't begin now.'

The deep, husky timbre of his voice, combined with the tantalising exploration of his skilful fingers caressing her face and neck, was already working its magic on Beatrice.

Julius considered his wife, seeing the set of her chin that brought a smile to his lips. 'I hope there isn't going to be a battle, my love. I wouldn't like to have a fight on my hands—not tonight. In order to make you understand that we are husband and wife, that from this night on we will share a bed, share our bodies, there is no other way.'

Beatrice started to protest, but his finger came across her lips and shushed her. Bending his head, he placed his lips close to her ear.

'I want you to relax, my love. There will be a drifting of the senses, soft kisses, an initiation into the art of love, moving towards a climax that will please us both, which is what I want,' he murmured, taking her face between his hands and kissing her sweet lips, lightly to begin with, offering her love, then deeply and tenderly. After a few moments of tense passivity, she placed her hand on his chest and began to kiss him back.

Raising his head a fraction, he asked, 'Did it concern you that our wedding was not the grand affair most young ladies dream of?'

'I didn't want a grand affair. I was perfectly satisfied the way it was.'

'You made a beautiful bride. You are so lovely your beauty blinds me. But that is not what this is about.'

Tilting her head to one side, relaxed by his kiss, she managed a teasing smile. 'No? Is it not more important to have a wife who is pleasing to look at than an ugly one?' she provoked.

'Ah—but it is not the face that is important, Beatrice.' Very slowly he walked round her, deliberately, examining her as she stood rooted to the floor, not touching her with anything but those amber eyes—and they were enough, boldly evaluating her assets. He halted and, bending his head close to her ear so that the warm breath caressed the back of her neck, said softly, 'When I was a youth, I was given some sound advice from a very wise man.'

Unable to move, Beatrice swallowed audibly, nervously, her heart beating wildly. 'What was that?'

'Never to buy a mare with a blanket on.'

'And—who was this wise man?'

'My father.'

Beatrice shivered under Julius's unrelenting gaze. He watched her with such a slow, unhurried regard that her skin burned from its intensity. 'It's a little late for that, don't you think? Perhaps you should have taken his advice.'

'I'm sure you're right, but, as you say, it's too late for that. You belong to me now. You are my wife and a husband may do as he pleases with his wife.' His voice softened until it was almost a whisper. 'Anything he likes. Now—shall we take off those clothes and see what we have?'

For a moment Beatrice shrank back, her green eyes darkening in fear, and Julius almost turned away, for before God he would not force her. Then, as he had hoped she would, her chin came up, her soft lips tightened and her eyes blazed her defiance, but she turned and presented her back for him to unbutton her wedding gown.

He worked downwards until the garment hung open. She shrugged and it fell to her feet, revealing a sheer, shimmering white-silk petticoat, the shoulders temptingly bare. The petticoat hid nothing from him and Beatrice saw the hard glint of passion strike sparks in his eyes as they moved over her. Her full, ripe breasts swelled against the silk that moulded itself to her bosom and the delicate peaks thrust forward impudently. He saw the inward curve of her waist, amazingly small without any tight lacings, the trim and seductive roundness of her hips and the lithe grace of her limbs.

Julius's breath caught in his throat. He had already realised that beneath all her clothes Beatrice was what every man dreamed of: a vision of incomparable beauty. His long fingers freed her body from the rest of her flimsy garments until she stood naked to his gaze.

The hardest thing Beatrice had ever had to do in her life was to stand calmly before him and let him look at her as he was doing now, when, feeling like a caged animal newly caught, she wanted nothing more than to find a way out. He stepped back, still smiling, but with a new fire kindled in his eyes. His gaze was direct, challenging, sweeping from her trim and shapely ankles, passing over her slender legs, and then more leisurely over her magnificent body, which was lustrous shades of honey and amber in the flickering flames of the candles and the fire. The triangle of curling fair hair at the base of her belly was now a mysterious dark enticing shadow, her breasts rose tipped and exuberant. His gaze passed on to her face. She had not flinched as she submitted herself for his perusal, but her eyes were large and hot and expectant, and a flush swept up her long shapely legs, her slender curves, staining the glowing flesh right up to her face.

Julius's lips spoke no word, but his eyes clearly expressed his wants. The bold stare touched a quickness in Beatrice that made her feel as if she were on fire. It flamed in her cheeks and set her hands to trembling as she stared back at him. Out of consideration for her obvious embarrassment, Julius extinguished the candles burning close to her, before taking his time in stripping himself naked. He unbuttoned and removed his shirt and laid it over a chair with his cravat and slipped out of his breeches and undergarments, tossing them atop the shirt.

When he was totally naked Beatrice stared at a certain part of his anatomy in horror, her face as white as the cravat he had just removed. She had always known men were different, but this was the first time she had seen one naked. Appalled by the size and colour of what she was seeing, she wanted to turn her head away, but found that she could not. Raising her eyes, she gazed at the rest of him. He was bathed in a light cast by the remaining candles and was aglow with deep golden shades that rippled along his hard, lean frame. His body was strong, proud, savage, determined and eternally masculine. Beatrice was no less shaken by the sight of him than by his slow perusal of her a few moments before. They weren't touching, but they generated enough heat between them to light a fire.

As Beatrice dragged her gaze towards the bed, her eyes lit on her nightdress where the maid had left it draped over the quilt. She made a move to get it, but Julius stepped in front of her.

'Please allow me to cover myself,' she said, unable to keep the desperation out of her voice.

'Now why would you want to do that?'

'Because I never go to bed without wearing my nightdress. As for you—you seem to have an aversion for wearing clothes which I consider to be most indecent,' she uttered with quiet reproach.

Julius chuckled softly, delighting in her innocence. 'There are times, Beatrice, when clothing can be a hindrance. One's wedding night is one of them.' His eyes again caressed her from top to toe, touching her everywhere. 'A man finds them troublesome when a wife wears them to bed.' He held his arms out wide, his lips smiling about his white pirate's teeth, proud of his nakedness. 'This is what it's about. A man and a woman alone. No maidenly blushes, no resistance, no fumbling with nightgowns.'

The colour deepened in Beatrice's cheeks and she tried to quell the trepidation that had arisen. When she met his eyes the shock was sharp, for she suddenly realised the moment had arrived when she must pay her dues. Would he seek vengeance cruelly and cause her pain? How could she have cast herself into his grasp so recklessly? She made a move towards the door, but his hand shot out, his fingers fastened about her wrist.

'Oh, no, my pet, there is no way out. Besides, you cannot leave the room undressed. You'll likely set the servants all agog. It's time for bed.'

'But I'm not in the least tired.'

'Good,' he said, his whipcord arms coming slowly around her. 'Neither am I,' he murmured thickly against her throat.

The warmth of his body pressed full against the coolness of Beatrice's own. The jolt of surprise she experienced had nothing to do with revulsion, but rather with the bold, manly feel of him. The alien hardness was a hot brand against her thighs. His face lowered. His mouth was scalding upon her breast and she was devoured in a searing, scorching flame that shot through her like a flaring rocket.

'Oh, Julius,' she panted in a whisper. 'Please— don't...' She could not draw breath. 'Please—stop...'

Leaning down, he swung her up into his arms and carried her to the bed, promising himself every step of the way that their loving would be so perfect for her that she would never fear it again.

His strength was unexpected. He carried her easily, turning her and taking her down with him. His lips caressed her neck and ventured downwards until they were warm and moist upon her breast, rousing her to a heat she had not thought possible. She told herself she should resist what he was doing, that she didn't want this, but she knew it would be useless, for she was no match against the power of his arms and shoulders, imbued with even greater strength by his charged emotional state.

The body that Julius's own so fiercely desired lay beneath him and his uncontrollable hunger for her took command. He managed to free one hand and cup her breast. Her hair was spread out on the sheets, adding to her wild beauty. Her lips responded to his. While he held her firm so that their bodies were touching, his experienced mouth parted hers and flirted with her lips, her tongue, his hands caressing her body, her breasts, circling the rosy crests with his thumb until they stood proud and firm. Beatrice shivered with delight and clung to him—but suddenly, feeling her modesty about to be invaded when his hand slid boldly up the inside of her thigh, her wakened senses alarmed, she gasped and began to pull away as if she had been scorched.

'Please—stop it. I can't do this. I don't want to do it.'

Blindly, the tears sprang from her eyes. His hard thighs were between her own, bringing his virile organ inexorably closer to the gateway of his desire.

Julius immediately knew how apprehensive she was and, although she resisted, he held her hips against his. Such was his desire, he was tempted to mount her and seek his release, but he fought it, determined to take her slowly, to cause her as little pain as possible.

'No,' he said gently as she tried to wriggle from beneath him. 'Don't pull away and I'll do my best not to hurt you.'

But he did hurt her when his manhood, swollen and hard, touched her in brief dalliance, then pressed into the delicate softness of her. A quicksilver pain shot through her and Beatrice bit her lips to keep from crying out, hiding her face against the base of his throat. Her nails dug into the soft flesh of his back,

but he seemed not to notice as his mouth touched her
ear and with utmost care he began to move.

For a while the pain was fierce, but like the most
violent of storms this passed, all the more quickly for
its furious nature, and afterwards, as she lay against her
husband, she could not understand why her breasts and
her belly quivered in hot anticipation for the moment
when he would reach for her again.

Their second union was so very different. Even as
she tried to turn from him, Beatrice felt the betray-
ing moisture from her loins and she could resist no
longer. This time there was no pain. It was forgotten
in the heat of motion and the sensation of Julius fill-
ing her, thrusting, touching all of her. Surprised, she
felt herself respond to him and swell against him in
pulsating waves of pleasure as he brought her body to
life. And then bliss as a wonderful aura burst around
them. Deep inside the sensations started to build and
expand through her as his life-giving seed erupted and
spilled into her, warming her, combining their minds
and souls in physical release and the act of love.

She knew then what it was to be a woman, the hard,
powerful body of a man pressed against her, his manhood still swollen and warm, still moving, but gently
now. The pulsating contractions continued to build
until the heat slowly subsided and left her body quiv-
ering with the after-effects. The parting of their bodies
was jarring, like a bereavement from which she could
not imagine recovery. Unbidden tears came to her eyes
and she turned away, burying her face in the pillow,

weeping silently so he would not see. How could she explain to him how she felt? Everything was changed now. Nothing was the same—she wasn't the same. She wanted nothing more than to revel in this new discovery of herself and the fullness of the moment. Wanted desperately…what? What did she want? If only she could understand what had happened to her. What had she done? What had *he* done to her? Suddenly she knew a feeling of loneliness, for she had found such pleasure—a pagan pleasure in his arms—and something else, something dangerous to her, a feeling that shouldn't exist, but it did. For what she wanted more than anything else at that moment was for him to speak her name in that tender tone—and to say *I love you*.

No matter how hard she tried to conceal her tears, Julius heard her muffled sobs. As if her need to hear him speak communicated itself to him, he spoke, but not with the tone or the words her heart yearned for. He spoke quietly and without emotion.

'I apologise if I hurt you. I tried very hard not to. It would have hurt no matter who took you the first time.'

She shook her head and drew an unsteady breath. 'No, you didn't hurt me.' Misery engulfed her. The words he uttered were a long way from saying *I love you*, which was what she wanted him to say. At that moment she sorely wished he would go away, for his presence wreaked havoc on the serenity she so desperately sought.

Julius reached out his hand to draw her back into his arms, but when he heard her say, 'I would like to sleep now', he hesitated, then withdrew it, sensing she wished to be left alone, yet reluctant to do so. He wanted to test her honesty and ask her again, for her to reassure him that he hadn't hurt her, but he did not want her to tell him that she hadn't felt all the things he had when he'd taken her. He lay still, listening as her breathing slowed and she drifted into a deep sleep.

Hearing some imperceptible movement coming from his own chambers, he was wide awake at once. In one fluid, easy motion he got out of bed. The sight of the rumpled sheets so like a battleground brought back the sensuous memories of their lovemaking. All the emotions, the crashing waves of a tortured sea, surged and eddied in his mind. His gaze lingered on his wife a moment, thinking she was asleep. He felt a great wave of surprising tenderness wash over him. How vulnerable and utterly lovely she looked—how incredibly beautiful she was with her hair spilling over the pillows and gleaming in the pale dawn light.

He had done his level best to hurt her as little as possible. He was tempted to lean over and lay a hand on her naked shoulder before thinking better. Remembering her tears, he backed away from the bed, telling himself she would not miss him and would be simply relieved that he had spared her the unwanted task of another nocturnal pursuit.

In his own room Julius heard a controlled knock on the door. Opening it, he was presented with a footman holding a small silver tray with a letter on it.

'A message has arrived for you, sir. The courier

said it was urgent, otherwise I would have waited until morning to give it to you.'

'Here, I will take it.' Julius tore open the letter and read it quickly. The news was bad. Cursing silently, he strode to the door to issue orders to have his valet wakened to pack his bags.

Feeling the man beside her stir, through half-closed eyes feigning sleep, Beatrice heard the bed creak as Julius moved away from her and returned to his own chambers. She opened her mouth to call him back, but the thought that he might not want to strangled the words in her throat.

Drawing the sheet over her nakedness, she rolled on to her back. The movement caused her some annoyance, for in certain parts of her body she was sore and bruised, yet at the same time that small electrifying pulse, which surged just at that part of her that ached the most, flared in the most amazing way.

Immersed in her reflections, feeling languid yet clear headed, she stared up at the canopy. What Julius had done to her had left her bemused and possessed by him. She had not expected her body to respond to his in such an overwhelming way. He had done things to her that should have disgusted her; instead she had clung to him, encouraged him, even, her treacherous body glorying in it, the evidence being the red-black smears of her blood on the sheets—a sign of his entry—his gain, and her loss.

Chapter Seven

Beatrice was unable to quell the anxiety she felt as she left her room after breakfasting in bed. She did not relish the idea of confronting Julius again right now, when her emotions were still so raw and all over the place. But that was not to be. He was in the morning room waiting for her. He was dressed immaculately, fastidiously even, the cut of his expensive jacket setting off the powerful width of his shoulders, his legs smooth and shapely in the well-tailored perfection of his dove-grey breeches. His dark hair was smoothly brushed, his handsome face drawn.

This man she had married was compelling, resolute and complex, for would she ever know what he was thinking unless he told her? He was also arrogant and proud, and she believed he would fight for what he wanted, for what he believed in, and she had no doubt that he believed that he could master her, subjugate her, turn her into the wife he wanted.

With what she incorrectly imagined was his supreme indifference to her, he lounged against the fireplace, his hands in his pockets, his face carefully blank, his eyes directed away from her, as if he couldn't be bothered to look at her face.

Beatrice stared at him, her mind screaming for him to look at her. Her heart beat agonisingly with yearning, despairingly. She could not help but admire the fine shape of him, how she had come to know and like the male beauty of his naked body which overwhelmed her. She liked the hardness, the darkness of him, the width of his shoulders, the narrow grace of his hips, his flat, taut stomach, the long shapeliness of his legs. Yes, she loved all this—though it also disturbed her that she should want to see him like that again. She wanted to feel his arms about her body, his lips on hers, kissing her the way a man does when he loves a woman. But Julius had been unable to wait to leave their bed. In short, he didn't love her. He never would and she must accept that and learn to live with it, no matter how hard that would be.

Closing the door, she moved to stand in the centre of the room with more confidence than she was feeling. 'Good morning, Julius,' she said stiffly.

He glanced at her and nodded. 'Good morning, Beatrice.' His voice was clipped. 'I trust you slept well after I left.'

'Yes—perfectly,' she replied, thinking this man bore no resemblance to the one who had made love to her with such passion. This man was a stranger to her, a cold, forbidding man who looked at her with cold blatant uninterest. How could he be so nonchalant after the night they had spent together? At that moment all she could remember was her husband making love to her in a thousand tiny ways. Now his detached tone caught her off guard; his expression was as if he were studying an interesting document instead of his own wife.

Julius straightened and, with his hands behind his back, turned and strolled to the window, where he stood looking out. 'I have to go away for a while.'

Beatrice stared at him in surprise. She hadn't known what to expect when she had entered the room, but it certainly wasn't this. Had she been such a disappointment to him, then? She felt her cheeks burn. He might as well have torn her heart out, but even worse, he dashed all her hopes, her romantic dreams.

'Oh? Am I allowed to ask where you are going?'

'Portsmouth. I received a message earlier. It appears that two of my vessels returning from India were badly damaged in a storm coming through the Bay of Biscay. One of the vessels is missing. Several of the crew on the surviving vessel lost their lives and there has been considerable damage to the cargo.'

'I see—and—you have to go yourself?'

'I have agents capable of assessing the damage, but I would like to see it for myself. There's a loyal crew and thousands of pounds worth of cargo on the missing vessel, so it is imperative that I locate it.'

'And do you expect to be gone long?' she enquired, staring at his stiff back.

'No longer than necessary—two weeks at the most. Meanwhile you are to remain here—where Lady Merrick can keep an eye on you.'

'I don't need to be kept an eye on, Julius,' Beatrice replied, unable to hide her resentment. 'I am quite capable of looking after myself.'

He spun round and looked at her. 'I am sure you are, but Lady Merrick will be company for you in my absence. Were I to send you to Highfield you wouldn't know anyone. I intend to take you down there on my return. Here you will find plenty to occupy your time. I want you to familiarise yourself with the house and the servants. Hayes, the butler, and Mrs Keeble, the housekeeper, will be on hand to answer your questions. I'd prefer it if you didn't ride out just yet. None of the horses here are suitable.'

Beatrice bristled. 'I'm sure there must be one. Your horse would suit me perfectly. As you know to your cost I am an accomplished horsewoman—and it will need to be exercised in your absence.'

'No, Beatrice. Absolutely not.' He was adamant. 'You possess abundant courage, that I know—the kind of courage needed to fearlessly manage high-spirited horses—but apart from the grooms exercising my horse, he remains in the stable. Understand that. Besides, I shudder to think of the form of dress you would choose to wear. You would scandalise society if you rode through Hyde Park as you do in the country, astride in your breeches.'

'It is much more natural and comfortable to ride that way. I see nothing wrong with it,' she argued.

'You wouldn't, but ladies don't ride astride. It isn't done. Aside from any other consideration, just think of the damage it would do to my reputation if I were to allow my wife to ride in such a manner.'

'I'm fast coming to think,' Beatrice returned, 'that this reputation of yours is invented by you as a convenient excuse to prevent me riding out in public.' That riposte earned her a distinctly steely glare. Before he could think of a comment to go with it, she said, 'As you know, my own horse is still at Standish House. Could I not arrange for it to be sent here?'

'I don't see why not,' he said, having seen for himself how devoted she was to that horse of hers. 'I'll instruct the head groom to take care of it. Perhaps you should write a brief note to Lady Standish for her to authorise its removal from her stable. If she refuses to comply with your request, I shall take care of it myself on my return.'

'Thank you, Julius. I would appreciate that.'

'As my wife, I have no doubt people will want to make your acquaintance. Constance will be happy to assist you in the making and receiving of calls, and the ordering of more new gowns from your dressmaker will keep you busy.'

'Yes, although I have enough dresses and fripperies to last me a lifetime. I suppose it will be pleasant to have Lady Merrick's company on occasion—even when you return. Normal married couples cannot exist on a diet of love alone. And that description can hardly apply to us, can it, Julius?' she remarked, unable to conceal the hurt she still felt when he had left her bed so soon after making love to her.

Julius looked at her steadily. His face was expressionless, his eyes hard and empty, an emptiness that told Beatrice nothing of what he felt, then he said, 'It doesn't become you to be sarcastic, Beatrice. And as far I am concerned, you will hardly find me lacking in husbandly duties—as it will be my pleasure and yours to discover when I return.'

Duties, Beatrice thought bleakly. Was that really all their marriage meant to him—all the passion, the sensations he awoke in her that made her almost delirious when he made love to her? Despite the distant attitude she had adopted afterwards, which had been a form of self-defence, last night she had become aware that something was happening. Something awe-inspiring and frightening had happened to her in that split second it had taken her heart to acknowledge it. And she could do nothing about it.

Julius certainly didn't care for her and she had no intention of making a fool of herself by telling him she was beginning to care for him. He didn't give a damn and, in truth, she could hardly blame him. He would more than likely find it highly amusing and tell her it was unfortunate for her. So though it cost her every bit of her strength and will-power, and her own bloody-minded pride, she would keep her feelings to herself.

'When do you leave?'

'As soon as the horses have been hitched to the coach.'

'I see.'

At that moment there was a rap on the door. Julius crossed the room and opened it, speaking quietly to whoever it was before closing it.

'It is ready. I must go.'

Suddenly Beatrice wanted to cry and she didn't know why. Was it because she would miss him, would miss their sparring and the time when they would be alone in her room? How she longed for it now. He must never know how she felt. How he would laugh if he knew. She swallowed her tears and rallied.

'Then what can I say other than to wish you a safe journey, Julius.' Her voice was low, husky with an inner emotion she did her best to keep under control. Looking at him quickly, she caught a puzzling, watchful glint in his eyes—keen, eager, as though he hung on her next words, hoping she would say—what? She didn't know. 'I hope things are not as bad as you imagine when you reach Portsmouth.'

Her husband looked at her. Wearing a new morning dress, a creation of apple-green twill that emphasised her slender shape and set off the copper and gold of her hair, she looked like an alluring, enchanting temptress. He looked into her green eyes and his hands clenched at his sides as he fought the impulse to rebuke her for holding herself from him after their lovemaking, as though she could not bear for him to touch her again. And yet there had been moments in their second union when he had heard her sigh and her lips had been soft and she had returned his kisses, her hands caressing and clinging instead of clawing as though to steady herself as the climax washed over her. At that moment she had been totally his, dazed and submissive, a woman—his wife.

The urge to go to her, to take her in his arms and wrap her around him like a blanket and lose himself in her, to kiss her and tell her that he needn't leave her, that all she had to do was tell him she didn't want him to go, that she wanted him to stay with her, was strong, but, knowing the chances of her doing so was remote, without another word he turned on his heel.

His composure held tightly about him, raking his fingers through his hair and Beatrice's heart, he went out.

Restless in spite of the desultory mood which had gripped her ever since Julius's departure, over the following days Beatrice wandered about the house. It was the most opulent she had ever seen. Julius had bought it ten years ago with his newly acquired fortune. No expense had been spared. It had been decorated and furnished to his taste with every kind of luxury.

She did her best to acquaint herself with the servants and to familiarise herself with the running of the house, and the sphinxlike butler and Mrs Keeble were patience personified in telling her all she needed to know. Never having involved herself in domestic matters at Standish House, which she had considered tiresome and of little consequence anyway, and having no idea of what overseeing a large house and servants entailed, Beatrice was quite out of her depth.

She worked harder than she had ever worked before, but the multitude of responsibilities and tasks that confronted her daily as mistress of the house, rather than wearing her down, left her pleasantly exhausted and satisfied. She could not help, however, thinking of Julius, and missing him, very much aware how much he had got under her skin. Lady Merrick, who called on her most days, assured her that time would soon pass and he would return, but the confidence with which she spoke, while comforting, also left Beatrice more than a little fearful.

What would happen when he came back? Would the emotional chasm between them become an insurmountable obstacle? Was it possible that they could find a way of living together, or was there nothing there on which to build? There was little time for such thoughts until the day was done. But then, in the solitude of her bed, in the quiet of the night, her thoughts turned on themselves in a confusing mix. At these times she could stand the constriction of her room no longer and walked through the connecting door to pass a lonely vigil lying on his bed, wishing desperately for his return and the touch of his hands.

When she was not involving herself with household matters, Lady Merrick would whisk her away on excursions to the popular tea gardens of Vauxhall across the river and Pancras Wells. Beatrice went on her first river boat and went to admire the flowers at Kew and visited the museums and art galleries. In the afternoons they sometimes took advantage of the clement weather and drove in Hyde Park in the Merrick barouche to see and to be seen, often descending to join the numerous people fashionably strolling the lawns.

Shortly before her husband was expected to arrive home, a letter arrived addressed to her. It was from Julius. She stared at the bold handwriting in surprise, wondering what he could have to say to her that was so important he had to write to her. The letter was brief and to the point, its content making her heart plummet. Circumstances had arisen that meant he had to leave for Portugal on a matter of urgent business. He had no idea how long he would be gone—possibly weeks—and she was to remain in London until such time as he returned.

Beatrice was unprepared for the desolation that overwhelmed her, but she refused to be downhearted. And if Julius thought she was calmly to remain in his house doing whatever wives were supposed to do, then he could think again. Already she was tired of London and longed for the freedoms of the country where she could lose herself in the joy of riding a decent mount— and Larkhill wasn't all that far away. Suddenly elation swelled inside her and she smiled audaciously as she was presented with a new objective. Half of her was glad Julius wasn't here so that she could claim back her old home, and that half was starting to enjoy her new status and married life.

And so, the day after she had received her husband's letter, with a small contingent of servants and having sent a note to Lady Merrick informing her of what she intended, she left for Larkhill.

The days Beatrice spent in her old home were like the golden days of her childhood. The main rooms were furnished with pieces Julius had had sent down from London. She was like a child as she wandered from room to room, beset by so many wonderful memories. The house was filled with shadows, all hazy, dream-like as she moved about. How wonderful it would be, she thought, if she could remain at Larkhill for ever, but realistically she knew this was not possible. When Julius returned he would take her to Highfield, which was to be her home, but as long as she could visit Larkhill she would be content.

On her third morning while the dew was still on the ground and brilliant rays of early morning sunlight spilled across the lawn, she was pleasantly surprised when George paid her a visit. She met him on the drive, delirious with joy when she saw he had her precious Major in tow. After she had reacquainted herself with her mount, she turned her attention to her handsome cousin.

'Aunt Moira forbade me to have any further contact with either you or Astrid, George. I shudder to think of her displeasure should she discover you have been here.'

George shrugged, unconcerned. 'It was most unfair of her to do that. And anyway, I came to see you, not the other way round. We've missed you at the house. It isn't the same without you. You really did put Mama's nose out of joint when you up and married Chadwick. She accuses you of stealing him away from Astrid.'

'I suppose it must look like that to her, but in real-ity it wasn't. The whole Lord Chadwick affair was your mother's scheme from the start, a brazen bit of matchmaking in her eagerness to secure for Astrid only the best. It was unfortunate for her that Julius never had any intention of offering for Astrid, so I cannot be accused of stealing him away.'

George frowned, his expression anxious as he studied his cousin's face. 'You are happy, aren't you, Beatrice? You've no regrets about what you did?'

'No, none, George, truly. How can I not be happy when I have all this?' She opened her arms wide to embrace her beloved Larkhill, laughing joyously. 'I may not live here since Julius's home is in Kent, but I can still visit.'

'You do look radiant, Beatrice,' George said on a serious note. 'Chadwick must be doing something right.'

She flushed prettily, remembering her wedding night and all that had transpired. She was impatient for Julius to return so they could live like a properly married couple. 'Julius is a most attentive husband,' she said softly. 'He is away just now—searching for one of his ships that disappeared during a storm in the Bay of Biscay, which is the reason why I'm here now. How is Astrid? Well, I hope?'

'You will be surprised to learn that my dear sister is soon to follow you up the aisle.'

Beatrice stared at him. 'You mean Aunt Moira is to allow her to marry Henry Talbot after all?'

George wasn't smiling anymore. His concern for his sister was plain. 'Don't you believe it—no one so lowly. She's to wed Lord Alden of Alden Hall in Essex— before Christmas, if Mama has anything to do with it.

She's determined not to let him slip through the net.
You must have heard of him since he was a friend of
Father's.'

'Lord Alden? But—he's an old man—an extremely
stout, lecherous old man as I recall.' Beatrice remembered how Lord Alden had a tendency to grope the
female servants if they ventured too close. 'He's old
enough to be Astrid's father.'

'Exactly. Fifty-five, to be precise—and far too old
for Astrid. Naturally she is averse to the marriage and
spends most of her time weeping in her room.'

'Poor Astrid. Then she mustn't marry him. She's
in love with Henry—and he with her. As head of the
family, it is within your power to stop her marrying
Lord Alden.'

George shook his head. 'I've tried, but you know
Mama. Since you left her temper has become much
worse. She will not be crossed or argued with and
refuses to listen to reason. She's determined to do this,
Beatrice.'

'But she cannot force Astrid to marry him.'

'You're wrong there. When Mama has a bee in her
bonnet about something, she's as immovable as the
Rock of Gibraltar. She won't pass up the chance of
Astrid being a countess. Losing her game with you
has increased her determination.'

And her spite, Beatrice thought crossly. She sighed
deeply and linked her arm through George's, in perfect, amiable harmony with each other as usual. 'Yes,
I imagine she has. Come inside and have some break-
fast with me—bacon and eggs are on the menu, and

kippers, too—and if we put our heads together we'll try to work out what is to be done. Astrid cannot marry that man.'

Julius looked out of the carriage window, wishing the driver would go faster. He'd left Portsmouth at first light and now the sights and sounds of London were all around him. It had taken him two months to track down his stricken ship, which had managed to limp into a small port in Portugal, and a further two to have the cargo transferred to another vessel and to oversee the repairs before it was deemed seaworthy enough to embark for England.

Now he was impatient to be home and considered the shock his sudden arrival would cause to Beatrice. Had she changed in his absence? he wondered. Had she been lonely? Had she missed him? More than once it had occurred to him that she might resent having him return, that she might be enjoying the single life to the hilt, but that idea was nearly as repugnant as the idea that she might have found another on whom to bestow her affections.

What surprised him most was how much he had missed her. In his mind's eye she glowed like a light. Every day and night he thought of her, conjured up her image in his mind, trying to imagine what she was doing, how she looked, tracing every curve of her face in his mind, remembering her magnificent green eyes and the soft sweetness of her lips. He relived every minute he had spent with her, recalling every word, every inflection, how it had felt to hold her, to make love to her.

They would not remain in London. He would take her to Highfield. He was eager to show Beatrice her new home. She would be happy there—they would be happy together. They would make their marriage work. They had to. If he wanted his family name and the title to continue, he must start providing heirs. He wanted his life to have meaning, to have a real marriage—meaningful and lasting, a wife and children and love—not the empty relationships that passed for marriage in society.

He wanted Beatrice more than he'd wanted anyone in his life. At thirty-one years of age and after more affairs than he cared to remember, he had fallen victim to an outrageously spirited, beautiful girl who blithely incurred his displeasure, amused and infuriated him as no other woman had ever done. He had started off determined to gain the upper hand, but somehow she had managed to get him by the throat.

He was driven by a ridiculous eagerness to see her, as if his life depended on it. At last the carriage pulled up outside his house and he got out, smiling to himself when he saw the Merrick carriage in front. No doubt Constance was calling on Beatrice. He was glad his young wife had had company in his absence.

He let himself in as Constance was on the point of leaving. In the process of pulling on her gloves, she stopped and stared at him in shocked amazement.

'Why—Julius! You're back! Why didn't you let us know you were arriving today?'

He grinned, embracing her warmly. 'I thought I'd surprise you. It's taken me longer than I expected tracking down that damned ship. How is Beatrice? She is well, I hope?'

Lady Merrick became flustered as she considered how best to explain Beatrice's absence. 'I—I expect she is—but...'

He was no longer smiling as servants began moving quickly in all directions to inform those who didn't know that the master was home. 'Expect? What are you saying, Constance?'

'Beatrice isn't here, Julius. She's—at Larkhill.'

For a moment Julius was unable to absorb the full shock of what she said. In a low, deadly voice, he said, 'What did you say?'

'That Beatrice is at Larkhill.'

'But I specifically told her I wanted her to remain here in London until my return. I was under the impression that she would do just that.'

'Oh but she did—at first,' Lady Merrick said defensively.

'When did she leave?'

'Shortly after she received your letter telling her you would be away for some time.'

'And have you heard from her since she left?'

Lady Merrick shook her head. 'No, but then I didn't expect to. I called today on the off chance, thinking she might have returned.'

Furious with Beatrice for refusing to yield to his authority, Julius strode into the drawing room and poured himself a large brandy. Sinking into a chair, he drank deep, but the fiery liquid did nothing to soothe his raw nerves.

Having followed him, Lady Merrick saw the harshness in his taut features and sighed with helpless understanding. 'I know how displeased you must be about this, but can you really blame her? London is all very well, but Beatrice is a country girl at heart. Be honest with yourself, Julius. It must have crossed your mind that she would go to Larkhill.'

'As a matter of fact it didn't. When I told her to remain here I expected her to abide by my wishes. How dare she even consider disobeying me? How dare she? The conniving little… I should have realised it was no small task expecting her to remain in London when that damned house beckoned.'

In dumbfounded amazement, Lady Merrick stared at him, beginning to understand the reason why he was so furious with Beatrice. It was unbelievable that Julius, who had always treated women with a combination of easy indulgence and amused tolerance, could have fallen victim to the same kind of feelings that affected the rest of the human race. Apparently this self-confident, invulnerable man had lost his heart to his own wife.

She suppressed the urge to smile. 'Did you not realise that with Beatrice's need for control, such an order would only make her feel pressured into defying you? What do you intend to do about it?'

'Right now I can think of several things that are appealing—one of them being to wring her neck and another to go after her and drag her off to Highfield and put her under lock and key.'

Lady Merrick sighed and shook her head. 'I can imagine what society would make of that—more grist for the mill.'

'I don't give a damn what society thinks,' Julius said curtly, which was not the truth. In this case he did care; he was furious at being made to look a laughing stock by being unable to keep his wife under control. 'I know just how to handle my errant wife, believe me.'

Leaning back in his chair, he closed his eyes and took a long, harsh breath, trying to bring his temper under control. Beatrice would either bend to his will or he would break her to it, but either way she would learn to behave herself, he decided with cold resolve. For a few minutes he considered going down to Larkhill and confronting her openly with the ruthlessness that she deserved, then discarded the idea. He would make her come to him and he knew exactly how to do it.

Beatrice and George trotted into the stable yard at Larkhill, having spent a wonderful morning riding in the crisp November air over grassy tops of hills, meadows and shallow valleys. George was the first to notice the small elderly man walking about the yard, a younger man in tow, notebook in hand. In dark, sober suits they seemed to be inspecting the buildings. On seeing them they stopped what they were doing and began walking in their direction.

'I say, Beatrice, it looks as if you have visitors.'

Beatrice held her horse in check and watched

the strangers approach. 'Who are you, sir,' she said, addressing the older of the two, 'and what are you doing here?' She was somewhat bemused by their presence.

'I am Mr Sinclair of Sinclair and Lawson, estate agents, and this is my clerk, Robert Denham. I believe you must be Lady Chadwick, Marchioness of Maitland.'

Without taking her eyes off him Beatrice nodded. 'An estate agent? Forgive me, Mr Sinclair, but I have made no arrangements for an estate agent to view Larkhill. I think you must have made a mistake. Perhaps it is some other property you wish to see in the area. If so, I am sure I can direct you to it.'

'Oh, no, my lady. It is Larkhill I have been instructed to view.'

'On whose instruction?'

'Lord Chadwick—your husband, Lady Chadwick.'

Beatrice froze. A premonition of dread gripped her heart. Perfect months of dreaming away the days at Larkhill—golden days, happy days, days filled with joy and contentment, of riding with George and basking in the memories of her childhood—turned into panicked confusion.

Julius was back.

She stared at Mr Sinclair in utter disbelief, her mouth agape. A wave of dizziness rushed over her. She gripped her riding crop and for a moment could not speak at all. She was utterly stunned, crazed confusion charging through her veins.

'But there has to be some mistake. There must be.'

'There is no mistake, Lady Chadwick. Your husband

has instructed me to do a valuation on the estate with a view to selling. I hope you don't mind that I have made a start, but with such a large property to inspect it will take up most of the day. I did call at the house and was told you were not at home.'

The yard seemed to spin and Beatrice began to panic. She felt powerless, completely overwhelmed, thwarted, cornered. What a fool she had been. Why hadn't she foreseen that the blackguard would do something like this? Jolting herself out of her shock, Beatrice dismounted, handing the reins to a groom.

'Then please do continue, Mr Sinclair,' she said tightly, knowing better than to countermand her husband's instructions. 'Please excuse me.' Walking quickly towards the house, Beatrice could feel her face harden with anger. She knew why Julius was doing this. It was a means of gaining power over her. But it wasn't going to work. She glanced at George as he tried to keep up with her. 'I must leave for London at once. Julius cannot do this. To sell Larkhill—why, it's unthinkable.'

'He has every right,' George said gently. 'In truth, Beatrice, I'm surprised he hasn't done so before now.'

'But he can't,' Beatrice cried. 'He can't. Otherwise what was the point of it all?'

'Did it never occur to you that he would do it?'

'No—no, it didn't. Oh, George, what a stupid, blind fool I've been. But all is not lost. I'll go to him, speak to him. I have to make him see that he cannot do this.'

'Of course you must, but—you won't forget about Astrid, will you, Beatrice?'

She paused, looked at him and, seeing his worried look, her expression softened. 'How could I? Astrid is always in my thoughts. I am so concerned about her. I'll speak to Julius. I am sure he will know what to do.'

Beatrice's disbelieving dread increased with every mile that took her to her husband. She suddenly found herself at war with herself. Half of her was besieged by the wild joy at the thought that the man who had obsessed her thoughts since she had first laid eyes on him was home at last, and the other half was indignant and furious that he intended to take from her the very thing that had brought them together in the first place, without any discussion on the matter.

Oh, but Julius Chadwick was a sly one. By blatantly ignoring her feelings, without so much as a by your leave, like some wicked puppet master it was his way of telling her that he had taken control of her life and there was nothing she could do about it.

On reaching the house she hurried inside. She was met by Hayes in the hall. In stentorian tones he welcomed her home and informed her that her husband was in his study, working.

'Oh. Well, that's too bad. Tell him I'm here, will you, Hayes, and that I want to see him.'

'As you wish, my lady.'

Hayes crossed the hall to do her bidding. Breathing rapidly, Beatrice waited, her hands on her waist, the toe of her foot tapping impatiently, her eyes glued to the study door, behind which lurked the man responsible for her fury. She heard Hayes clear his throat and then proceed to tell Julius that his wife had arrived home and wished to speak to him.

Julius's low voice vibrated with annoyance. 'Tell my wife to go to her room. I will be up to see her shortly. In the meantime I have important work to attend to.'

Furious at being ordered to her room like a mindless piece of chattel, without further ado Beatrice marched to the wood-panelled study and pushed her way past Hayes. Julius was sitting at his desk, dictating a letter to his secretary. His head snapped up, his gaze riveting on her, and his expression went from shock to relief to cold anger.

'Beatrice!'

Putting a tight rein on her temper as she walked across the carpet, Beatrice could not take her eyes off him. He looked just as handsome as ever, just as ruggedly virile and formidably large. She refused to admit, however, that his chiselled male perfection had any effect on her. With unarguable logic, she said, 'I apologise for disturbing you, Julius. Obviously you consider me of less importance than your business concerns, but after an absence of four months, I'm sure you can spare a few minutes to speak to your wife.'

With deadly calm, Julius laid down his quill and turned his gaze on his secretary. 'Leave us, will you, Harry?' he said curtly. 'We'll finish this later.'

When Harry and Hayes had left the room Julius turned his attention on his wife. He took one look at her face and knew that his ruse to bring her back to London had worked. What he read in her face was a mixture of fury and dread. Little did she know that he had been waiting for her, that he knew that when Mr Sinclair introduced himself and informed her of his reason for being at Larkhill, it wouldn't take long for her to come hurtling back to London. He was not disappointed. In fact, she had made it faster than he'd imagined.

There was an air of barely controlled impatience about her that fairly crackled. Her hair hung in a tangled pennant of glossy waves. She was flushed. Her eyes had a luminous quality, green and dazzling, of a woman who had spent weeks in a state of bliss and contentment and with no wish to have it spoiled by a returning husband. It maddened him and fascinated him and made him desire her all at the same time, but he controlled the urge to drag her off to bed and looked at her in chilly, fierce reproach.

'Since you're here, I suppose we'd better get this over with now rather than later.'

Beatrice's head was whirling as she cast about for words. Until then she had thought she remembered exactly how he looked, but she was mistaken. His tan jacket clung to his wide shoulders and his thick hair was brushed back from his wide forehead. His face was one of arrogant handsomeness, with its sculptured mouth and striking amber eyes. But now she noticed the cynicism in those eyes and a ruthless set to his jaw. She searched his features, but found no sign that this forbidding man had held her and made love to her with seductive sensuality on their wedding night. Now everything about him exuded ruthlessness and brute strength.

She moved to stand directly in front of him, her hands clenched into fists. 'You know why I have come back to London, so don't pretend you are surprised to see me. How could you do this?' she cried in brazen confrontation. 'I find it contemptible and completely underhand.'

Julius loomed over her, holding himself completely still, his eyes boring into hers. When he spoke his voice was icier than an ice floe, and his words chilled Beatrice more than that. 'What I find underhand is for you to disobey me. It was foolish of me to expect to find my wife waiting for me to return home, to fling herself into my arms and shed tears of joy at my safe return. And if you're about to tell me how sorely you've missed me, the fact that you left for Larkhill as soon as my back was turned is a little incongruous. If you want to soften my attitude towards you and win my forgiveness for disobeying me, then you will have to think of something else.'

The sweet drift of happiness Beatrice had felt on waking at Larkhill that morning shattered away and her heart hardened and her face turned mutinous. 'Win your forgiveness?' she exploded, her colour rising with indignation, anger and confusion warring inside her head. Julius had never cared about her and he had no right to act like a self-righteous, outraged husband. 'And why, pray, should I want your forgiveness? I don't want it.'

'Oh, yes, lady, you do.' His voice was soft, mild

even, but there was a core of iron in it which told Beatrice to beware. His face was like granite, his mouth stern and his eyes had darkened in their fury.

'The way I see it, I have done nothing wrong,' she persisted. 'Your forgiveness is the *last* thing I care about.'

Julius caught his breath and his jaw clamped with the grinding resolution which had kept him always in control of those with whom he dealt. Show no one your thoughts, had always been his rule, but this rebellious wife of his had a habit of pushing his temper beyond his control.

'Beatrice,' he said, 'if you're wondering how far you can push me, you've just reached your limit. I expect you to understand the rules.' His eyes challenged her dangerously. 'The idea of being defied by my own wife is unthinkable. As long as you behave yourself I am willing to let you enjoy the full benefits of your position as the Marchioness of Maitland. So think very carefully before you make the mistake of defying my orders in the future. You'll regret it, I promise you. I can be ugly when I am crossed. You would do well to remember it.'

Anger at being spoken to like a recalcitrant child poured through Beatrice. She could not believe that this was her husband speaking to her, that he was worse than she remembered—more arrogant, more dictatorial and completely heartless. Despite the cold tingle of alarm his silken voice caused in her, stripping away some of her confidence, she lifted her chin.

'You cannot bully me into compliance, Julius. I can

see that my removing myself to the country has upset you, though I cannot for the life of me see why. What did you expect me to do—sit about all day and slowly go out of my mind?'

'Other wives seem to find plenty to fill their days.'

'Ha,' she scoffed. 'Running their husband's house— in the kitchen and the pantry, discussing menus and counting linen, and when all that is done sitting by the fireside embroidering samplers and darning socks. When you left I did all that and found it tedious.'

'For two weeks, Beatrice. You did that for two weeks, before you went haring off to Larkhill.'

'And why not?' she persisted. 'I miss the freedom of the country—my horse. London is horrid in the summer. Most people take themselves off to the country.'

'The Merricks don't. They reside in London all the year round.'

'Only because Lady Merrick likes London and likes being around people. Besides, they don't have a country residence to retire to.'

Julius stared down at the tempestuous young woman, her face both delicate and vivid with her stormy eyes and soft lips, and he suddenly saw her as she'd looked in the garden at Standish House, her enchanting face turned up to the night sky. As they'd discussed the stars there had been a softness about her, an elusive gentleness that was as fragile and vulnerable as the delicate flowers that surrounded her. She was still that same young woman, completely female, sensual and she was his wife. He had made love to her, but he did not possess her, for the sweet, wild essence of her still belonged to her.

She was not a conventional woman. She was young, naïve and vulnerable and could not be blamed for rebelling against the restrictions which held her. She was not submissive or pliant and was unwilling to be moulded to the whims of others. The fury within him lessened and, as he looked down into her glorious eyes, his stomach clenched at the thought of hurting her.

'For the time I have been away you have had more freedom than most, Beatrice, and now I have returned I would like to see your defiant heart more involved with household affairs.'

She accepted his words coldly, her head high, her cheeks flushed. 'Anyone would think you married me for my domestic accomplishments, when we both know different. It may have escaped your notice, but I haven't had a great deal of experience with being a wife. So if you have finished reprimanding me, *my lord*, I have a matter of my own to raise with you.'

'I know.' Satisfied that she was adequately chastened, Julius perched his hip on the edge of the desk and folded his arms across his chest.

'You cannot mean to sell Larkhill,' she said, unable to keep the desperation from her voice. 'Julius, you can't.'

'I don't need Larkhill. It means nothing to me.'

'But it does to me,' she flared with a sudden impassioned flourish, her eyes blurred with tears. 'It means *everything* to me. You know that. Why do you have to change things? Why are you doing this? Why do you have to hurt me? Is it to punish me for manipulating you into marriage? If so, then would you please find some other way of doing it instead of selling Larkhill.'

'I have already decided,' he said firmly. 'The matter is settled. As soon as I have a copy of Mr Sinclair's valuation, the Larkhill estate will be put on the market. I am hoping for a quick sale.'

For a moment Beatrice's mind could not adjust itself to the fact that he really was going to go through with it. How could he do that? How could she live and never see Larkhill again? At least at Standish House she had still been able to see the fields, the tall trees, the low, wet meadows, the quiet places only she knew about. Resentment of Julius burned in her heart.

When she spoke her voice was low and trembling with contempt. 'What a cold, unfeeling blackguard you are, Julius Chadwick. This is nothing short of tyranny. You are enjoying every minute of what I am going through. Because of what I did, you will naturally want to torment me as much as possible to pay me back. Little did I think when I named the forfeit after beating you in that race that you would do this to me.'

'Then you should have had more sense. You should have foreseen that I might call your bluff.'

'Well, I didn't. Why didn't you tell me at the start you might do this? Why let it go so far? Don't you see it was a way out for you? When you asked me to back down I would have done so at once and disappeared out of your life for ever.'

'Perhaps I didn't want you to disappear, Beatrice. You intrigued me. I had just returned to England after a long absence and I realised that to continue the line I must have heirs, and to have heirs I needed a wife. I was considering searching for some high-bred débutante. I hadn't started looking and then you came along with your outrageous challenge. The moment I laid eyes on you I knew you were different. I am not just referring to your beauty—I've known beautiful women before and quite frankly they bored me to tears. I had no intention of selling Larkhill when I met you. It is a valuable property. The land yields well. I would have been a fool to get rid of it then.'

'It still is. I may have made it difficult for you to refuse to honour the forfeit, but I did not believe you would be so petty or mean spirited as to retaliate and sell a property that is still viable merely to punish me.'

'And if I had told you I meant to sell it, would you really have backed down?'

'Of course I would. Without Larkhill there was no point in any of it.'

Relinquishing his perch Julius stood up and moved closer, a cynical twist curling his lips. 'You never fail to amaze me, Beatrice. You are the only woman who has not been drawn to me by my title or my gold. All you care about is that damned house. Well, all your scheming has come to nothing. No matter how much money it brings in every year from the rents and the land, the sooner it's out of our lives the better. The mistake is yours. Accept it. There is no going back so you will have to learn to live with the consequences of your actions—however painful that will be.'

Beatrice looked at him for a long time and then she

nodded slightly. 'Yes—yes, you're right, Julius. The mistake is mine.' Without another word she turned from him and went to the door.

'Where are you going?'

'To have a bath and a change of clothes.'

Julius's strong mouth began to smile. It turned into an audacious grin, his temper replaced by something else. 'That's the first sensible thing you've said since coming home. It will be my pleasure to get you out of those clothes.'

Chapter Eight

Beatrice spun round, shocked by the implication of his words and that he expected her to tumble into bed with him after all the hurtful things he had said to her. 'Shame on you, Julius,' she retorted, her cheeks aflame. 'I have not been in the house two minutes and already you are thinking of...'

His black brows crept upwards and with a defiant look he sauntered towards her with the predatory grace of a panther. When he spoke his voice was silky smooth. 'What, Beatrice? Of what am I thinking?'

'Of—of bedding me after all you have just said... Can you not think of anything else?' Her heart was pounding with wild confusion and she was flustered now he was so close.

She was determined to deny him, but inside her that treacherous spark ignited. Trying to deny her attraction to him was useless. There was a churning sensation in her stomach, like the fluttering wings of a captive butterfly, and a mounting heat swept through her and her body began to stir.

Julius chuckled softly, wondering why, from the very first, she'd had the power to attract him—wondering why he felt this consuming, unquenchable need now to possess and gentle her without breaking her spirit.

Placing a finger beneath her chin, he tilted her face to his. 'I'm afraid not, my love. But then after an absence of four months and relatively a new bridegroom, it is not unusual.'

She swallowed and quivered when his finger ran over the curve of her cheek, knowing that in no time at all she would lose her ability to resist him. 'Please allow me to leave, Julius.'

'I will,' he breathed, his whisper fraught with wicked seduction, 'in a moment.' He bent his head to kiss the place where his finger had been before, teasing her senses into a wild awakening for him. Beatrice closed her eyes, unable to move. 'I know you want me.' Taking her arms, he drew her against the solid wall of his chest. 'I intend to see if I can still make you respond to me as you did before I left your bed on our wedding night.'

'Please don't,' she gasped, turning her head aside, drowning in humiliation at the brutal reminder of how wantonly she had behaved then.

By the time his lips caressed her earlobe, she was overcome with the need for his kiss. Unable to stop herself, with a low moan she turned her face to his and offered him her mouth. He claimed it immediately and she revelled in his embrace, despite her earlier determination not to let this happen. Ending the kiss, he held her fevered stare before lowering his head to her breast. She watched in hazy silence as he gathered her waist in his hands and gently kissed her breast through her gown, his warm breath permeating the fabric. Her heart slammed into her ribs and she could not have uttered a word of protest if she had wanted to when his lips moved on to the V-shaped neckline and he pressed fervent kisses on the exposed flesh.

She rested her hands on his wide shoulders as his mouth travelled upwards, brushing along the sensitive column of her throat, her ear and the curve of her cheek. She made no effort whatsoever to stop him when he pushed his fingers through her hair and held her head firm, taking her lips once more. All thoughts beyond this moment and this man fled. His lips moved over hers with a flowing, demanding passion, an insistence that she kiss him back that was almost beyond denial.

What he was doing to her was more than Beatrice could withstand. With a silent moan of despair, she yielded to his kiss, parting her lips beneath the sensual pressure and, at that moment, his tongue slid between them, invading her mouth and taking possession of her. Lost in a stormy sea of desire, confusion and yearning, she felt him relinquish his hold on her head and splay his hand across her lower spine, forcing her closer to him, moulding her melting body to the hardening contours of his. She could feel the taut strength of his legs and thighs pressing intimately against hers. His other hand cupped her breast, his thumb brushing back and forth across her sensitised nipple, an action that was overwhelming. He could do with her what he willed. Her body was open to him. He could take her there and then, and he surely knew it.

The ardour with which Beatrice was responding to his kiss had a devastating effect on Julius's starved body. Desire flowed through his bloodstream like wildfire, pounding in his loins. Fighting back the urge to lay her down on the carpet and ravage her there and then, he dragged his lips from hers and drew a long, steady breath.

Her heart still pounding, her mind still reeling with pleasure, Beatrice closed her eyes and rested her head weakly on her husband's chest and felt him press a gentle kiss on her hair. At last she found the power to raise her head and open her eyes; she looked at him with a haziness similar to that of drinking too much wine.

Julius took a step back, satisfaction in his eyes and a worldly smile. 'You are an exceptional woman, Beatrice. No more foolish talk of not wanting me. I think I have just proved a point. Now go and get your bath. I will be up to see you shortly.'

Beatrice turned from him and somehow made her legs carry her to the door. Slipping out, she went to her bedchamber, spent and breathless, and even more confused than she had been before. She leaned her back against the door and closed her eyes, trying to regain her wits. Julius had uncovered a wanton streak in her she never knew existed and there was nothing she could do. Beneath the caressing boldness of his hands and his lips, she was his woman, and though she was honest enough to admit her treacherous woman's body came alive—not against her will, but willingly—it was with a heavy heart. As intoxicating as it was, she realised it was a completely separate thing from what she really wanted—an intimacy of the heart with Julius.

Her feelings for her husband overrode all else. Everything else faded into insignificance—even Larkhill didn't seem so important any more. She could already feel his control closing around her, suffocating her. His rank, his strength, his intelligence, his power, his ability to still her protests with his lips—all this made Julius a powerful man indeed. She could feel herself sliding into his grasp and was steadily losing the will to control her own destiny.

Julius sauntered into his wife's bedchamber. Having bathed and dismissed her maid, Beatrice was seated at her satinwood dressing-table, her elbows on the surface, her forehead resting on her hands. Even with her hair shining like newly minted gold in the sun, she looked the picture of heartbreaking dejection. She hadn't heard him enter. He started to turn away and leave her to her privacy, then, with a sigh, he changed his mind and went further into the room. Closer now, he realised her shoulders were shaking with sobs and he felt a surge of remorse, cursing himself for behaving like an insensitive, blundering idiot.

He was barely able to believe his own selfish

callousness. He should have been gentler with her, more of a husband than a hard-bitten businessman with a bitter past. His churlish display had upset her, alienated her, and he regretted that. He hadn't meant to make her cry. Being the cause of her misery, he knew he was in for a delicate round of diplomacy.

'Beatrice?'

She started violently at the sound of his voice. Snapping her head up, she dashed her tears away with the back of her hand and, picking up her hairbrush, began brushing her hair vigorously.

'What do you want?' she managed to say, her voice flat.

'To apologise.'

This was not what Beatrice had expected. Her eyes met his in the mirror and her lips twisted wryly. 'You? Apologise? Is the callous attitude you used on me earlier supposed to be endearing? Is this what I am to expect in the future if I unwittingly transgress?'

'This is how I am, Beatrice. I am not perfect.'

'No, you're not.' She sighed despondently, tired of the argument. 'It doesn't matter. You were right. I've been a fool, a stupid fool for thinking that by marrying you I would bring Larkhill back into my life, and now I shall have to live with the consequences of my stupidity.'

Julius's heart turned over when he looked at her reflection in the mirror and saw the wounded look in her glorious green eyes. Going to stand behind her, he stilled her hand and took the brush from her, taking on the task of brushing the long silken mass himself.

Beatrice made no move to stop him. She just sat quietly, watching him through the vanity mirror. The image of his tall, masculine frame occupied with such a feminine task enabled her to manage a weak smile.

'You missed your vocation, Julius. You would have made a good lady's maid.'

He grinned leisurely. 'I would be only too happy to stand in when your maid is absent.' He paused and gazed into her eyes. 'Why were you crying?'

'Because I couldn't help it. I am ashamed of myself. I was crying for my own ineptitude, my incompetence and my inability to manage my own life.'

'I don't agree. I think you have a natural talent for all three. You're being too harsh on yourself, Beatrice. Your aunt made it clear that you were not particularly welcome in her house, therefore you had no desire to stay where you were not wanted. But without means where could you go? You yearned for your old home, which was the only place where you had known happiness, and you saw me as a means of getting it back. I cannot blame you for that.'

'You don't?'

'No, I don't.' He experienced a feeling of comprehension, for while he had been struggling with his own life, her world had also been falling apart. At least now he had an insight of what lay behind her fear and dread, and what had driven her to do what she had.

'Nevertheless, I can see how, by my actions, I have humiliated and embarrassed you. I should not have done that. I thought of no one but myself. You can divorce me if you like. I wouldn't blame you.'

Julius stiffened. 'Is that what you want?'

She sighed dejectedly, looking down at her hands. 'It no longer matters what I want. The choice is yours, Julius.'

Putting the brush down, Julius turned and walked slowly across the room to the window, where he stood looking out. Divorce! It was unthinkable. He could not imagine having to go back to the way his life had been before he had met Beatrice—back to the darkness, the loneliness, the endless isolation, the despair, though he would never admit it to anyone. To be with Beatrice now, to have known her as a husband knows his wife and then to have her walk away, that would reduce him to a wretched creature who had been cast out. Whatever it took, he knew he would do anything to keep her with him.

Recovering his composure, he said firmly, 'There will be no divorce.'

Beatrice stared at her image for a moment as relief washed over her. Closing her eyes, she tried to gather her thoughts, to know what to say, what to think. Julius had never spoken of how much he cared for her, not even pretended to. She wasn't certain of his feelings—she wasn't certain of her own, either. All she really knew was that the sight of his hard, handsome face and the bold amber eyes never failed to make her entire being feel tense and alive. She liked being with him, she liked it when he kissed her and when he made love to her. Added to his other attractions, she knew that Julius had a depth of character other men lacked. She was confused as to how she should feel and think, but that didn't really matter one way or the other, because she *was* going to love him. It was happening and she couldn't stop it.

Julius came up behind her and his hands settled on her shoulders. In the mirror she watched him bend his dark head, felt his warm lips against the curve of her neck sending tingling sensations down her back.

'You're very beautiful, Beatrice. I suppose you don't want to hear it, but it's true. I feel we are well suited to help each other. A rare jewel. That's what you are.' She was very still, unable to move as he drew her hair aside and placed a kiss lightly in the nape of her neck, before whispering in her ear, 'And quite irresistible.'

She wanted to contradict him, but her tongue remained silent. The rest of her body began to sing and her pulse raced at the warmth of his breath on her neck.

He looked deeply into her eyes, wanting to show her what he felt when he looked at her, not just what he saw. 'Will you do something for me?'

The raw emotion in his voice registered on Beatrice and she felt her bones begin to melt. 'What? What is it you want?' she asked with a nervous tremor in her voice.

Julius raised his head and his lips curved in a smile, while striving to keep his raw hungry need to be inside her at bay. 'I know exactly what I want; if you come to bed with me now, I'll show you. I want to see you naked on the bed with your hair spread across the pillows. I want to look at your face while I touch you and make love to you, because I badly need to know how you feel.'

Mesmerised by the seductive invitation in those eyes and the velvet roughness of his deep voice, Beatrice stood up and wrapped her arms around her husband's neck, knowing that, for him, this was a moment of atonement. Julius swung her into his arms, driven to try to make amends to her in the only way he knew how. Carrying her to the bed, he lowered her gently onto the quilt and followed her down, his lips finding hers in a long, deep kiss.

When he could finally tear himself away from her to remove his clothes, Beatrice watched him unashamedly, glorying in his magnificent body. Slipping out of her robe, she slid beneath the covers and waited for him to join her. When he did, he gathered her to him.

'You're trembling,' he said in the gentlest of voices.

'I know,' she admitted nervously. 'I don't know why.'

'Don't you?' he asked softly. 'Perhaps this might help,' he murmured, placing his hungry lips on hers to still their tremor, tasting the hot sweetness of her mouth.

Feeling as if her heart would surely burst with what was inside her, Beatrice made a tiny, smothered sound of desire and answered him with a melting kiss of her own. It was enough. Julius gathered her tightly to him, pulling her against his full length, clasping her against his rigid thighs while his lips were both rough and tender. When he lifted his mouth from hers, she felt an aching sense of loss that was replaced by sweet torment as he slid his mouth down her neck to her breasts, nuzzling them slowly before his lips closed tightly over her taut nipple. She moaned in helpless pleasure, desire streaking through her, her hands tangling in his hair, her back arching in helpless surrender.

Deliberately taking his time, Julius slid his hands over her like a connoisseur, caressing with skilful reverence, claiming every inch of her for his own, heating her skin and making her ache with soon-to-be-fulfilled yearnings. Eager to do some exploring of her own, Beatrice heard the quickening of his breath as her fingers inched tentatively over his bare flesh, savouring the sculpted hardness of his chest and abdomen. His hands slid lower, curving around her hips, his lips trailing lower and nuzzling closer to the curly triangle between her legs. Beatrice gasped, tilting her head back, her hand gripping his shoulders, her head pounding like a maddened thing, filled with a mixture of excitement and impatience for him to take her.

Julius felt her escalating desire. All his cool control stripped away. Desperate for her, he pulled her beneath him as though he could not withstand another second of denial. Lifting her taut buttocks to receive him, he entered her.

Beatrice opened completely to him, moulding her hips to his as he began to move, presenting him with a gift of surrender, unwittingly driving him to unparalleled agonies of desire, her surrender answering something deep within his soul. Wanting all he had to give, something wild, raw and primitive and savage built inside her, racing through her veins with wrenching pleasure, the undulant waves of his taking increasing to a crescendo of resounding power. Nothing either of them felt was suppressed or hidden, there was just exquisite joy.

They reached their climax in wild, wonderful, burning unison. Julius's body jerked convulsively again and again, and he clasped her to him, feeling the tiny, shudders of her body as she rung the last pleasure of her orgasm from him. Breathing hard against her cheek, his heart raging in frantic tempo with hers, his body merging into hers, his seed deep inside her, he was more pleased by what had just happened between them than by any other sexual experience of his life. It was also, he thought, the most profound moment of his life.

When reality returned and his breathing evened out, he moved on to his side. Beatrice's hair spilled over his naked chest like a drift of satin and he raised a hand to smooth it off her face, feeling humbled and blessed by her unselfish ardour—and relieved that this time she didn't turn from him. Content and sated, their bodies succumbing to the dreamy aftermath of complete consummation, they remained that way for several minutes, then Beatrice stirred and draped a leaden arm around his waist. Julius tipped her chin up so that he could gaze into her eyes.

'How do you feel?' he asked softly.

Beatrice's long, curling lashes fluttered up and her eyes like two languid green pools gazed into his—this man, her husband. She had not sought his love, she did not expect it, and she certainly had no right to it, but at that moment, more than anything she had wanted in her life before, she wanted it.

'I feel like a wife,' she whispered. 'Your wife.'

He laughed huskily. 'Which is exactly what you are, my love. My wife in every sense. And I feel like a husband,' he said, with tender solemnity. 'To think I actually believed there was no such thing as marital bliss.' Relaxing against the pillows, he revelled in the simple joy of having her in his arms, her head resting on his shoulder. 'How incredibly stupid I have been.'

'No, you are not stupid,' his wife declared loyally, turning her face up to his. 'Although I would dearly like to know what has given you reason to think that.' She observed a tightening of his features and something in his eyes warned her not to press, but she was not to be put off. Placing her lips against his shoulder in the gentlest caress, her heart aching, she wished he would open up to her. 'As your wife I would like to know something of your past, Julius—your parents. Will you not tell me?'

'Time enough for that,' he replied, closing his eyes.

Beatrice wriggled on to her stomach and propped herself up on her arms, her face only inches from his. 'Please be open with me, Julius. I want to know the nature of the man I married. I have always been forthcoming about myself—and you witnessed for yourself the misery of what my life was like at Standish House. I too find it hard to speak about my deepest feelings, but I would willingly do so with you. Despite all my efforts to keep you from seeing my many insecurities, you have a habit of pulling them out of me. I think that is because now I am your wife, I want you to know who I am. I know you are a very private person, Julius, and I respect that, but if you cannot open up to me as I am willing to do with you—even if it's just a little at a time—then we have no chance of happiness until you can begin to share yourself with me.'

For a moment he did not move, nor did he reply. Then he opened his eyes and met her direct gaze. From the very start, despite her outward show of confidence, as he had gazed into those soft green eyes he had sensed in this brave, unspoiled girl a great capacity for love that made him hope that in time his own most secret yearning would be fulfilled. It was a yearning he had never known and never thought he could have until Beatrice had thrust herself forwards and challenged his spirit. He now felt that he could tell her something of his past without revealing the dark secret he kept locked away in the furthest corner of his mind.

'It is the way I've always been,' he said in answer to her question. 'I cannot change the way I am.'

'I would not expect you to do that, but it is not unnatural for a wife to want to know about her husband. I know you've had a difficult past—indeed, we have both suffered because of what our fathers did,' she said, knowing that whatever she said now might determine their whole future. 'Lady Merrick has told me a little about your life, and you, if you remember, when you brought me to London. I know of your achievements and how they made you rich, but your family remains a mystery to me. Why, Julius? Why won't you tell me? I know it is largely down to your father. Is it because you are ashamed? Because if so, I will tell you now that I don't care who your parents were.'

Rage blazed in Julius's eyes for a moment, but then he sighed resignedly. 'Yes, Beatrice, I suppose I am ashamed, but there is more to it than that.'

'Please tell me?' she asked softly.

'If you insist on knowing, I will tell you. Until his demise my whole life revolved around my father. He was a greedy man. It was not in his nature to live his life in modest comfort. He was the Marquess of Maitland, once a name to gain admittance into the highest political and social circles. He was also the worst in a long line of gamblers, falling deeper and deeper into debt running into tens of thousands of pounds. Everything of value was stripped away to pay the bills and his gambling debts. It was sheer hell for my mother. She was constantly at her wits' end. He was not a good man, nor was he kind—especially not to my mother. He also drank heavily and treated her very badly.'

Beatrice watched, her beautiful eyes wide with shock as pain slashed across his features. 'That must have been awful for her—and for you, having to witness it.'

Reaching up he pushed her hair casually over her shoulder. 'He was a brute. The banks were threatening foreclosure on loans he could not hope to cover. Nothing remained against which capital might have been raised. I had a personal income, but Father took it all. He stole and gambled away every penny. Even the properties were gone—pledged against loans he could not hope to repay.'

'Lady Merrick told me it was some money given to you by your grandmother and your own intelligence and good sense that enabled you to succeed. I admire you for that.'

'Yes, God bless her. Without her—without that money—I could not have done it.'

Beatrice smiled. 'Oh, I'm sure you would have found a way. Is your grandmother still alive?'

He hesitated, and for a moment Beatrice thought he wasn't going to say more. When he did, his deep voice was strangely hesitant, almost as if he was testing his ability to talk about it. 'She died shortly before...'

'Before what?' Pain slashed his features once more. She touched his cheek. 'Julius, please tell me.'

He turned his head to one side and quietly said, 'Before my mother.'

'There—was a fire—at Highfield. Your parents...'

He turned and looked at her once more, a fierce light having entered his eyes. It was so hard to say these things, even harder than he had thought it would be, each word an ocean of pain, and he felt as if he were a youth all over again.

Beatrice did not say anything, but simply listened as the words carried on pouring out of him.

'Both my parents perished. Only days before, Father had suffered badly on the stock market and it went from bad to worse when he tried to recoup his losses at the tables. On the night of the fire, finally realising his dreams of greatness were shattered, he returned to Highfield. Arriving late at night, he thought he was alone in the house. My mother was supposed to be visiting a friend. Unbeknown to my father, she was feeling unwell and decided to put off her visit. She was asleep when he returned.'

Beatrice's heart quaked and her soul was beginning to hurt at the forlorn air around him. 'Julius, what are you saying? Surely you don't think he set fire to the house deliberately—that he—'

'What? Committed suicide? That he killed my mother?' He spoke with glacial calm. 'How would I know? How would anyone know that? Some say it was started accidentally. Some say it wasn't. The fact that he dismissed all the servants before the fire started speaks for itself,' he finished grimly.

'I'm so sorry,' Beatrice whispered through a blur of tears, and all the sympathy and warmth in her heart was mirrored in her eyes. Once she had foolishly thought she knew what a broken heart was like. How wrong she had been, for it was only now breaking for this man who had to live with the knowledge that his father might have killed his mother. 'You must have been out of your mind with shock and grief. I can understand why you didn't want to talk about it.'

'All their married life my father crushed my mother. I loved her down to the depths of my soul and could not forgive him for the hurt he dealt her by his actions. I was appalled by the enormity of his debts and that, along with what he might have done to my mother, was the moment when I truly think I began to hate him. Can you imagine what it is like to do that, Beatrice? That was also the moment when I began to hate myself for harbouring such feelings.'

He fell silent and after a moment he looked at his wife, as if remembering she was there. He saw some of the horror in her eyes, and said, 'Now you know my deepest secret. You are right. You are entitled to know all this, but God help me, Beatrice, until this moment I could not tell another living soul how I felt.'

Beatrice didn't know what to say. How could any words suffice? 'Thank you for telling me, for sharing that with me.'

'Thankfully I was then in a position to pay off my father's debts and lost no time in having the part of the house damaged by the fire rebuilt. As far as I was concerned, that was the end of it.'

He said that, Beatrice noted, with deadly finality. It was as if he'd resolved matters to his complete satisfaction in his own mind, and nothing and no one could ever intrude on the place where he had put his parents to rest.

'After that I threw myself into my work, travelling east and west to try to forget.'

'And—Larkhill?' she whispered tentatively. 'You haven't mentioned how my father came to lose it to you.'

Apart from a tensing of his body, Julius's face remained expressionless. 'I would prefer not to go into details of that night, Beatrice. Suffice to know that after paying off the mortgage I placed the estate in the hands of an agent to run in my absence. The first time I saw Larkhill was when I went to assess it for myself. In all honesty I had no idea you existed. I didn't know your father had a daughter. If I had known it would bring me face to face with you and the pain of your loss, not for the world would I have gone down there.' He met her gaze. 'How do you feel now you know the whole sorry story?' he asked, gently smoothing the tousled curls with his hand. 'Are you wishing you'd never laid eyes on me? I wouldn't blame you.'

'Please don't think that. I'm glad you've told me. I cannot imagine what would have become of our marriage if you had not shared this with me. It's too big, too important to have let it stand between us for the rest of our lives.'

'And there will be no more talk of divorce? In for a penny, in for a pound?' he murmured, encouraged that she didn't pull away.

Beatrice swallowed the lump that had risen in her throat and, lifting her head, she gave him a wobbly smile. 'Yes, something like that.'

'And you have no concerns about the position of being my wife—about what that entails?'

'Tell me what it is you expect your wife to do.'

He upturned her face to his, gazing deep into her eyes. 'Always remain by the side of the marquess and desire him as you do now with all the passion you are capable of—all the days of your life.'

Beatrice tilted her head to one side, her heart pounding so hard she believed he must hear it. 'I already do that, but will the marquess continue to desire his marchioness with the same amount of passion he asks of her?'

He cupped her cheek in his hand, loving all the subtle nuances of feeling conveyed in her expression.

'I believe I could manage that—in fact, I believe the marquess already does.' He wiped a tear away with his thumb. Only then did she realise she was crying.

'Oh, Julius! I pray God you are sincere, for I could not bear it if you weren't. I—I love you, you see...'

His face hardened and he pressed his finger to her lips, silencing her. 'Don't say it, Beatrice,' he said with quiet, implacable firmness and a caution he had always maintained when it came to affairs of the heart. 'Already you have given me far more than I could ever expect. Do not give more than that.'

Beatrice lowered her eyes and said no more about it, but his rejection of her love hurt more than she imagined possible. She accepted that she loved him, that he gave her great joy, and it broke her heart to think he might never reciprocate her love. Looking at him once more, she put her face close to his, studying it intently, looking to see if there were any more secrets. As though he suspected that she was trying to see into his mind, there was a darkening to his eyes which after a moment seemed to disappear like a cloud blown away by the wind. There was nothing to see, but she could not explain the tiny *frisson* of doubt that would not leave her.

'Please don't lie to me or hold anything back, Julius. We must both agree to set a pattern of honesty and frankness for the future. You married me because I made it difficult for you to refuse—and I married you because I wanted to bring Larkhill back into my life.'

'What are you saying?'

Raising her head, she met his gaze. 'That things

change in the most peculiar way. Not for one moment did I think I would end up feeling like this when I challenged you to that race. When I first realised I had feelings for you I told myself I was deceiving myself and continued to do so. I do not know when those feelings began, but what I do know is that they are feelings so much stronger and deeper than anything I have ever felt before.'

'You are right,' he murmured. 'Things do have a way of changing. But I'm beginning to like the result of your scheming. I would like you to know that from the moment when I first laid eyes on you I wanted you—badly, my love.'

Beatrice jerked her head back and gave him an indignant look. 'You did? You should have told me.'

Julius chuckled and rolled her on to her back. 'What? And spoil the fun? Not in a million years,' he said, kissing the tip of her nose.

Beatrice laughed at his unprincipled determination to get what he wanted and his complete lack of contrition for it. 'Shame on you, Julius Chadwick. Have you no principles at all?' she demanded.

He pulled her further down the bed and covered her body with his own. 'None whatsoever,' he told her before taking her lips in a kiss that she was unable to resist, and their bodies joined once more in a dizzying union of delight.

After their loving, with a feeling of well-serviced bliss lingering in his body, Julius was enjoying looking at his wife seated at her dressing table. She had slipped into her robe, which was nothing more than a wisp of satin and lace and ribbons in a delicate shade of peach. His eyes lingered on the thrust of her breasts as she raised her arms and attempted to bring her tousled hair into some kind of order. He admired the long graceful line of her back and the fall of her golden hair. As he watched her his throat went dry. Dear Lord, she had been beautiful before, but now she was glorious. Before they had married she had seemed wholesome and innocent, but now she seemed different, like a young woman who had come into her own. She glowed and bloomed and seemed softer somehow. In the mirror her eyes were drifting, dreaming, and she looked like a woman whose senses were fulfilled, physically and emotionally.

When she stood up and stretched languidly, like a cat beneath the sun's warmth, the slender, graceful length of her was outlined beneath her robe. The fabric strained over her breasts, rich and full. Her figure was taut and trim, yet he saw the slight roundness of her belly as her robe clung to her.

All at once Julius felt unbalanced by the strength of his emotions. Was it possible that his wife was with child? Doubting his suspicion, he cautiously looked again. No, the swelling was there, noticeably. He was perfectly still as though the slightest movement might disturb his thoughts. He wondered if she knew she was with child and, wondering if she did know, why she wasn't telling him of his impending fatherhood?

He did his best to calm himself. Should he tell her he knew her secret? Should he wait for her to tell him of her own accord? The child would make a difference to their marriage, he realised that, and he and Beatrice must try to shape some solidity into their lives—for the child. *The child.* The mere thought of a child growing inside Beatrice warmed his cold heart until it glowed with something sweet and loving. He felt a thrill of anticipation race through him and his heart gave a leap of excitement. He wanted to reach out for her, to touch and caress that little mound, but his pounding heart told him to be cautious, not to rush things.

He glanced at her face. She seemed preoccupied, troubled, suddenly, and he wondered if she might be considering how best to tell him of her pregnancy.

'Is there something you wish to tell me, Beatrice?' he prompted with peculiar gravity.

On a sigh she turned and looked at him. 'Yes.'

His heart soared. He waited in hope and expectation for what she was to say.

'It—it's Astrid, Julius. I am so concerned about her.'

Dumbfounded, Julius stared at her. 'What? Astrid?' He sounded stupid. That wasn't what he'd wanted to hear. 'What about Astrid?'

'Aunt Moira is forcing her into marriage with a man almost old enough to be her grandfather. Oh, Julius, I have to help her.'

Julius swallowed down his immense disappointment. 'You may speak freely. Please tell me the facts. What is the name of the prospective bridegroom?'

'Lord Alden. I am sure you are acquainted with him.'

'I am. And has Astrid asked for your help?'

'No.'

'Then do you think you should interfere?'

She stiffened. 'Interfere? I would not call concern for a dear cousin interfering. I'm at my wits' end trying to work out what to do.'

'Have you spoken to her?'

She shook her head. 'No, I have not. Aunt Moira will not let her see me. I've seen George on occasion and he is powerless against his mother.'

'Lady Moira cannot force Astrid to marry against her will.'

'Yes, she can. Astrid is terrified of her. She is cowed by her mother. She will do what she is told to do. But George tells me that she is suffering greatly. She is making herself ill.' Moving towards the bed, she sat beside him, moving closer when his arm came round her, and in a small voice, she said, 'Julius—could you, perhaps…?'

Annoyed that she should feel such concern for her cousin when he was riven with questions about her condition, he lifted his head and looked at her in that lofty manner so characteristic of him. 'And what would you have me do? Leave it, Beatrice. Do not interfere in this.'

Beatrice held his gaze, stung by his words, but determined to stand her ground to the bitter end. She felt that she was fighting for Astrid's very life. 'Do you doubt the seriousness of my cousin's plight?'

'I think it might have been exaggerated. Married to Lord Alden, Astrid will be mistress of one of the finest houses in the country and she will find him a generous husband. Beatrice, I will not become involved in this. I will not be used.'

'And so Astrid will have to suffer a miserable marriage to a lascivious old man so that your good name might be preserved? Shame on you, Julius.'

He looked at her through narrowed eyes. Beatrice stared back at him, outwardly calm while her emotions became a turmoil of anger, fear, exasperation and compassion—and a deep, abiding love for her husband.

Julius scowled, knowing that what she said was right—Alden was a lecherous old man and he couldn't blame Beatrice for wanting to prevent her gentle cousin from marrying him. 'All right, Beatrice,' he said more agreeably. 'You win. I promise I will give the matter some thought.'

Gently pushing her away, he tossed back the covers. Swinging his long, muscular legs over the side of the bed, he stood up and proceeded to dress, a reluctant smile tugging at his lips when he saw his wife's face light up with joyous delight. Utterly defeated in this, laughing softly, he strode round the bed and caught her to him, kissing her lips before turning for the door.

'But think on, my love. Do not strain the bonds of husbandly affection beyond this. Now I will leave you to dress and see you at dinner.'

On a sigh Beatrice sank on to the bed. 'Julius,' she said softly. With his hand on the door handle he turned and glanced back at her, hearing the emotion that clogged her voice. 'Thank you.'

He smiled. 'For what?'

'For everything.'

The smile faded from his face, replaced by an expression so intense, so profoundly proud that he could not speak.

Over the days that followed, instead of repairing to Highfield, Julius decided to stay in London for a few weeks to be close to the offices where he conducted his business and for Beatrice to enjoy the position of prestige in society she was entitled to. For the first time in his life he enjoyed the company of a woman—taking her places, showing her off and lavishing expensive gifts on her.

When the novelty of their unconventional marriage had run its course among the members of the *ton*, they became a favoured couple, much sought after for any social occasion. Invitations arrived at the house in large numbers. They went through them together, laughingly inventing excuses to decline some of the invitations so they could spend their time together in serenity and seduction.

Beatrice's days were filled with contentment. Her nights were spent in Julius's bed and the primitive, wild splendour of his lovemaking. He would linger over her with painstaking tenderness, making love to her slowly, prolonging her release, until she had to plead with him to end the wonderful sweet torment. Other times he would reach for her in hunger and take her quickly. She came to learn there was a baseness to him, too, when he would take no denial, when his kisses could be fierce and demanding, his passion all-consuming, leaving her breathless but thoroughly content in the warm security of his embrace.

He taught her many things, one of them being to show him what she wanted. He also taught her the power she had over his body—and how to use it. Always an avid learner, Beatrice put her new-found knowledge into immediate and highly effective use; but, when not stirred to impassioned heights, she would simply nestle in her husband's arms, feeling the brush of his lips on her brow or a nuzzling kiss against her ear. He was the husband that women dream of having for their own and Beatrice was still stunned by the realisation that he was hers.

Among a society where it was considered unfashionable for husbands and wives to spend all their waking hours together, the Marquess and Marchioness of Maitland—who were rarely seen apart and were clearly very much enamoured of each other in a way that went beyond wedlock—made it fashionable. With collective sighs of envy, society had to admit that they made a striking couple, the marquess incredibly handsome, smiling that lazy approving smile at his beautiful young wife, who seemed to have the ability to make him laugh in a way no one had ever heard him laugh before. And the marquess clearly adored his wife and didn't care if the whole world knew it. Theirs was a most unusual marriage.

Chapter Nine

Ever since Julius had noticed Beatrice was pregnant he had floundered in a sweet morass of unbelievable joy and hope that would not let him rest—hope that this child would give them an anchorage to settle down. It was so unbelievable. Some instinct warned him not to let her know he knew her secret—if she knew herself. If she did, he was waiting for her to tell him of her own accord.

It was on their wedding night when she had conceived—over four months, yet still she had not said a word. For the first time in his life he was completely bemused by what went on inside a woman's head. Why hadn't she told him? A woman must know when she was pregnant—surely? He had been waiting for two weeks, scarcely leaving her side—not that he wanted to—so he might be available when she finally revealed her condition, which couldn't be long.

The matter came to a head when her horse was brought from Larkhill and she came into the drawing room in her riding habit, her face lit up with excitement. She intended taking Major for some exercise in the park, despite the fact that rain-filled clouds covered London and already heavy splashes could be heard against the drawing-room windows. Julius came alert instantly. He could imagine his wife's idea of exercising her mount—more like a break-neck gallop clearing any obstacle that confronted her.

'I don't think you should,' he said, putting his newspaper aside.

'Why ever not?' Beatrice said, pulling on her gloves. 'Major will be feeling so frustrated after the journey. A good blow out will do him the world of good. We both need the exercise. Come with us if you like. I'd love it if you would.'

'No, Beatrice, not today. Besides, it's raining.' He spoke softly, patiently, while squaring his broad shoulders and preparing to do battle, knowing his refusal to allow her to ride would more than likely send her back into the stubbornness, the mutinous obstinacy she had shown at the beginning of their relationship.

'Don't be ridiculous, Julius. Since when did a little rain put you off?' Picking up her crop, she walked to the door.

'Beatrice,' he said, getting to his feet. 'I said I would prefer it if you didn't ride today.'

Hearing a warning note in his voice, she turned and looked back at him, her dark scowl telling him not to start ordering her about—or trying to. 'But I must ride.

I can't sit about all day, as you have had me do ever since I came back from Larkhill. I shall go out of my mind if I don't get out of the house. You can't deprive me of the pleasure I get from riding.'

'I have no wish to, but what if your horse takes it into his head to bolt?'

'He won't—and if he did I can deal with it. I do know my horse, Julius. You of all people know that.'

'Nevertheless I would prefer it if you did not ride him,' he told her firmly, tempted to say that he didn't want her gallivanting about Hyde Park taking risks. This was his child and, by God, he was going to see it born. 'I've told the grooms they are not to saddle him. When he needs exercise they will do it.'

'Goodness me, aren't you the fierce one today,' she remarked crossly. 'I might as well tell you now that I will not take orders from you or a groom, and if necessary I shall saddle my horse myself.'

'I don't think so,' he said, going to stand in front of her, trying to put some warmth into his voice so as not to antagonise her. 'What if you were to take a tumble?'

'I won't.'

No, he thought, she wouldn't. She was the best horsewoman he knew, but his judgement was tempered not with admiration, but with fear.

Perplexed by his refusal to let her ride and his strange mood, Beatrice frowned up at him. 'Julius, what on earth is the matter with you? There's nothing unusual in my riding out—and I promise to take one of the grooms with me if that's what's worrying you.'

'No, it isn't that,' he replied sharply. 'You can hardly

expect to get up on that horse and go galloping in the park when you are in a delicate condition. Have you not the sense to safeguard your child—our child?'

She stared up at him in disbelief, then laughed, thinking he was being ridiculous. 'Forgive me, but I'm not sure I take your meaning. Child? What are you talking about?'

'That I know you are pregnant, Beatrice.'

'I am? How do you know?'

'Your own body provided me with the announcement of my impending fatherhood.'

'A baby? But—I can't be. I mean—I feel so well. In fact, I've never felt better in my life. When you're having a baby you're… Oh dear! I think I may have put on a little weight but—a baby?'

Slowly shaking her head, feeling as if her legs were about to buckle under her, she sank into a chair, trying to get her head round what Julius had said. Could it be true and, if so, how could she possibly not have known? Her monthly fluxes had always been irregular—although now she came to think of it she'd seen nothing for—how long?—three months. Her breasts were tender, but she had thought that was just blooming womanhood. Her stomach was still taut, yet her clothes had seemed a little tight of late.

'Dear me, if I am with child then—then I must be four months,' she whispered. 'It must have happened on our wedding night.' She placed her hands to her scarlet cheeks. 'I cannot believe I didn't know.' Her eyes flew to Julius, who was gazing down at her with all the love and tenderness he felt for her there in his eyes. 'But I might not be. It's not certain.'

'We'll get the doctor to confirm it,' he murmured, squatting down beside her and taking her hand. 'But I do think you are, my darling. You really didn't know?'

Smiling while close to tears, she shook her head. 'No—but you did. How stupid is that?'

Getting to his feet, Julius laughed softly, pulling her up and gathering her to him. 'Not stupid, my love. Just a little—naïve, I think. But think about it—how wonderful it will be,' he murmured into her sweet-scented hair, the mere thought warming his heart.

'How long have you known?' Beatrice asked, her cheek against his hard chest, still unable to believe it and yet at the same time feeling a thrill of anticipation race through her. Her heart gave a leap of excitement in her chest, for Julius was acknowledging it and, even more wonderful, was saying he did not mind.

'Since the night you came back from Larkhill. I wanted to ask you, but I felt you might want to choose your own time to tell me. You would have told me, wouldn't you—had you realised it yourself?' He smiled wryly when she turned her face up to his in dreaming contemplation.

She returned his smile tremulously. 'I could hardly not, could I?'

'And you are not unhappy about it?' he said, as he traced his finger along the elegant curve of her cheek.

'Deliriously happy,' she murmured, her eyes aglow

with love. 'And you were right to tell me not to ride. I would not wish to harm the baby.'

'You won't—if you ride at a gentle pace. I'll accompany you tomorrow. Hopefully the sun will be shining by then.'

'It already is,' she said, wrapping her arms around his neck and pulling his head down to hers. 'For us.'

'I have something to give you.' Disentangling her arms, he went to a table. Picking up a flat packet which looked as if it might contain papers, he brought it to her.

Beatrice took it, looking at it and then at him in bemusement. 'What is it?'

'My belated wedding present to you.'

Tentatively she opened it and pulled out some papers, yellow with age. She was hardly able to believe what she saw. 'But—these look like the deeds for Larkhill. But I—I don't understand.'

'They *are* the deeds, Beatrice. I told you I had no intention of keeping the estate. I have made the property over to the person to whom it rightly belongs. You.'

When Beatrice realised what he had done, she was overwhelmed with gratitude and love. Reaching her arms around his powerful shoulders and burying her face in his neck, she murmured, 'Thank you so much. I can't find the words to tell you how much this means to me. I really don't deserve you.'

The naked anguish in her voice brought a constriction to his throat. Threading his fingers through her hair, he framed her face between his hands and gazed at her. '*I* don't deserve you, my love,' he whispered hoarsely. 'Dear God, I don't.'

Some days later, Julius had business to attend to at his offices, so Beatrice was alone when an unexpected and unwelcome visitor arrived. It was mid-morning, too early in the day for visitors, so Beatrice was surprised to see her Aunt Moira. Beatrice felt a chill steal across her heart when her aunt breezed into the room. She gave no greeting, save a slight inclination of her head.

Beatrice received her with the utmost politeness. 'Aunt Moira, this is an unexpected surprise. I hope you are well. I had no idea you were in London.'

'Why should you?' Lady Standish began in her authoritarian, yet ladylike way. Without being invited to do so she sat, stiff backed, her hand resting on her brass-knobbed walking cane. 'This is not a social call, Beatrice. I am here out of necessity, not because I choose to be. You will understand the reason why I am here.'

Sitting stiffly opposite, Beatrice looked at her aunt with unaffected astonishment. 'Forgive me, Aunt, but I don't.'

'I have come to fetch my daughter home. I assume this is where she is hiding out.'

Beatrice stared at her in disbelief. 'Astrid? But—she is not here.'

'No?'

It was clear her aunt did not believe her, but if Astrid was not at Standish House and she had not come to

Beatrice, then where was she? 'No, Aunt Moira, she is not. When did she leave home?'

'Three days ago. She left the house to visit a neighbour for a musical afternoon and did not come back.'

'Then—is it possible that she might have met with an accident?'

'No. Enquiries were made. Some of her clothes are missing, which tells me she has run off.'

'But—this is alarming. Where is George? Did she not confide in him?'

'George has been in Brighton for the past two weeks. He is due back tomorrow. As yet I have not informed him that Astrid is missing.'

'Then I think he should be told. But—why would you assume she has come here?'

'Where else would she go?' Lady Standish said in an angry tone. 'Don't pretend to be ignorant of it,' she accused scathingly. 'She is here, isn't she? You are hiding her. I know it.'

'Indeed you are mistaken, Aunt Moira,' Beatrice answered. 'When I left Standish House you forbade me to see Astrid and I swear I have not.'

'Do not trifle with me, Beatrice,' Lady Standish said. 'You may have married a marquess, but you are still a nobody.' Her eyes had taken on a wildness as she looked around at the luxurious green-and-gold room. 'Just look at this place—look at you. Your scheming has paid off admirably.'

Beatrice bristled with indignation at the affront. 'My father was a gentleman as well you know, Aunt Moira. I do not consider myself beneath Julius. In our marriage we are equal. Astrid is my cousin and I am worried about her.'

'Astrid is not your concern. Untrustworthy, that's what you are. You are together in this. I know you have been down to Larkhill. I am also aware that George visited you there. You are all in it together—scheming against me—all part of the same wicked conspiracy.'

'There is no conspiracy.'

Lady Standish banged her cane with impatient outrage, her voice rising. 'Do not contradict me. If you know anything at all, then I demand that you tell me. I am entitled to know where my daughter is.'

'Clearly Astrid doesn't think so, otherwise she would have told you. If you do not believe me when I say she is not here, then please feel free to search the house. May I remind you that this house also happens to be my home and should Astrid come here for whatever reason, I would not turn her away.'

Lady Standish looked as though she had been pole-axed. Both hands gripped her cane fiercely, the knuckles white, her eyes staring icily at her niece.

'Perhaps if you had not insisted that she wed Lord Alden,' Beatrice went on, 'she would not have run away.'

'But they are engaged. It is an excellent match and it is my wish that they wed.'

'Clearly Astrid has an aversion to the match—as great an aversion as she had when you aspired that she marry Julius,' Beatrice told her tightly, struggling to keep her anger under control. 'Julius has spoken to

Lord Alden on my behalf—since George told me what you intended I have been exceedingly worried about Astrid. Julius has explained to Lord Alden Astrid's fondness for another man. From what Julius has told me, he is reconsidering the marriage.'

Lady Standish's face was chalk white, and when she next spoke her voice shook with fury. 'And you denied there was any conspiracy. Lord Chadwick had no business, no business at all, to interfere in a matter that does not concern him, and neither have you. How dare either of you disregard the arrangements I have made for my own daughter? This is too much.'

'I did so because I happen to care for Astrid. I was deeply concerned when George told me you were forcing her to marry a man she does not care for. Where have you looked for her? Have you seen Squire Talbot? That is the obvious place. Is Henry at home? If he is absent and his father ignorant as to his whereabouts, then I would say that is a clear indication they have run away together.'

Her aunt's body was visibly shaking with anger. 'If that should prove to be the case, then believe me when I say that her ambition will never be gratified.'

'Astrid's ambition has always been to marry Henry.'

'And I forbid it,' she replied, her voice brittle. 'Any alliance between Astrid and Henry Talbot will be seen as a disgrace. She will be censured and slighted by everyone connected to us. I will not have it. You do know her intentions, don't you?'

'No, Aunt, I do not, and if I did I would not tell

you—not if it meant Astrid would suffer further heart-ache.'

'Your defiance does you no credit. How dare you address me in this impertinent manner? You will pay dearly for this,' she warned Beatrice with a fixed stare. 'God help me, you will pay the price of what you have done to me. I will not be beaten.' Struggling to maintain her composure, she stood up and crossed regally to the door, where she turned and looked back, her piercingly cold eyes regarding the beautiful young woman, whose eyes were filled with contentment. 'So it's true what everyone is saying,' she sneered. 'Your union with Lord Chadwick is working out against all the odds. I believe you have put on a little weight, Beatrice. Marriage clearly agrees with you.'

Beatrice lifted her head and met her stare for stare, reluctant to disclose her pregnancy to this cold woman. 'Yes. Julius and I are very happy.'

'And so you should be—after the trouble you caused securing for yourself a most advantageous marriage, you despicable, scheming girl. I know he sent someone to assess Larkhill for its value, which implies he might be going to sell it. It will serve you right if he calls your bluff. You should have thought he might do that when you propositioned him.'

'Julius no longer owns Larkhill, Aunt Moira. He has made it over to me. So you see, I have achieved everything that I set out to do.'

'Really? Your scheming is not worthy of congratulations. You think you know Julius Chadwick, don't you? Perhaps you would not be so cocksure if you knew what the man you married is guilty of.'

Perplexed, Beatrice stared at her. 'What do you mean? What are you saying?'

'Ask your lying, two-faced husband,' she uttered viciously. 'He knows.'

'Knows? Knows what, Aunt Moira?'

'The truth. The truth about how your father died.'

Beatrice laughed a little nervously, then her heart began to beat with a new intensity, as though perceiving she was about to be told something that had been hidden from her. 'What are you talking about?'

A slow smile stretched the older woman's mouth, a smile that was pure evil. 'Why, Beatrice, that your husband is a murderer. After he took Larkhill from your father and found the estate was mortgaged up to the hilt, he killed him.' Her smile became one of satisfaction when her niece's eyes widened in deepening incredulity. 'There, you have it.'

Pain and disbelief streaked through Beatrice and a tiny hammer of panic began to pound in her head. 'No. You are lying.' She swallowed past a constriction in her throat. Something inside her had begun to die. 'This is preposterous,' she uttered shakily as terror began to hammer through her. Everything in her recoiled from believing Julius was capable of such evil. She knew in her bones he would not do something so wicked as to kill her father and then marry his daughter. None of it made sense. Julius couldn't do that. He wasn't a murderer—but then, how would she know?

'I know you are bitter about what I did, when I challenged Julius, but to say…that—why would you say such a cruel thing?'

'Because it's true.'

Her entire body vibrating with horror, a scream of hysteria and denial rose in Beatrice's throat. But then she recalled what her aunt had said before Julius had taken her from Standish House, that when she came to know the true nature of the man she aspired to marry, how he dealt with those who dared to cross him, she would learn to hate him. Was this what she had meant?

Facing her aunt, she felt each of her enraged words as if it was a blow to her head. 'I do not believe you. Unable to live with what he'd done, my father killed himself.'

'If that is what you want to believe, then do so—it's what your husband wants you to believe—but do you know that for a fact?'

'Yes,' Beatrice answered implacably.

'And I have reason to know,' her aunt said with equal implacability, 'that the man you married shot him.'

Beatrice was trying so hard to concentrate and not to give way to the terror of her aunt's accusation that she dug her nails in her palms. 'I cannot—will not—believe this. I will speak to Julius. He has to have a chance to deny this—this slander, to explain.'

'He has no defence. Your mother knew—in one of her more lucid moments she told me when she came back from London, before she took to her bed and turned her back on the world.'

Beatrice's blood already ran cold, but those words froze her heart. 'My mother,' she whispered. 'She told you that?'

'She was there. She saw Julius leaving the house. I promise you, Beatrice, I do not lie.' Her smile was one of venomous satisfaction. 'Think about it. How does it feel knowing you are married to the man who killed your own father?'

Lady Standish made to leave. Beatrice watched her, feeling quite ill to have confirmation of something she had sensed, but could never put her finger on—that when Julius had opened up to her he had not told her everything. His betrayal of her trust was like a stab in the heart.

A tremor of fury rippled through her, and with a sudden spurt of anger, she said, 'And what does that make you, Aunt Moira? If, as you say, Julius is a murderer, how could you bear for him to marry Astrid? Was your greed for title, wealth and power so great you were prepared to sacrifice your own daughter on the altar of matrimony with a man who is capable of such evil? Where were your principles then?'

Lady Standish looked at her hard before raising her head and leaving the house.

Drowning in a black pool of despair, Beatrice couldn't stand it. She understood everything her aunt had said, but she could not seem to move or feel. Was it really true that Julius had killed her father? If he had, how could she bear it? She was in pain, a constant searing pain that would not ease.

Mechanically she moved to the window, her arms wrapped round her waist in an agony of suffering, staring blankly at nothing. Feeling sick to the stomach, she tried to collect her wits. What on earth should she do? She didn't think she could confront him just yet, to look into the harsh, handsome face she adored and hear that beautiful baritone voice. And yet could she stand the uncertainty of not knowing the truth? Could she go on living with him, spending days and nights together, pretending—living with the lie that would be their lives? Or could she bear the torment of living without him?

But as she considered the awfulness of his crime, she could not believe he had done this to her. Anger began to burn in her breast. If what she had been told was indeed true, how dare he make a mockery of her faith in him? Little wonder he had been so secretive. Little wonder he had wanted to conceal what he had done. She told herself to be fair and give him the benefit of the doubt, but deep down she knew there was some truth in it.

She had half a mind to seek him out at his place of business and demand that he tell her what he was playing at, but no doubt he would prevaricate and lie and continue treating her like the stupid idiot he took her for. If he had gone to great pains to conceal the mystery, then how could she think he would oblige her and tell her the truth now?

Resentment burned through her. They had an agree-ment to be open with each other, to be on equal terms, to tell each other the truth in all things, yet, despite his promise, her husband had persisted with his deception. How dare he conceal something as important as this from her? There was nothing equal in what he had done. She wanted answers and explanations and noth-ing would stop her from finding out exactly what had happened.

When Julius arrived home he went into his study to look over some papers. He was seated at his desk and just about to raise a pre-dinner brandy to his lips when the door was flung open and Beatrice came in like a hurricane.

'Good Lord!' he spluttered, dabbing his chin where the brandy had splashed. 'What's got into you? Beatrice? I'm always glad to see you, but could you not knock or…?' His voice died away in bewilderment at the sight of the expression on her face and he placed the brandy glass on the desk.

Beatrice knew she must look odd. How could she help it when the words she wanted to speak—shout—at him were roiling at the back of her throat in an effort to get out, to tear him to pieces in her fury?

'What have you done?' she managed to say at last.

Julius's face showed astonishment. 'Done? What have *I* done? What can you mean? I have merely come home after concluding a successful day's business and come in here and poured myself a drink, which, if I am allowed to, I shall relax and enjoy.'

'Stop it, Julius. Don't you dare pretend you don't know what I mean.'

'My love, believe me, I haven't the slightest idea.'

'Then you should.'

'You do seem to be annoyed about something…'

'*Annoyed!* Dear Lord, annoyed doesn't half-describe what I'm feeling right now you—you blackguard, so will you stop prattling on and tell me the truth or I swear I shall scream,' she uttered vehemently.

He was getting annoyed and it showed in the narrowing of his eyes and his scowl. Julius Chadwick was not accustomed to being called names of any sort or brought to task about anything; though he adored this woman and knew he always would, he was not about to let her throw her weight about like a street woman looking for a fight. He didn't know what had awoken her temper, but something had and it seemed it was aimed at him.

'It's you who are prattling on, Beatrice,' he said irritably, 'and unless you tell me what all this is about I cannot answer your accusations over something I know nothing about. Is something wrong?'

'Yes—yes, you might say that.' Looking at him across the desk, she rested her hands on its surface and leaned in, her face on a level with his. 'It's about honesty, openness and trust. Stupidly I thought we had agreed to that in our marriage. I now find I have got it so very wrong. How can I trust you when you are up to your eyes in deception? This is not the marriage I agreed to when I came back from Larkhill.'

'And why is that?' His voice was icy.

'My father, Julius.' She met him look for look and her eyes were green ice. 'I want the truth about the manner of his death, and who better to ask than the man who killed him.'

For a moment his face took on an expression of total incomprehension. He frowned as though he were doing his best to unravel her words, make sense of them, then his face hardened when realisation of what she was accusing him of hit him.

'Who told you?' He spoke mildly, but his amber eyes had sharpened.

'Aunt Moira.'

'And when did you see your aunt?'

'A short time ago. She came to tell me that Astrid is missing and accused me of hiding her here. She also told me that not only did the man I married take Larkhill from my father, but that he also killed him. I have to ask you if there is any truth in this, Julius. And please don't lie to me.'

'Do you believe I am capable of such an act, Beatrice?' He was watching her warily, having schooled himself well in the necessity for restraint in trying circumstances like the one he now faced.

'Before my aunt came here I would have said no, never in a thousand years would I have believed you could do anything so—so vile. I don't want to believe it, but it would appear that my mother bore witness to the whole sorry affair—and my mother was not a liar.'

'I'm sure she wasn't, but perhaps she mistook what she saw.'

'Did she? Then perhaps you can explain what did

happen that caused my father to lose his life. Either he shot himself or someone murdered him. Tell me the truth—if you can.'

Julius got up and walked round the desk to stand in front of her, where he stood looking down at her upturned face. Despite the fact that they were hurling daggers at him, her eyes were also full of hope that he would deny he'd had any part in her father's demise. But he could not alleviate her doubts. Telling her about her father and the manner of his death would change the whole picture for her and he knew she would not be pleased with what she saw. It might make it worse. Maybe she would be better off not knowing the burden that lay so heavily on him, that there had been times when he thought he would be crushed by it. Unfortunately after her aunt's visit, she now knew half of the story and would assume the rest and assume wrongly.

His face became tense and he looked away. 'I'm afraid I can't do that.'

'Then tell me this—did my mother see you leave the house that night?'

Julius pushed his hand through his thick hair. His face was becoming dangerous and the gentleness, the concern, was replaced by grinding anger. His eyes darkened and he spoke through gritted teeth. 'Damn it, Beatrice. Can't you leave it?'

'No, Julius, I cannot. Don't you understand? Ever since my father died I believed he had killed himself and that my mother—who found his body—was so shocked she retreated into herself because she couldn't bear to live without him and the knowledge of what he had done. Now I know that she couldn't bear to live with what she had witnessed—that he did not die by his own hand—and, being the gentle person she was, she was too afraid to speak out. I have a right to know what happened and I demand that you tell me. Were you there? Did she see you leave the house shortly after my father was killed?'

Julius looked at her hard, seeming to consider very carefully what to say next. At length he said tightly, 'Yes, Beatrice, she did.'

Beatrice stared at him with eyes wide with horror. She had hoped and prayed he would deny it, that he would tell her there was no truth in what her aunt had told her and that what she had said was merely the rantings of a vicious old woman.

'Then you have deceived me most cruelly,' she uttered with a rage that was buried bone deep. She stepped back from him, as if she couldn't bear to be near him. 'How could you? When I married you I did so for no other reason than to gain access to Larkhill. The opportunity was too beautiful for me to resist. Suddenly you were more to me than the whole world, more than my own future, more than fortune. I would have been a fool to turn away from what you could offer me—and then I fell in love with you.' She gave a hard, contemptuous little laugh which bordered on hysterical. 'How stupid was that? I now find that the one man I have ever loved is worthless, utterly vicious and corrupt, without principle and without honour—a man who killed my own father. Do you think I could ever forget that? No, Julius, that memory will burn within me as long as I live.'

Julius's hand went out to her. His face was strangely gentle and his amber eyes softened and were filled with compassion and warmth. They told of his own regret, not that her father was dead and that she truly believed he had killed him, but that it should give pain to her.

But Beatrice would have none of his concern and her cold, narrowed eyes told him so. 'Don't touch me,' she spat.

He drew back his hand. 'Your father did not shoot himself—I can tell you that—but there is more to it than that, Beatrice.'

'Then tell me.'

'I—I cannot tell you,' he said haltingly, finding it almost impossible to think of that night when his whole world had fallen apart, let alone speak of it. For a moment his mask slipped and Beatrice glimpsed fleetingly his inner pain, that he seemed deeply troubled and genuinely at a loss. But then the mask was back in place.

'But if you want me to believe you, you must.'

'I—cannot.'

'Then if you cannot defend yourself, I am not interested in anything further you have to say.' She turned from him and walked across the room to the door. 'There is nothing more to be said. I want to be by myself—to think about what I'm going to do—away from here. Away from you.'

Julius's eyes narrowed. 'Just exactly what is that supposed to mean?'

'That I'd rather die than live in the same house as the man who killed my father. I am going to Larkhill—without you. I suppose it was your guilty conscience that prompted you to return it to me.'

'No, it was because I wanted very much to give you back the equivalent of what was taken from you.'

'Then I suppose I must be grateful for that at least.'

'I am sorry, Beatrice, if I have hurt you. I regret that, but please believe me when I say that I desire only your peace and happiness. Do not forget that.'

She turned and looked at him. 'It is not enough to say you're sorry, to try to make amends, hoping to wipe out everything you have done,' she said, stiff with pride and anger. 'You should have thought of all this before you robbed my father to add to your own fortunes and then killed him. Now it is too late, do you hear, too late! How can I possibly remain married to you knowing this? I will keep Larkhill, but I would rather die a thousand deaths than take anything else from you! Can't you understand that I hate you?'

She flung the last words in his face and had the bitter satisfaction of seeing him whiten. She triumphed in it, rejoiced in it, hoping for some sign of weakness which would put him absolutely at her mercy, but Julius Chadwick was a man of steel and did not know how to weaken. He merely shrugged and turned away from her.

'I shall leave for Larkhill at first light. Please don't try to stop me.'

'I won't.' The fact that she had been so quick to believe the worst of him cut through his heart like a knife, leaving him with a dark sense of having been betrayed. He knew that by not telling her everything he was being unreasonable, but he just couldn't help himself. Even if their marriage had been a travesty at the beginning, he had become comfortable with the idea of her being his wife and was reluctant to let her go.

'Go if you feel you must—after this I am sure you can't wait to leave me, but I will never divorce you,' Julius continued dispassionately, immune to the wrathful expression on her beautiful face. 'We will discuss the course of our future at a later date, but until then we have a child to consider and it will be raised by both a mother and a father.'

One look at his face convinced Beatrice that he was absolutely furious with her. Not only were his eyes glinting with icy shards, but the muscles in his cheeks were tensing and vibrating to a degree that she had never seen before.

She drew an infuriated breath. 'As you said, we will discuss the course of our future another time. Goodbye, Julius.' With that she swept out of the room, leaving him staring after her. She did not see the move he made towards her, or his look of angry pain and suffering, or hear the sigh of bitter defeat he uttered when she closed the door.

With a sense of burning betrayal and seething anger at her husband's terrible crime, fighting back scalding tears of hurt, Beatrice hurried to her room—to pack, she decided, for if he wasn't going to tell her the truth, she would not remain in the same house as a liar and a murderer.

In her wretched suffering she lay awake, hearing sounds of her husband moving about his room behind the closed connecting doors. It went on all night, which told her that he too was unable to sleep. She wanted to call out to him, wanted desperately to feel his arms around her, but she could not do it.

Dawn found her huddled in the comforting warm refuge of her cloak as the coach left the house. On the point of leaving, a letter addressed to her was delivered. It was from Astrid. Not until the coach had left London behind did Beatrice open it. It was as she had expected. Astrid had run away with Henry Talbot. They were in Scotland, at Gretna Green, where they had married. Astrid went on to tell her that they were deliriously happy. Things would be hard for a while since they had no money, but Henry's parents had agreed that they could live with them for the time being.

Beatrice was happy for Astrid and sincerely hoped her cousin would find happiness wed to the man of her choice. She could well imagine how the news would be received by her aunt and had no doubt that she would turn her back on her daughter and cut her off without a penny.

It was raining hard and clouds the colour of pewter brushed the rooftops of London, the streets blacker than midnight. The roads were bad, as bad as Beatrice had expected when she'd embarked on this journey, and the rain showed no sign of relenting. But she was oblivious to the cold and the discomforts of the journey the closer she got to Larkhill.

She had closed her eyes and listened to the pounding hooves of the horses and the pounding of her heart. The familiar pain of betrayal was still present, but after hours of thoughtful contemplation in a more rational frame of mind she had the feeling that something was not quite right. Had she really married a monster, a murderer? In her mind she could see Julius smiling down at her, hear his voice filled with need. Could the man who had held her so tenderly and loved her with such unbridled passion really have killed her father? Was he really capable of doing that and then making that man's daughter his wife?

Nothing rang true. In the confused and heated aftermath of her aunt's disclosure, when her emotions had veered between hysterical panic and shaking irrationality, when she had questioned him and accused him so fiercely, his replies had been tentative, almost painful, and she began to suspect that there was something he had not told her—that even now he was deliberately keeping something from her. He had not denied murdering her father, but then, he hadn't admitted it either. He had admitted being there at the time, but that didn't mean he was responsible.

Recalling the moment when the mask had slipped from his face and he had seemed at a loss to know how to answer her questions, she asked herself why. She knew it was not out of coldness.

It was out of fear.

But what was he afraid of? Himself? It was strange

how that one look she had seen on his face could cause everything to shift, to put everything into place. Julius wasn't a murderer. She wasn't mistaken in that. She had been too ready to judge. Had she misjudged him? And if she had, would he ever be able to forgive her?

As the coach swung up the drive to Larkhill, she vividly remembered her confession to him of how she had fallen in love with him and how quickly he had silenced her. She had known he did not love her, but there were times when he made love to her that gave her reason to believe he was coming to that conclusion. She wished she hadn't left him. She wished she was with him now so that she could tell him she was mistaken and apologise for being too ready to condemn him.

By the time the coach stopped in front of the house, so convinced was she of Julius's innocence that she was tempted to tell the driver to turn and head back for London, but out of consideration for the tired horses and driver, she decided against it. She would spend one night at Larkhill and then she would take a leap of faith all the way back to her husband.

Chapter Ten

The man who stood at his bedroom window watched his wife climb into the waiting coach. The hood of her cloak protected her head from the driving rain, denying him one last look at her lovely face. As if she sensed he was there, she paused and raised her head in that regal way of hers, the crisp wind flirting with the cluster of curls escaping their confines, before dropping her eyes without looking back, gathering her cloak about her and climbing inside.

His face impassive, Julius watched the coach pull away, but inside everything was shattering, bleeding, draining the life out of him, for without Beatrice it had no meaning.

He had been a fool not to tell her what she wanted to know, but, dear Lord, apart from James and Constance Merrick, he had never told another living soul about what had happened on the night Beatrice's father had died. He would tell her, that he had decided. He would tell her every sordid detail, no matter how painful, because he now realised that he wanted her more than he had ever wanted anything in his life.

Beatrice had become a part of him which he could not deny. She was like burnished steel, strong and audaciously bold—her eyes blazing with defiance, fighting him, challenging him. daring him with her outrageous forfeit, determined not to have what was hers denied her. Her heart was the sweet centre in the headlong strength of her mind and body and, quite simply, now that he knew her and could see her for what she was, he loved her. He would fill her days and nights with joy and pleasure, until she loved him as much as he loved her. For he did love her, and his heart swelled as he admitted the truth to himself. He could not lose her as he had lost his mother.

Telling her the truth would be difficult, for he found it hard to expose his inner self, but Beatrice would understand—like no one else she would understand. It would take a while to earn her trust after this, he decided, but some day she would surely find him worthy of it.

Driven by a fierce eagerness to see his wife, it became clear to him that if he did not go after her, his energy would be spent in waiting and tearing himself to shreds.

The night was dark and Beatrice was restless in her bed. The wind was high, but the rain that had been falling for two days had temporarily abated. A figure made its way with stealth-like caution towards the house, halting when it reached an iron gate that opened on to the kitchen yard. The figure paused to take stock of things before proceeding. A deathlike stillness hung over the house, which seemed to moan in sorrow over its impending doom. A chain was lifted from the gate and the earthbound shadow slipped through the opening and dashed towards the outbuildings that joined on to the house.

The night's depth of darkness was impenetrable, then the wind changed direction, and the clouds allowed a shaft of moonlight to sweep across the yard. Concealed beneath an enveloping cape, the figure scuttled into the interior of a shed. Gloved hands hastily struck flint to steel over a small mound of gunpowder, and sparks shot outwards and upwards until a sudden blaze flared up. Several minutes later the figure re-emerged and ran the way it had come, looking back only once to watch flames leaping from the building, the wind whipping them towards the house.

Having been travelling for hours, impatient to be at journey's end, Julius willed the coach to go faster. The well-matched team lunged forwards, taking their duties seriously, as the driver drove them at a breakneck pace along the mired roads, swerving madly around bends and not even checking their stride when the wheels caught a rut. Only a couple of miles and he would be at Larkhill. A deep sense of relief surged within him. The wind rushed by the coach and once again heavy splashes of rain began pelting the windows. Pulling up the blind and gazing out, Julius wondered at the reddish glow of heat in the night sky, while a rolling mass of grey billowed above it.

Cold, congealing horror suddenly seized him as memories of another fire—a fire that had robbed him of his mother—almost overwhelmed him. The fire was in the direction of Larkhill. Dear God, he prayed silently, don't let it be the house—don't let Beatrice have come to harm. His fears were confirmed the closer they got. He was relieved to discover it was the outbuildings that were on fire, but being connected to the house, it was only a matter of time before the whole lot went up if it was not checked.

Spurred to action, he leapt from the coach and ran towards the blaze, ignoring the searing sting of flying ash. Along with members of the small staff Julius retained at Larkhill, men from the surrounding area, alerted by neighbours who had not retired for the night and had seen the blaze, were trying to fight the flames to stop them reaching the house. There was no hope in saving the outbuildings. They were succeeding, for mercifully the rain aided them in their task as it came sheeting down once more.

The urgency of the moment pressed upon him and his tone conveyed his growing anxiety for the occupants of the house as he enquired as to their safety. On being told they were still inside, he ran towards the front door.

Torn from her uneasy dream, Beatrice came upright with a gasp and stared about the dark room in wide-eyed panic. Something had disturbed her. A sudden chill shivered along her spine as she pressed back upon the pillows, trying to listen above the howling of the wind. Her heart suddenly lurched. Was that smoke she could smell?

'Beatrice...Beatrice...'

'Julius!' The name flared through her brain as she realised it wasn't part of any dream. It was Julius! She threw herself from the bed and ran out of the bedroom. As she reached the top of the stairs her eyes swept the hall, anxiously searching for the man who had called her name. Someone was pounding on the locked front door; a moment later it crashed open—and there, right below her, was a very tall, dark-haired man. Her heart gave a leap, missed a beat, then began to thump madly as a pair of penetrating amber eyes looked straight into hers. Momentarily stunned by his arrival, she saw the bitter regret carved into his handsome features and the aching gentleness in his compelling eyes.

'Julius!'

Immediately she flew down the stairs and ran across the hall towards him. He caught her up hard in his arms and listened as the words came tumbling out.

'Thank goodness you've come. But why did you? I intended to leave in the morning to return to you. I couldn't bear it, leaving you like that. I know you didn't do it, Julius. I know you didn't kill my father—you couldn't do that, and I don't know why you said you did, but...'

'Hush, Beatrice,' he said, holding her away from him to look into her face. She was flushed and breathing hard, her hair dishevelled from sleep and utterly lovely. He saw tears shimmering in her magnificent eyes; one of them traced unheeded down her smooth cheek. 'What is this?'

'I know you're innocent. I know you didn't do it.'

Gently he traced his lean fingers along her cheek and, with a raw ache in his voice, said, 'What made you realise that?'

'I worked it out for myself.' Her heart in a tumult of emotion, Beatrice clung to him once more, burying her face against his chest. 'I do believe in you, Julius,' she whispered fiercely. 'Forgive me for doubting you—I didn't mean to, I didn't want to, but I was so angry and confused. I will support you in anything you do. I trust you implicitly. I love you so much.'

'That's all I need to hear.' His arms tightened round her, his impassioned whisper strained with feeling. 'We'll talk later, Beatrice. Then you can cry in my arms all night if you wish and, while you do, I'll tell you how sorry I am for everything I've done and said that has hurt you. And when I've finished doing that, you can help me find a way to forgive myself.' He held her away from him. 'I have to go. I promise I'll explain everything, but in the meantime there's a fire to put out.'

She sprang back in alarm. 'What? A fire? Oh—I thought I could smell smoke. Where? Is it the house?'

'It's the outbuildings. Hopefully it won't get to the house. Men from the village were already working on it when I got here. Thankfully the wind's changed direction and it's raining hard. With a bit of luck it will be put out.'

'But how did it start—do you know?'

'Not yet. The time for questions will come later, but I would like you to get dressed all the same. Best to be prepared should the wind change direction again.'

A part of Julius's urgency seized her and when he disappeared through the door she took the stairs at a frantic pace.

The fire was put out and the night grew still once more as Julius went to join Beatrice in the master bedroom. She was in his arms before the clock had spent another second. Lowering his head, he kissed her in stormy tenderness before closing his eyes and burying his face in her sweet-scented hair as his arms fairly squeezed the breath from her. When he raised his eyes to meet hers, his lips smiled.

'I thought I told you to get dressed.' His voice was hoarse with emotion, for Beatrice was attired in nothing but her nightdress, her wonderful wealth of golden hair tumbling down her spine. 'Do you intend to spend your life disobeying me?'

Beatrice leaned back against his arm and smiled with joy as she caressed his soot-smeared cheek. 'I did not disobey you. When I saw the fire had been put out I decided to get undressed again.' Her dark eyes took on a pleading look. 'Come to bed, Julius.'

The sound of her voice was so sweet, Julius almost pulled her down on to the bed. Instead he sighed and gently disengaged her arms. 'Later. I want to talk to you first. There are things I want to tell you.'

Feeling an unexpected lurch of dread, Beatrice swallowed her disappointment. 'Can't it wait until morning?'

'I would prefer to get it over with. Until you know the truth it will always be there, lurking between us.''

'How did you become so wise?' she asked with a tender smile.

'If I were wise, my darling, I would have told you everything at the beginning. Keeping it to myself has only made matters worse between us. I can see that now.' Removing his coat and loosening his neck linen, he took her hand and drew her to the fire. Sitting beside the hearth, he drew her on to his knee, sliding his arm about her waist. 'I want to tell you everything about the night your father died. I promise it will be the truth.'

Beatrice gazed at him, warding off an icy chill. 'I sincerely hope so, Julius. You didn't kill him, did you?'

'No. And before we go any further I want to tell you that Constance was right. I never gamble. I never have—only with business investments. The game of cards that was to be the destruction of both of our fathers took place at a private gentlemen's club. There were few present to witness the outcome. Your father lost Larkhill to my father—not to me.'

'I see. Were you present?'

'I arrived when the game was over. My father was more excited than usual. I didn't know why until later. I was deeply shocked and wanted him to return it. He wouldn't hear of it and told me not to interfere.'

'You should have told me this. I'm sorry that I made you suffer for it. My father should never have put Larkhill on the table.'

'Don't forget that he, too, was desperate. Nor did I kill your father, Beatrice. My father did.'

Beatrice didn't say anything. She simply sat on his knee, listening as the words began pouring out of him.

'My father couldn't believe his good fortune when he won Larkhill. He genuinely believed it would be the answer to all his problems. When he checked its value and found it was heavily mortgaged he became demented. He began drinking—in fact, he became a walking, drunken nightmare. He swore revenge on your father. I arrived at the house when he was about to leave with the intention of confronting your father with a loaded gun. He was so drunk he didn't know what he was doing. He became violent, so violent that I had to lock him in his room. I don't know how he got out—his valet, I suppose, though he denied it.'

Combing his fingers through his dishevelled hair, he looked at Beatrice. He must have seen the horror in her eyes, for he said, 'I think you can guess what happened next. I knew where he had gone and hurried after him. Your parents had rented a small house in Charing Cross. The hour was late and when I arrived the deed was done. Your father was dead, shot in the head, and my father stumbling out of the door. He had thrown down his gun. I left it there. The house was quiet—I had no idea your mother saw me and would naturally believe I had killed him.'

'That was what she told Aunt Moira, on one of

the rare occasions that she spoke. She had found my father's body, you see, and so deep was the shock that it affected her health.'

'And your aunt told no one?'

'No, I don't think so. Why she kept quiet about it is a mystery—unless she meant to use the knowledge against you at a later date.'

'She could try, but there are people who would testify that your mother was an ill woman, that her mind had become somewhat unstable following the suicide of her husband. I have restored the Chadwick good name, earning the respect of those in the upper echelons of society. I doubt anyone would listen to the rantings of an aged and bitter woman.'

'I sincerely hope not. Now that we have resolved matters between ourselves, I would hate to have you cast into prison.'

Julius kissed her forehead. 'I am not going anywhere, my darling, I promise you. After leaving your father, when I got back to the house, James and Constance were there. They had seen my father arrive home and were worried by the blood on his clothes and the state of his mind. He was quite demented, almost boasting of what he had done to your father. I told them everything that had happened and swore them to secrecy. The next day when my father was sober, he remembered nothing. I did. It was like a nightmare, like a dream in a delirium, so infamous I could scarcely believe it.'

Beatrice stared at him in horror, hardly able to take in what he had told her. 'I knew there was something you weren't telling me, but I had no idea it was anything as shocking as this,' she whispered. 'But—I don't understand. Why did you let me go on thinking it was you? Why did you let me go on thinking the worst of you?'

'Because I was ashamed of what my father had done,' he answered, choosing his words with care, his conscience smarting with the irony of trying to protect the reputation of his undeserving father while—at least where Beatrice was concerned—damaging his own. 'Everyone believed your father had shot himself because he could not bear the shame of losing Larkhill. No one stopped to question whether or not the weapon found at the scene might not be his. It was assumed that it was. Nothing on earth would have compelled me to reveal the truth about what had happened and only my determination prevented an almighty scandal at the time of your father's death. Some scandals dim with time—that one wouldn't.'

'So you covered it up and were prepared to let me— and my mother—live the rest of our lives believing my father had killed himself.'

'In that, my love, I am guilty—and deeply ashamed for my weakness. I am truly sorry and beg your forgiveness.'

'You have it, Julius, for I understand why you acted as you did. But do you realise what could have happened to you had my mother spoken out?'

He nodded grimly. 'I can only thank God that she didn't. I couldn't tell you. I thought you'd be better off not knowing the burden that lay heavily on the man you married.'

'What I don't understand is why you felt you had to protect your father, after all he had done to you and your mother? He was undeserving of your sacrifice.'

'Like I said, I was ashamed—and at the end of the day he was still my father,' he said, speaking quietly, the pain of his father's crime evident in his eyes. 'It was hard enough for me to accept he had been a failure, without having to tell the whole world he was a murderer. Shortly after that he, too, was dead. As far as I was concerned it was over—I had no wish to resurrect a time that was painful for me. I saw no harm in letting the world go on believing I was the culprit who stole your home—things might have been different had I known about you. As things turned out, it was fortunate for you that Larkhill was one of the few properties I managed to save being taken over by the bank. That was the only good thing that came out of it—and meeting you.

'The behaviour of my forebears—their addiction for liquor and gaming—has been difficult for me to take. I hoped it was not hereditary—that I would not turn out like them or any offspring I might sire. When I agreed to marry you I knew you were entitled to know all this, but dear God, Beatrice, I could not tell you. I cannot blame you if you hate me for what I've done. I deserve it.'

With tears clogging her throat, Beatrice wrapped her arms around his neck. 'I don't hate you, Julius. Never that. I know I said I did, but I didn't mean it. I love you so much—more than anything on earth.'

When she drew back her head, Julius reached out

and wiped a rogue tear away with the tip of his finger. 'Bless you for that.' He took a deep breath. 'I can't remember when I came to love you. I think it was from the very start—when you challenged me to that damned race. You were feisty, stubborn, an outrageously brave and gorgeous girl who challenged my spirit, blithely incurred my displeasure and refused to yield to my authority—and, much, much worse than that, you mocked my equestrian skills. That was unforgivable,' he said with a teasing smile. 'But despite all this your smile warmed my heart and the touch of your lips heated my blood. So you see, my love, I have loved you from first sight and cannot imagine my future without you.'

Beatrice's eyes filled with tears as she gazed at him and smiled tremulously. 'I'm glad you've told me at last. I wanted so much to believe you were innocent. I wanted it so badly to be true, and in my heart I knew it. I love you, Julius Chadwick, and I don't know what I would do without you.'

'I'll see that you never are, sweetheart.'

Suddenly she moved slightly and a look of wonder lit her eyes. Her hand went to her stomach and a smile touched her lips. 'Oh,' she whispered, 'how odd.'

Julius frowned, bewildered by her remark. 'What is?'

'Our baby. Oh, Julius, I do believe it moved—like a butterfly fluttering its wings.'

A lump of emotion swelled in Julius's chest as she took his hand and pressed it against her stomach. With a feeling of awe, he, too, felt the gentle movement of their child.

With her cheek against his chest, she whispered, '*Now* will you take me to bed?'

Without saying a word he swung her into his arms, cradling her tenderly against him, brushing his lips against her forehead. He carried her to the bed and laid her down, intending to give her so much pleasure that she'd be able to forget the misery he'd caused her.

As dawn settled its pinkish shroud upon the land, the circling, confused wind that had battered the earth with a sheeting rain for most of the night had abated. The countryside grew quiet in hushed relief. The very air seemed to hang in breathless suspense, while wraith-like vapours shifted aimlessly among the trees and shrubs and filled low hollows on the land. The house, bounded on three sides by tall, gaunt trees, seemed to merge with the landscape. Apart from a tired, thin spiral of grey smoke rising from the outbuildings to the rear, nothing moved and nothing stirred, not even the lovers, their bodies entwined beneath the covers.

Now the truth was out at last, the shadows between them had gone away. After all their years of loneliness, they were no longer alone. They had each other now. They were together, in spirit as well as in flesh—as one, as though they had found the bits that were missing from themselves in each other.

They remained at Larkhill for a further week, during which time Julius arranged for work to begin on rebuilding the outbuildings. The cause of the fire remained a mystery, until a grim-faced George paid them a visit.

'It was my mother,' he said without preamble. 'I'm sorry, Beatrice, but unable to bear the thought that you had finally got what you wanted, she paid someone to destroy the house.'

Beatrice, seated on the sofa, was clearly horrified. Though she knew her aunt wished her ill, she could not believe she would go so far as to want to destroy Larkhill. 'Does you mother really hate me as much as that?'

'She couldn't stand knowing you had won, that you had indeed secured Larkhill for yourself. She wanted to hurt you the only way she knew how. I'm so sorry, Beatrice.'

'Aunt Moira can be very cruel.'

'Yes, yes, she can. When she learned her scheming had failed to destroy Larkhill, she could not hide what she had done. In her fury she could not stop herself telling me. I could not believe it myself. I can only thank God that apart from the destruction of a few outbuildings, no one was harmed and the house is still intact. I—would appreciate you not taking this further, Beatrice. No good would come of it.'

'We won't,' Julius answered for her, 'providing Lady Standish stays away from my wife.'

'She will—I shall make sure of that. It may surprise you to know that she regrets her actions and is more than a little ashamed. She didn't mean to harm you, Beatrice. Having seen you in London earlier, she had no idea you had come down to Larkhill. She knows how much Larkhill means to you. She meant to hurt you by destroying it. I have her word that she won't try anything like that again. You need not fear. She—will shortly be moving to the dower house.'

His hesitancy and the sudden warmth that lit his eyes brought a knowing smile to Beatrice's lips. 'Then that can only mean one thing. You are to be married, George?'

He beamed at her. 'I am. Leonora has consented to be my wife.'

'That's wonderful news, George. And does your mother approve?'

'Leonora has all the requisites that are important in my mother's scheme of things. But whether she approves or not is neither here nor there. I chose my own wife, not my mother.'

'Then I wish you every happiness, George. But what of Astrid? Has she returned from Scotland?'

'She has, although I haven't seen her yet. Henry and Astrid are living with Henry's parents. It's just a temporary situation, until they've found somewhere they can afford to live. As you know, the Talbots are not wealthy. Astrid's dowry will help, but she will find that her standard of living will be somewhat reduced and nothing like what she has become accustomed to.'

'She is happy, George. That is what counts.'

He smiled at her. 'So it is, Beatrice. So it is.'

The following morning Julius didn't accompany Beatrice when she went to call on Astrid and put his wife's excitement down to her eagerness to see her cousin. In fact, she had seemed strangely preoccupied and somewhat secretive ever since George's visit, which puzzled him. Everything became clear when she returned and told him she was ready to leave Larkhill, that she wanted him to take her to Highfield where she was impatient to take up her new life.

He gazed at her suspiciously. 'Of course. We'll leave right away if that is what you wish. You'll have to decide what you are going to do with Larkhill. The house shouldn't be left empty indefinitely.'

She hesitated, searching his face. 'It's not mine any more,' she told him. 'It belongs to Astrid. I wanted her to have it.'

Julius nodded slowly. This was the last thing he had expected her to say, but he knew she would have given the matter serious thought and that the decision to part with her beloved Larkhill would not have been taken lightly. 'You are sure?' he asked.

Beatrice took a deep breath. 'I'm sure. I know it will be safe in Astrid and Henry's hands.' And she was sure. She would always remember the look of joyous disbelief and gratitude on her cousin's face when she had offered Larkhill to her. That alone made it all worthwhile. 'I would be grateful if you would take care of the legalities, Julius. You know all about these things. All I want is you—to live with you wherever that may be.'

'And you will not regret it?'

'No. There is nothing that can be bought or sold or bartered that I would want. The only thing I want cannot be bought—and it is not the ownership of Larkhill. It is you, Julius. Only you.'

Overcome with emotion at what she had done, he put his arms around her and drew her close to him.

She lifted her face to his kiss and breathed in the warm, masculine smell of him, tasted the warmth of his mouth as it came down on hers. All the love that had been accumulating through the lonely years of her childhood was in that kiss. Julius felt it in the soft lips. With unselfish ardour she offered herself to him and Julius took what she offered hungrily, feeling it flowing through his veins and mingling with his blood until the joy of it was shattering.

'I love you,' she whispered. 'I belong with you— wherever that may be.'

He sighed, his eyes adoring her. She was everything he'd ever dreamed she could be—and more.

The next six months were spent in wedded bliss at Highfield Manor in Kent—a magnificent estate that surpassed anything Beatrice had ever seen. It was at Highfield where Julius and Beatrice's son was born. It was also at Highfield where they received news that Lady Standish had died in her sleep. Beatrice did not grieve for her aunt and chose not to return to Standish House for the funeral.

After twelve months of mourning, Julius and Beatrice did attend George's wedding to Leonora Fenton and they stayed at Larkhill with Astrid and Henry.

With its acres of corn and green meadows filled with cattle and sheep, Larkhill looked loved and well tended and prosperous. Beatrice's heart soared with affection and gratitude to Henry, who had done all this, but she no longer considered it her home.

When George and Leonora stood at the altar to speak their vows, Julius's gaze riveted on his wife standing next to him. The sight of her still continued to have a devastating effect on him, but here, in the church, caught in a shaft of light piercing the stained-glass windows, expecting their second child, never had she looked so radiantly beautiful or so serene. Every muscle of his body strained to endure the torment of her nearness. But it was a torment he welcomed, an agony he didn't want to be spared. And he knew that having her beside him was all he could ever want for the rest of his life.

* * * * *